DAVID DREEPEL

A NOVEL

MARLI SIEBURGER

Cover Design & Layout: Summer Morris, Sumo Design Studio
Printed in the United States of America.

To my husband,

John M Harbig II

BOOK ONE

THE CHILDREN OF NORDACHE

CHAPTER
I

"WHO ARE YOU?" ASKED the ancient man dressed in a stylish white tunic that tenderly, brushed the fine beige sand. He carried a serene tone of voice and appeared extremely calm. His hair, in catches, covered his shoulders as it moved gentle with the breeze which blew through the land at the moment. His mysterious blue eyes openly, delivered a peaceful look. On his right hand he held a lovely wood cane, wore sandals on his feet and seemed familiar with the environment around him.

"I am David…. David Dreepel" responded the twelve-year-old boy."

"David Dreepel, the son of the great, Magno Dreepel, from Nordache, the Province of Jarmayra?

"Do you know me?" replied the boy.

"I know you more than you can imagine. I know you from the very beginning. Before you even had a name. From an abstract time created inside labyrinths of perhaps flawless imagination."

"If you know me why did you ask, who am I?"

"I want to hear you say your name. Something of great importance for our first encounter and future relationship."

"Why do you know me?" asked David.

Now, fully trapped by the desire to hear more. He seemed surprised with the sudden presence of the ancient man.

"I am your creator. Call me Nicolas Toscapela, the author of your destiny. The beginning and the ending, the authority and knowledge, the architect and the destroyer. I am the first and last whisper in your fortune."

Promptly, David repeated in his mind all that had been said. The instant became important for a slight reflection and too much was told for one minor question. While David listened to the echoes of these words, the ancient man remained close. He also enjoyed the silence for he wished David Dreepel would catch the meaning of his announcement.

As the quietness persist, perplexing David's thoughts, the ancient man entertained himself writing with his cane, four letters on the soft sand— D.L.O.T.

"I don't believe in the proclamation of power you claimed to have," explained David Dreepel, "You may know my father for reasons that I don't know, but being my creator seems absurd."

"Oh! I knew you would not believe me," replied the ancient man. "David, David, David. My dear Dreepel! You have vigorous strength, tenacious courage and superb intelligence. Do you see these letters on the sand? Use the power of your brain. Four letters and four children. They are the letters of…?"

DAVID DREEPEL

"Our names?"

"Yes," responded the ancient man.

The unexpected revelation lessened the hostility that began to grow among them. David Dreepel sent a perspicacious and inquisitive glance to the children next to him. His mind traveled fast wishing that his encounter with this strange man, ended quickly and forever.

"I assume that only David Dreepel knew his name. Am I right?" asked the ancient man.

"Yes," the other three children answered in agreement.

"Good."

"Yes. As a matter of fact—*good,*" replied David Dreepel, sharply, "Very good. At least I know my name. Because we have found ourselves here and I think that like me; they also didn't know from where they came and why we ended in such a desolated place."

Nicolas Toscapela, the ancient man, slowly, moved near David. He spoke kindly. "Patience, David Dreepel; patience and perseverance. Only this place is deserted, not the others. My dear Dreepel, your journey will be a delightful encounter."

"Journey? What kind of journey? What strange conversation is this?" asked David with a trace of frustration tainting the tone of his voice, totally confused.

"The journey of your life," explained Mr. Toscapela.

David wobbled his head distrustfully and lifted his shoulders hopelessly. His life crashed into a chamber of obscurity and his thoughts seemed to float inside a never-ending course.

"If you know me, as you alleged, why don't you explain, in an open way, what I am doing here. Why do you know my father and why this tale about a journey? I feel completely lost inside my own existence and they do too. These children must feel the same way. We have no clue of what is going on."

"Okay, Dreepel. This is how I am going to call you from now on," said Mr. Nicolas Toscapela. Then, almost touching each one with the edge of his cane he proceeded, "You are David Dreepel, twelve-years old. She is Olivia Viglianco, also twelve-years old. Lucas Lambert, eleven-years old, then this young girl, Tess Viglianco. She is ten-years old, and is Olivia's sister."

David brought a weak smile to his lips. "Thank you! Now, aside from our names, we know our ages," he added with a glimpse of satisfaction adorning his face. "I don't know how, but yes, it seems that you know us. Please continue. Tell me more."

"I transported you here."

"You what?"

"I brought you here," repeated Mr. Toscapela, gladly and glancing around; ready to inform them whatever they wanted to know.

The children also exchanged a long, intriguing look, without uttering a word. They understood that Mr. Toscapela was either lying to gain their sympathy, or playing odd games with them.

"Why, Mr. Toscapela?" asked Lucas in a kind tone of voice. "Why did you transport us here?"

"Because this is the place I have chosen to start the fascinating journey David Dreepel had asked for."

"Really. Did I ask for it?"

"You did....And now,...well...now, it is too late to go back."

The obscure manner the ancient man talked and explained things only forged perplexity in the children's minds. The more they listened to Mr. Toscapela, the quicker they deepened into an endless confusion. They appeared in this place out of nowhere, didn't know each other and couldn't remember anything from their past.

Olivia Viglianco came forward objectively. She also had questions. "Mr. Toscapela, tell us our stories. Where did we come from and what has happened to us before we got here. Please have a little bit of compassion. We're four children lost in…, in …, in time?"

"And… place," articulated Tess, eagerly to make herself present us well.

"Yes," snapped Lucas. "Tell us the truth about this encounter. For example, what is the name of this place? It's so quiet and isolated. It only has the ocean and sand hills. What's the name of it?"

"Gargatuela," said Mr. Nicolas Toscapela.

The children instantly, mocked their faces.

"Gargatuela?" snapped Olivia and Lucas in perfect harmony.

"Yes… the Dunes of Gargatuela. The god of the ocean created this place. According to the legend he fell in love with the Gargatuela Moon and after that he crafted this place for her to come down to meet with him. When this happened the ocean turned into a man and the moon into a woman. For three days, only dunes of sand and a dark sky depicted the landscape of this place. The sand hills represent the years they have been seeing each other."

"During the entire year, they only saw each other for three days?" asked Tess.

"Only for three days. This place can't be without ocean or moon. They have to return."

"Wow…" uttered the children.

Then, gradually, they silenced. Their minds drifted away from

Mr. Toscapela for they spent some time examining the furtive, stillness of the place.

"Mr. Toscapela, who are you? Are you a god? Or a magician?" inquired Olivia, kindly.

"If you say that a creator is god, then yes. I can be a kind of god. I am a man with interesting vision and flamboyant imagination."

Lucas' curiosity ran wild and he questioned freely. "Why did you choose the Dunes of Gargatuela, to meet with us? Does it hold some magic?

"No," answered Mr. Toscapela. "Sooner or later, I would have to establish this meeting between us. The first contact we must have, before the story begins. And I chose to do this in a peaceful and quiet place. I wished to keep our first encounter as the most remarkable we could possibly have. The Dunes of Gargatuela holds the stillness and mysticism we all deserve for such a meaningful moment."

"What is the name of the ocean god?" asked Tess.

"Estanbulo."

The children repeated the god's name and laughed.

"Have you seen him?" added Tess.

"No. Gods like to live separate from people. Their lives extend beyond eternity and the incognito aspect of it must remain protected."

"Estanbulo…?" repeated Tess laughing again.

"A moon…Gargatuela…?" remarked Olivia derisively.

The instinctive criticism stopped the fruition of the dialog and only the sound of strange names lasted to enlarge the seconds. A flawless silence wrapped them, until…, Lucas Lambert commented.

"Imagine… four children with a mysterious life."

"And an ancient man claiming to be my creator." stated David Dreepel.

"That's right Dreepel," replied Mr. Toscapela. "And I… am the ancient man holding the magic dust which controls everything. There is nothing that you can possibly do, to change it. I bet you are eager to know what would be next in your journey, am I right?"

"Yes," answered David, promptly.

Like David, Olivia also wished to know what would be next and who this ancient man was. Moving closer, she asked, "Mr. Toscapela, where are you from?"

"I am from a very distant place called Woodmera. No one knows its location, only me."

"Why?" inquired David Dreepel.

"Because I decided to keep it a secret. No one will ever be part of it, but me. In Woodmera began my entire existence. There, nothing will be lost. Everything will be moving to another dimension, life happened in perfect satisfaction and no one will ever damage it."

"Oh! It's too much mystery," said Olivia. "None of it makes any sense. Our lives have no farther importance. No one cares about us."

"Yes. No one cares," cried Tess. "I only want to know more about me and my sister."

"Me too," replied Olivia. "Please Mr. Toscapela. You said David is from Nordache. Where is Nordache?"

"Yes. Where is Nordache," inquired Lucas.

The ancient man removed from his mind the thoughts he had been engaged with and for an instant studied the children. He understood their frustration. He decided to comfort them. He knew that sooner or later; he would have to do that.

"Okay children. The big moment just arrived; the starting time. Let's take a trip to the City of Nordache, in the Province of Jarmayra."

Kindly, Mr. Toscapela asked them to gather around him. Then, he closed his eyes and spoke in a strange language. A language from the past, a language from clever wizards, or maybe ancient gods. The children did not understand a word.

> In the name of what I can control. The ability of having the power of imagination, esoteric code D.L.O.T., two seconds fragmentation and incorporation, space... time folder... the future... City of Nordache... Province of Jarmayra... year 1979.

After that, Mr. Nicolas Toscapela extended his cane, drew a line on the sand and uttered the magic words. "DRIVABA...! ANAPOLENTRA...! MARGOREL...!"

Immediately, the line gained color. It turned orange and mysteriously lifted in the air, folded in half and in slow motion seesawed a couple of times. Next, the line extended once again, and gradually returned to the ground.

Mr. Toscapela looked at the children and said, "Children hold your hands and cross this line. You will arrive in another place and another time."

"Don't you come with us?" asked David Dreepel.

"No. You don't need me in Nordache."

The children grew apprehensive.

"Don't be afraid. You will be fine. We will meet again, but not in Nordache."

The children looked at Mr. Nicolas Toscapela one last time. Like magic, their lovely faces showed no distress and they lost the desire to ask questions. Silently, they crossed the line and disappeared.

Mr. Nicolas Toscapela, looked over the isolate place and smiled. He walked through the dunes until he also vanished. In the dunes of Gargatuela, the magic had begun.

CHAPTER
2

CITY OF NORDACHE
SECOND MOON

IN A PLACE CALLED Nordache in the Province of Jarmayra, planet My Jupiter; Lucas Lambert, Olivia and Tess Viglianco were sitting on the shore playing with the wet sand.

The calm, green, ocean appeared to be a lake just there, decorating the tranquil afternoon. The waves moved noiselessly, and slowly. The salt water barely hit the shoreline and the blue sky warmly covered the whole beach.

Around 12:00 o'clock the Lambert and Viglianco family went back to the house and sit outside to eat lunch. Samantha Lambert and Jessica Viglianco were cousins. Every year, they traveled to the south coast of Nordache, to the small island called Tee-Tee Cala, where Jessica had a house and they spent the whole summer at the beach with the children. Olivia, Tess, and Lucas, simply loved this time of the year.

Outside the house they sat at a picnic-table and peacefully, begun eating their lunch. The weather was hot, but enjoyable. All tables were located underneath enormous trees and pleasant shades, silently, protected the area.

The children occupied a table separated from the adults. Grandmother Amelia, the mother of Jessica Viglianco, was there with them. While having their soup, bread, and fruits, the children saw a grasshopper on the branch of the enormous tree under which they sat to eat. The first person to see the grasshopper was Tess, who at the time was only eight years old.

"Look... a grasshopper," she said."

The other children turned their heads and stared at the attractive, grasshopper. Its vigorous outlook almost scared them.

"Wow...! I think I never saw a grasshopper as big as this one," commented Lucas; now, only nine years old.

"Yes, unusual, almost the size of my hand," added Olivia.... She just turned ten years old.

"This grasshopper is beautiful," stated Tess, observing its eyes. "It seemed to talk to us."

"Forget about talking," remarked Lucas. "It is so cool that it can jump and fly at any time. Can you imagine how cool it would be if we could do that? Human's form of transportation is so poor."

The children quietly, observed the insect. What Lucas had said about human's form of transportation had occupied their minds for a few seconds. Grandmother Amelia came to the table and sat with them.

"What plans do my lovely grandchildren have for the afternoon?" she asked holding a happy smile, and wary look.

"I want to go back to the beach," said Lucas.

"Me too," added Tess.

Grandmother Amelia waited for Olivia's words. And… soon… Olivia spoke. She raised her head and said, "Grandmother, don't you want to know what we were talking about before you arrived?"

"Hmm…! Yes, Olivia. What was it?"

"This grasshopper," responded Olivia, turning her head toward the branch. "It's the most beautiful—" The branch was empty. The grasshopper has gone.

"Oh! Where is it?"

I think it has gone?" said Lucas.

"No," replied Tess, moving from the table, walking around, looking carefully to see it again.

"Grandmother," said Olivia, "It was a lovely green, green, grasshopper, you should have seen it. Almost the size of my hand."

Tess walked underneath the enormous tree trying to find the grasshopper. She strolled around the trunk of the tree, always looking up. The tree had countless of short and long branches, spread in different directions. Suddenly, Tess bumped into a boy sitting on the ground. He was about ten years old.

Oh! I am sorry," said Tess. "I didn't see you. I am looking for a beautiful grasshopper that was on the branch of this tree. Have you seen it?"

The boy just moved his head negatively. Tess looked up to the branches one last time. "I think my cousin Lucas is right. It has gone."

The boy silently, looked at her. Grandmother Amelia, Olivia and Lucas came closer. "Did you find it Tess?" asked Grandmother Amelia.

"No…. Lucas is right. It has gone."

"Maybe we scared it," added Olivia.

"I don't think so," replied Lucas. "It climbed up on the tree and cuddled into a branch between leaves probably, to take a nap. Since it was as green as the leaves, now it would be difficult to see it."

"Yes," added Olivia. "And this happens to be a big tree."

"Perhaps the grasshopper moved to the upper branches to do what you were doing; having lunch. Grasshoppers eat leaves," said the boy that was sitting on the ground under the tree. He spoke for the first time.

"Who are you?" asked Olivia.

"My name is David. David Dreepel."

"I am Olivia. She is Tess, my sister. Lucas our cousin. And Amelia my grandmother.

Quietly the boy shook his head.

"Do you like grasshoppers?" asked Tess.

"I do. This kind of insect belongs to the group called Suborder Caelifera. They are ancient chewing herbivorous, dating as far back as the Triassic period, which is around 250 million years ago."

"Wow…! You do know about grasshoppers, hmm?" commented Lucas.

Olivia observed the boy and asked, "Why do you know so much about—"

"Children… let's go," said Grandmother Amelia. She called the meeting off by saying that lunch was over and that they should go back to the beach to enjoy the rest of the afternoon. Nothing else was said. The children left.

At the beach, Lucas, Olivia and Tess jumped into the ocean and enjoyed the warm green water. They swam, ran, and laughed tirelessly. Then they decided to build a sand castle.

Grandmother Amelia had come to help them. She placed her knees down on the wet sand and said, "I always loved to build a sand castle. Do you know why? Because at night when I closed my eyes on my bed, I imagined how wonderful it would be if I really owned a castle like the one I had built."

"I want to build a deep moat around the castle to protect it from outsiders," explained Lucas. "I want to impress people with my castle so they can see the power of it from a distance."

"Hmm. I never thought about that," replied Grandmother Amelia. "That castle could be evidence of power?"

"I like that Lucas," added Olivia. "Water around the castle will keep robbers and pirates away. And you're right; a castle… just by being a castle… is powerful."

"We should put a bridge that opens and closes, so none of our enemies will get in," declared Tess.

Unexpectedly, Olivia saw the boy that was sitting under the tree. He stayed isolated watching them. He wore green summer shorts and a white t-shirt.

"Hey David… come. Come and play with us." Olivia called, moving her hand in the air indicating, *come… come.*

David Dreepel, came near them. He put his knees on the wet sand and began to help building the sand castle, as well.

"Lucas is building a deep moat around the castle to keep enemies out," explained Olivia.

"Yes," replied Lucas, "By looking at the castle, the enemies should immediately know that we have power."

For a few minutes the children worked in silence and grandmother

Amelia helped them. The afternoon stayed calm and a soft pleasant breeze constantly traveled throughout the shore.

Because they were talking about power, Grandmother Amelia asked, "If you could have power to control something Tess, what would you like to control?"

Tess stopped what she was doing, placed her pointed finger over her lips... thoughtfully. She then twisted her nose and frowned her forehead. "I would love to control colors. I want to be able to change the color of things at any time."

"Colors...?" exclaimed Grandmother Amelia. "Why colors...? Colors are not essential; their significance has no special eminence. I'd rather control something...,..., important."

"What Grandmother? What would you like to control?" asked Olivia with great interest.

"I would love to control fire, water, wind, the ocean, rain, rivers, or the clouds on the sky."

The children stared at the ambience. Obviously, Grandmother's words woke up their dormant mind and connected them with novel, intriguing ideas. A soft wind passed through and as slowly as the waves ran away from the shore, the extensive silence also vanished. Tess spoke again.

"Grandmother, I know what I want to control. I want to control the wind."

"Ah! Now, you make a good choice."

"My turn," replied Olivia. "I want to control fire."

"Excellent Olivia. You and Tess have in your hands two essential elements, wind and fire."

Lucas remained thinking. Grandmother Amelia, Olivia, and

Tess quietly waited for his choice. They knew he was connected with their conversation.

When Lucas spoke, he said, "I'd like to control the rain. I would love to use it to clean the ambience. Imagine... I could wash the planet with my power."

"Very good, Lucas. Very good." added Grandmother Amelia.

Since David said nothing, Olivia asked, "And you David. If you could control something, what would you like to control?"

Another critical silence ran through the moment. Apparently, David Dreepel did not expect participating in this quest. He gazed around and smiled for the first time. He tilted his head thoughtfully. "I like magic. I would love to be able to make things appear and disappear, make things small or big, and transport myself from one location to another with the power of words."

"Really?" uttered Grandmother Amelia. A magician? Incantation power.... How interesting!"

"How clever," replied Tess.

Then with a glare of contempt Olivia added, "Impeccable answer. I like that."

Grandmother Amelia disconnected from the children and the sand castle. For a few seconds, she flew away in the wings of this lovely fantasy. Magic.... The power of spells. She thought David Dreepel was a smart kid.

Lucas decided to challenge David and he freely said, "From where did you come from that you have such a terrific knowledge? A clever way of saying things and explaining facts? You introduced yourself with the MESOZOIC ERA, when you spoke about grasshoppers and easily jumped into MEDIEVAL TIMES, for the sake of magic—like nothing. Are you for real?"

David Dreepel looked at Lucas. "Of course, I am real you can see me. I don't understand why I know these things, but I can tell, I am a Homo Sapiens."

Lucas, Olivia, and Tess stared at each other.

"Lucas, what is Homo Sapiens?" asked Olivia.

"I don't know."

"Grandmother," called Tess. "What is Homo Sapiens?"

"Oh, children! Who said that?"

"David Dreepel."

"David, what have you been reading lately? This is a hard subject for a ten-year old boy."

"Grandmother, what is it," insisted Olivia.

"*Homo Sapiens* is the name of our specie. In Latin, it means *wise man*."

The children remained quiet, as if they were whispering secrets. Suspiciously, they studied David Dreepel with one question… two questions… three questions in mind.

"Do you speak Latin?" asked Tess.

"No," responded David Dreepel.

"So, we all are Homo Sapiens," stated Olivia.

"Yes…" replied Lucas, "We are like David and David is like us."

Grandmother Amelia left the children and walked to where Samantha and Jessica were sitting. The children remained at the shore working on their sand castle.

Some time went by and the children finished building the castle. As soon as they finished it, an incandescent brightness took over the shore and a forceful breeze intensified its grasp. Speedily, the breeze changed directions and ended its course at the ocean. As it traveled through, it changed the ambience, as the ocean and the people instantly disappeared. The children stayed alone in the middle of nowhere with their sand castle. They couldn't understand what was going on and they felt scared.

As they looked around trying to comprehend such a phenomenon, a beautiful young lady appeared next to them. She had abundant long, golden curly hair and she solemnly descended from above, floating in the air as angels without wings. In slow motions she descended until her shoes touched the sand.

"Good afternoon children," she said kindly, eyeing them. Attentively, she studied each one.

"Who are you?" asked David Dreepel.

"I am Leila Maglaja. I came from Lili Sandra. The land of incredible magicians. My mother and my father are magicians and I'll be one, too."

"Where is the ocean?" asked Tess.

"Oh! I made it disappear. I have a mission to accomplish and since I am learning to do magic, the noise of the ocean annoys me. So, for now, we will only have the shore and the sand castle."

"The shore and the sand castle?" asked Olivia.

"That's right. The shore and the sand castle."

"You said you're learning to do magic?"

"Yes. Any problem with that?"

"Of course… you're not yet a magician," answered Olivia.

Leila took a long breath, as she eyed the sky pleading. Her tolerance was diminishing by seconds. "We are not born magician, children. We need to study to becoming one."

DAVID DREEPEL

"I'd like to learn magic," said David Dreepel.

"Maybe one day you can do that."

"Yes. Maybe one day."

A beautiful yellow, red, and purple sunset appeared far away at the end of the land. Its bright colors impressed the children.

"Okay. Let's work. I am here for—" she opened the palm of her right hand and read, "David Dreepel, Lucas Lambert, Olivia and Tess Viglianco. Are these your names?"

"Yes," the children answered in conjunction.

"Good. I have to take you with me. We will be engaged in a great journey. First, we will go to the dunes of Gargatuela and from there we must travel to Bonahunta, in the Province of Normabell, which will be under the third moon; the Otela moon. The moon full of exciting surprises."

The children blinked their eyes displeased. Their minds crashed into a perverse labyrinth of illusory endeavor. They silently repeated to themselves. *Exciting surprises? Bonahunta? Normabell? And Otela Moon?*

Suspiciously Olivia commented, "This…. This is not happening, right? She's not for real. She's talking about strange things, dunes of Gargatuela and Normabell Province, in what planet is it? Then she wants to take us with her on this dangerous journey?"

"Why do you think it's dangerous?" asked Tess.

"I don't know," responded Olivia, "She made the ocean disappear and we don't even know if she can bring it back. Too much mystery. For example… the moon full of *exciting surprises.* Have you imagined if these surprises were unpleasant, dreadful, and cruel? If we go with her and something goes wrong. Who would save us?

The children remained quiet. Quiet and scared, vague, and lost, with the next question echoing their minds.

True…. Who would save us under the Otela Moon?

CHAPTER
3

BONAHUNTA, THE COVENANT CITY of My Jupiter and according to Mr. Nicolas Toscapela it was located at 97 degrees of Tona Quemia Galaxia and turned out to be the only city which had the Otela Moon every seven years.

So… when Leila said: *We have to go to Bonahunta, in the Province of Normabell, which will be under the third moon; the Otela Moon. The moon full of exciting surprises.* The children sunk into an abysm of complexity and they could only utter, "What…?"

And because they spoke in conjunction and in such a fast fashion, Leila Maglaja sent to them her most severe look which—at the moment—delivered the ardent heat of the fire inside her eyes.

"You all heard what I have said. We will go to Gargatuela, then… to Bonahunta."

"I am not going with you to places I don't know," stated Olivia.

"Yes… neither am I," replied Lucas and David.

"We don't know you," repeated Olivia.

A gentle breeze blew through the island and the warm touch of it messed with the children's hair. Silently, they enjoyed the pleasant air.

"And you Tess?" asked Leila, "What do you want to say? I believe that you, too, have something to say."

"I would love to go to these places you have said, but I don't know if it will be safe. You said you're learning to do magic."

Leila smiled. She loved Tess and her genuine answer. Olivia perceived that Leila became a fan of Tess. She knew her sister very well and felt that she had to protect Tess. Olivia spoke again.

"You came from nowhere, made the ocean disappear, began talking of fictitious places and confessed that you are learning to do magic. How do you expect us to believe… trust… or even give you credit for floating in the air like…, …, like…,"

"Like a kite," finished Lucas.

"Yes. Like a kite."

Leila gazed at the sand patiently. The absence of the ocean really calmed her. She realized that Olivia could harm her mission. Leila needed to conquer Olivia's trust.

Leila remembered her mother. Marcela Festalma Maglaja. She always taught Leila the power of common sense, the energy of the cosmos, the vitality of the soul and the infinite capacity of the mind. Her mother said that some of the reasons people lost their battles was because lack of sagacity.

Leila decided she would not lose her battle because of Olivia mistrust. No, she was a Maglaja and all members of Maglaja family had achieved their ambitions by believing in the power of their minds. If Olivia didn't trust Leila, Leila should trust herself to make Olivia change the course of her perceptions. And of course, with the supremacy she possessed to be used in this mission, she could do that.

In one of her classes, Leila learned that the mind of a child, travels fast, understands simplicity and accepts any illusory execution. They carried the honesty of their ingenuity and trusted originality. It was all a magician needed.

"Children, wait a minute," said Leila, "I know you don't trust me, but I have a mission to accomplish and I plan to do that, if you like it or not. If I don't accomplish this mission, I will probably never graduate as a magician. And being a magician is very important for me. You all need to understand that."

Suspiciously, the children exchanged cold looks. *She's not for real.* They all agreed.

"I can do something to make you trust me. And I am going to do it, right now."

"And what it would be?" asked Olivia, promptly.

"You will see," responded Leila.

"Yes... I want to see it, too" replied David Dreepel.

Patiently, Leila breathed in. She re-evaluated her idea. Then with a glare of pleasure she spoke.

"Olivia, do you remember the conversation you had with your grandmother when you were building this sand castle?"

"I do."

"Good."

"What did you say you would love to control if you have power?"

"Fire."

"Yes... fire."

"I am going to give you the power to control fire, for one minute. Only one minute."

The children frowned their eyebrows while repeating Leila's words in their minds. They seemed to make a good discovery. *Probably, we would be kids missing in action.*

"You will do what?" inquired Olivia.

"Don't say anything. Just look at the sand castle you have built," ordered Leila.

The children turned their eyes toward the sand castle. They watched attentively.

Leila brought an intense green light into her eyes and said, "ALCATEZY…! TELAVERTY…! CARTIERY…!"

In front their eyes all kinds of trees began to grow around the castle. They never had the size of real trees, but they were taller than the sand castle and rapidly lightning stroked the trees and they caught fire.

Shocked, the children stared at Leila.

"Go Olivia," said Leila, "Use your power."

"How?" asked Olivia.

"I don't know, my dear. Use your imagination. And remember, you only have one minute. Don't waste your time talking to me, because if you do that, you will lose the castle."

Olivia realized that she must act. And she did exactly like Leila anticipated. The mind of a child indeed, brings infinity surprises. Willingly to save the castle they had built, Olivia stretched her arms and pointed to the fire. Audaciously she ordered, "Fire… reduce to one single flame."

A portion of indulgent time…crucial quietness…and tenacious

expectation…ran through. Seconds passed, then the fire, magically began to rush from the edges toward the center until it converted in one single flame.

"Now, flame, come to the palm of my hand," commanded Olivia.

The flame lifted in the air, traveled, and stopped in the palm of Olivia's hand. Hurriedly, Olivia brought the hand close to her lips and blew it off.

Lucas, David, and Tess, crashed into endless astonishment. It seemed that a ghost suddenly took their breath away. They just witnessed a child doing magic.

"Wow… this…, was cool," finally Tess commented. Then, they returned their attention to Leila. Now they were not sure— *if she was not for real.*

"Olivia, I like the way you controlled your power," said Leila. "After all…, smart girl."

"I like it too," said Lucas.

"Now we can go with Leila, right?" snapped Tess.

"Of course," said Lucas. "It will be an exciting trip. Imagine, doing magic and seeing mysterious things happening in front our eyes. Nothing could be more exciting than that. Let's go."

Olivia quickly, shook her head left to right, disapprovingly. "Lucas… you and Tess are crazy. Going to these places can be dangerous. We may never come back. Bad things happen."

"Is it possible?" asked David Dreepel.

"Yes," said Leila. "In the field of *magic*, anything can happen *good* or *bad*. In every way; it is either, the power which controls the *good*, or the power which controls the *bad*. Magic means serious ventures, severe encounters, and genuine outcomes. Nevertheless, the intrinsic force controlling sorcery lies down in the core of magicians' hearts. In conclusion, even though only spirit controls curses, bad things can happen."

"See…," replied Olivia. "And don't forget that we will be under the power of a young magician. She didn't graduate, yet. She is learning. And these are her words."

"Okay. Enough," shouted Leila. "I am running out of time.

Immediately Leila raised her right arm, brought an intense green light to her eyes and executed the best magic the children had ever witnessed. She transformed the sand castle into a stone castle, and changed the size of it, so the children could fit inside without any problem. Next, without giving them any explanation, she replaced their beach clothes. She dressed them for their voyage.

David Dreepel was a beautiful boy. His angel face held two impressive, gentle, blue eyes, the most sensitive blue eye any person could ever see. An abundant amount of light brown hair evenly covered his head. Seeing him dressed in colorful Medieval costumes raised the children's curiosity to the next level. David Dreepel's new look, carried the image of a young magician.

Without delay, Olivia, Lucas and Tess, also had been dressed in attractive costumes as well. The neat style of medieval clothes, the glamorous hats, and elegant boots they wore, had transformed them into dignified children.

After she had swapped their beach clothes to Medieval costumes, Leila, with an imperative tone of voice, proceeded, "David Dreepel, Lucas Lambert, Olivia and Tess Viglianco; please, get into the castle."

The moment raised concerns and fears and the beat of time became high and dry. The children had met the fruition of another nightmare. They hesitated for a moment, because millions of questions invaded their minds in all directions. They lacked the power to do anything against Leila's order.

They looked around wishing for miracles; however, not even the ocean was present. They felt terrified and completely speechless. Nothing they could say would change Leila's intention. Her voice carried the vital sound of an expert magician. They just obeyed.

As soon as they entered the castle, Leila made it very small; the size of a souvenir. Then, she bent over, picked it up, shook the sand out of it and shuffled it inside the pocket of her dress. Slowly Leila ascended in the air. She went up… up… and up. Until, she faded between clouds.

THEY TRAVELED FOR TWO YEARS.

CHAPTER
4

CITY OF BONAHUNTA
THIRD MOON

IN BONAHUNTA, LEILA CHECKED the date and time on the palm of her right hand. It was Saturday, September 7th 1654, and the time was 10:00 am. Following that, a delightful smile adorned her lips. *The children will love it,* she thought.

The place where Leila had arrived was named Campos Vesulio. The green, flat land extended quietly, between gorgeous trees and perfect flower gardens. A couple of mountains edged one side of it and a noiseless river ran through in the back of the property. Leila found the location absolutely exquisite; a dazzling site for a castle.

After observing the ambience around her, she positioned herself in the center of the land, pulled the castle out of her pocket and carefully set it over the green grass. With a stare look, flaring off intense green lasers, she uttered her magic words and made the castle big, the size of real castle and she remained outside, waiting for the children.

DAVID DREEPEL

David Dreepel, Lucas Lambert, Olivia and Tess Viglianco, appeared at the front door. They stopped to survey the unfamiliar place and for a few seconds, they could only endure the beauty of it.

Doubtfully, they eyed Leila. Millions of bizarre thoughts occupied their minds. They wished to comprehend the magical aspect of this voyage, to at least, capture some portion of such fantasy. But no, they remained fearful wondering about what could be next.

"Children, welcome to Bonahunta," said Leila, walking toward them. "The city of infinite surprises, special nights, and dramatic moons. The legend of the South. The things that happen in Bonahunta, never happen in another city. Bonahunta, has the utmost benedictions any god could give away and the harsh curses any dark magicians can spell. And these last two things are exactly what makes Bonahunta… so special."

Apprehensively, David Dreepel asked, "Leila, where is Bonahunta located?"

"Bonahunta, is in the south part of My Jupiter planet, in the Province of Normabell, which now is under the influence of Otela, the third moon."

"Province of Normabell?"

"Yes," responded Leila.

"How big is it?" asked Lucas, willingly.

"It's big. About seven cities form the Province of Normabell. The largest and most notorious one, is Bonahunta. The Otela Moon appears in the sky of Bonahunta every seven years, and because of such phenomenon infinite surprises visit the city and during ancient times, it acquired the title of *Legend of the South.*"

"Did we change ages?"

"Of course, Lucas. We have been traveling for two years. Now, you're eleven years-old. David Dreepel and Olivia are twelve, and Tess just turned ten."

"In what year are we?"

"We are in 1654. A beautiful Medieval Era."

"No. This is impossible," snapped Lucas.

"Why?"

"Mathematics, Leila. Think about it. If we traveled two years toward the future, how come we arrived in the past?"

"Ah! Smart observation, Lucas. Let me explain what we have done. First, we traveled from Nordache to Gargatuela under my magic spell, and this took us two years. When we arrived in the dunes of Gargatuela in 1981; immediately, Mr. Nicolas Toscapela transported us here. He used *Surdrape Time Fold Passage*, which is his latest and extremely fast form of transportation. It took only a few seconds to travel from 1981 to this fascinating Medieval time."

"This is so cool," added Tess. So cool…!" She seemed enthralled with everything.

Leila waited for more questions, but the children remained quiet. They needed some time to catch up with so much mystery. Again, their lives held nothing but secrets.

Leila had decided to move on informing them what they didn't know. Assuredly she said, "My Jupiter is a huge planet. Even though the Province of Jarmayra borders the Province of Normabell, the distance between the city of Nordache and the city of Bonahunta is thousands of kilometers. Only special forms of transportation will allow people to travel such a distance in days."

"And I assume the Surdrape Time Fold Passage," added Lucas,

"A magic charm that only Mr. Nicolas Toscapela has the power to use, made such a travel possible."

"That's right Lucas," responded Leila. "He created it."

Now, the children remembered the ancient man in the elegant white tunic, writing D. O. L. T. on the sand with his wood cane.

"Of course, Mr. Nicolas Toscapela…," repeated David Dreepel. "He appeared from nowhere, used a unique kind of magic and in a blink of an eye, sent us to Nordache. I remember him."

"And he chose the year 1979 as the significant year in your life. The year you met Lucas, Olivia and Tess," stated Leila."

"Yes. Because in Gargatuela, we only knew our names."

"Strange area," added Lucas, "Sandbanks all over the place,"

The children brought Gargatuela to their minds. Silently, they agreed it was a dead site. Discouraged, Olivia studied their new reality. Following that she said, "Aside from Dunes of Gargatuela, this furtive way of traveling from one century to another in seconds… seemed to be a silly joke."

"It's cool Olivia," affirmed Tess.

"We'll have to understand… it's magic," replied Olivia. "We'll never know enough to comprehend the mystery involved in it."

Lucas felt bored. He walked away saying, "I don't know why David and Olivia insist in talking about things we will never understand. Look…. It's a beautiful morning. I want to see the city."

Leila heard him. She had been observing Lucas and saw he was not captivated with their conversation. "I think it's a good idea, Lucas. We should go to see the city."

Lucas and Tess, wanted to explore the city, but Olivia and David had so many questions to ask. They ignored Lucas and Tess wishes.

David asked, "Leila, under your spell what form of transportation did you use to take us from the city of Nordache, to the Dunes of Gargatuela?"

"I used what we call Zilcar Black Holes. They are the fastest form of transportation magicians can use. Once I reached certain level of elevation, I picked a Zilcar and traveled inside it. When I met you, in Nordache, the city was under the second moon, the *Elba Moon;* one of the moons that attracts the fastest black holes revolving the planet."

"I have never been involved with so much mysteries," stated Lucas. Now the conversation attracted him.

"Neither did I, Lucas," replied Olivia. "And I am not sure if we're safe here. There are lots of things that we don't know. And we remained under the spells of… I don't know what. And… Leila… Magla…

"Maglaja," responded Leila.

"Yes. Maglaja… is learning to do magic."

Leila kept Olivia's remarks to herself. She understood the pressure they were facing to endure the power of magic. The children had curiosity tormenting their minds and at this point, there was nothing that she could do to change the order of their spectacles.

Peacefully the children engaged into the excitement of exploring the land in which Leila set the castle. The green land enhanced their wonder.

"Leila, in what way is the city of Bonahunta?" asked David.

"That way," Leila pointed toward the left. "It's less than half mile from here. Just there, after the God Eller temple."

DAVID DREEPEL

The children looked at the tower of the temple. They breathed in the fresh air that gushed through. They had thoughts bouncing inside their minds. Again, they felt lost and confused.

"Okay Leila, tell us the truth," said Tess. "What will be next?"

"Now we wait, Tess."

"For whom?"

"Mr. Nicolas Toscapela. He is the master. At the appropriate time, he will arrive."

The children, switched glances, but said nothing. Leila invited them to see the river at the back of the castle. "I grew up swimming in rivers," she said.

They stopped at the edge of the river and watched it. The clear water ran almost soundlessly and it washed over the stones slowly, carrying away a school of small fish.

"Why did Mr. Nicolas Toscapela send us to Nordache," asked David? "And why did he select the year 1979?"

"Well… he selected Nordache because the city was under the Elba Moon, the moon which attracts the quicker black holes. He knew I'd need this kind of transportation to take you back to Gargatuela."

"Okay. It makes sense. And why the year 1979?"

"I don't know. Perhaps, because you needed to meet each other at certain ages? Why he selected this particular time to start your journey, probably, will be a forever mystery for all of us. From the very beginning, *you…*'David Dreepel' forged the course of all actions. When I gathered with Mr. Toscapela for this mission, he told me that Lucas, Olivia, and Tess did not know you. Before the encounter in Tee-Tee Cala Island, you weren't friends. So, the year 1979, became the chosen year. The year we all had met. And now... here we are."

David took a few minutes to discern what was said. He realized the meeting in Gargatuela was only to establish the first contact with Mr. Nicolas Toscapela. For some reason..., another mystery.

For a moment, the children remained quiet remembering the day they had met. They brought to their minds the island of Tee-Tee Cala, the sand castle and the lovely grasshopper.

David kept his conversation with Leila. He was eager to know more. "Why you can change the size of a castle, make the ocean disappear, create a fire, ascend and descend in the air and need black holes to travel?"

"We're humans. In magic there are many kinds of laws and limited power to those involved in it. I can't break down a human body in one place and blend it together in another, or perform the action of bending the time."

"Why not?"

"That power was not granted to me."

"Why? Because you're still learning magic?"

"Perhaps. Like I have told you before, the laws of magic hold the boundaries of its performances."

"Leila, all these rules of magic are very strange."

"I know, David, however all of them make a lot of sense. For example, the speed we would need to travel from year 1978 back to 1654 would be dangerous to our bodies. Humans would not resist such speed. That is why we need to bend the time. In black holes concept is different. We can only travel small distances and we didn't transcend any era. Remember, I made you and the castle small, but I never exited you, from the century."

"That's right. Would you have the power to use Surdrape Time Fold Passage, one day?"

"I don't know, David. No one knows if this kind of transportation would be available in the future. Maybe you should ask Mr. Nicolas Toscapela when you see him again."

"Oh! I will. He owes me lots of explanations. My existence remained hidden in a huge obscurity. It took two years to get from Nordache to Gargatuela. Then, in a blink of an eye, he had brought us to Bonahunta, during Medieval time. What could possibly, be next?"

Lucas and Tess became bored to death. "Leila, all this conversation is very interesting but, can we go to the city?"

"Of course, Lucas. Let's go."

Leila and the children walked happily to the city of Bonahunta.

Besides being the Legendary City, of the Province of Normabell, the city of Bonahunta, also gained the reputation of being one of the most beautiful cities in the south part of the planet. The majestic trees, edging both sides of the streets noiselessly, enhanced the peace of the ambience. At the center of the city, great tables full of merchandise appeared outside the stores to accelerate the daily trades.

Leila and the children entered the main street and felt amazingly surprised with the great festivities that were going on. Lots of people gathered on the streets to play music and to dance. Lovely jesters walked from place to place and venders approached visitors trying to sell their products. Leila said it was the first day of the fair.

The morning held a perfect weather. In one tent an old lady was selling flowers. When Leila and the children passed in front of her, Tess waved and smiled. The old woman waved back.

At the end of the street, Leila and the children stopped to watch the beautiful horses that came to participate in the knight's jousting games. They also saw some knights on the verge of starting their competitions.

Attractive ponies arrived into tents and stayed in exhibition to be sold. There was a stand and King James Lamarcus, his wife Claudia, and his lords were sitting to watch the martial games.

After the stand, Leila and the children turned around and began their way back toward the entrance. Tess saw a coin in the dust, she stopped and picked it up. Tess used her clothe to clean it. She shielded the coin in her hand and when they passed in front the old woman selling flowers, she went close and bought a flower. Tess carried the flower and gave it to Leila.

"For me?" asked Leila.

"Yes. Put it in your golden hair."

Leila left. "Thank you, Tess."

The other children just watched the exchange.

"Tess, how did you buy a flower?" asked her sister Olivia. "We don't have money."

"I found a coin on the ground."

"Oh! Lucky you," snapped Lucas.

Leila and the children returned to the castle, so the children could have something to eat. While walking, David Dreepel asked, "Leila, how often do they have this fair?"

"Every three months. They call it the Thomas Ganbari Fair. Lots of people come to see the attractions. Today is the first day, and only local knights participate in the jousting games."

Once again, they arrived at the entrance of the city. Quietly, they turned right and walked to the castle.

In Campos Vesulio, they entered the castle and found a man and a woman in the kitchen preparing lunch. Leila introduced them to the children.

"Children, this is Mr. Inbacula, and she is Mrs. Clenilde. They are the castle's caretakers. By the way… the name of the castle is Astafe."

"Astafe…?" replied Lucas.

"Yes, Astafe. It means *Sunset* in *Lastenia*," responded Leila.

"Lastenia…? What is *Lastenia?*"

Leila didn't answer. She waited to see what David would say.

"Lucas, *Lastenia* is the ancient language of My Jupiter," explained David. "For many years it remained as the official language."

"Is this true, Leila?" asked Lucas.

"Yes. This is very true."

"How do you know these things, David?"

"I don't know."

Lunch was ready and they sat outside in a large patio next to a garden full of beautiful flowers. The lunch consisted of bread, baked duck, and fruits. While eating, Tess said, "Leila, you look very pretty with this flower in your hair.

"Thank you, Tess. You're very sweet.

After lunch they walked on the bridge over the river and arrived in the woods, on the back side of the castle. In the woods they could hear the sound of the voices and the music that came from Bonahunta's main street.

"How long do you think it would take for Mr. Nicolas Toscapela to come?"

"I don't know David. It can be at any moment or…, it can take years."

"Years?"

"Yes, years.

"But—"

"Honestly David, it's his decision."

David held his frustration and for a few seconds endured it with sadness. "Do you know something Leila, Mr. Nicolas Toscapela is a very mysterious man. He said that I have asked for *this journey*. I can't imagine *how*? And *why*?"

"Hmm…! HOW…? Could be by articulating some words, right? And WHY…? Because of something that you really wanted.

David eyed Leila unhappily. Inside his mind, her words wobbled, then flipped and flapped. They mixed the connotations and shrank the possibility of new notions.

"With this kind of talking, you're not helping me to attain any evidence about myself."

"My dear David Dreepel can I give you one piece of advice? Stop your worries. Live the journey and unfold the mysteries."

CHAPTER
5

THE RASTAGA WOODS
THIRD MOON

LEILA AND THE CHILDREN advanced through the woods. The incredible tall trees strikingly made the planet small. The children enjoyed the place with tranquil expressions on their faces. Suddenly, an imposing rain forest welcomed them and the mysticism inside it was so overwhelming, that they moved on silently.

They walked closed to each other and in between the tall trees, wisely eyeing around as if nature communicated with them. Tess, who loves nature, felt in heaven.

The Rastaga Woods had invisible grottos. They called them Cristonelas Grottos. According to the ancient professors who studied them, they were a kind of phenomenon. People entered them without knowing they were grottos. Inside a Cristonela, the vegetation went dead, the soil became extremely dry, and the fog turned dense and very low. When people experienced these changes they realized they had arrived on the other side of the woods; a place where strange things materialized. According to the last studies, made ten years ago, three Cristonelas Grottos had been found in the Rastaga Woods.

The Cristonela's phenomenon was mentioned in the Bá-Onadi Book, which was the most important magic guide in the magic school of Lili Sandra. However, for some reason, Leila Maglaja failed to acknowledge how dangerous they could be.

Naively, Leila walked the children into these threatening woods and placed themselves into the most unexpected chain of events she could ever imagine.

Leila and the children strolled into one of the invisible grottos as if they were just walking around the trees. Abruptly, they noticed the change on the trees. They were tall trees, covered by a dense fog, and without leaves. They all noticed the yellow grass and dead vegetation on the ground. They looked at each other and they were scared.

Unexpectedly, Tess said, "Leila, do some magic for us. Show us that you are a fantastic magician. This place seems awesome for this type of things."

Tess' request surprised Leila, greatly. Tess was not afraid like the other children. She seemed optimistic about the place. Leila thought they should leave.

"No, Tess. I am not allowed to play with magic. Magic is a serious business."

"Oh Leila! I gave you a beautiful flower. Now give me something. Grant me…. A wish."

Leila measured Tess' words. She would love to please her; nevertheless, magic is not to play. Leila decided to take control of their actions. "I don't like this place. We need to leave… now."

"No," shouted Tess. "Look around. This is a mystic place, perfect for you to practice some magic. You want to become a magician, don't you?"

Leila breathed in a kind of insolence. She felt intimidated by Tess talking. She never saw Tess speaking in that tone of voice. That girl had been nothing but sweet. Silently, Leila wasted some time uncovering Tess' new behavior. And she did it observantly.

Leila decided to be smart and keep the calm. Avoiding to not lose control of her power, she suddenly asked, "Tess, if I would grant you a wish, what it would be?"

With a smile on her lips, Tess began to think. For a moment, she drifted away in the wings of her imagination. While Tess was thinking, Lucas spoke.

"No Leila, that's not fair. If you grant Tess a wish, you would have to do the same for us; David, Olivia, and I. We would love to enjoy whatever incantation you decide to perform."

"Children, I can't do that. I cannot play with magic."

"We are in the woods, Leila. Nobody would see us." Then using her lovely angel face, Tess begged, "Please…"

Leila became a fan of Tess Viglianco since the moment she saw her at the Tee-Tee Cala Island in Nordache. Their mutual fondness belonged to the very beginning of the journey. As for the moment, by analyzing what Tess just said, Leila accepted the statement as true. The place was deserted, mystic for any charm, perfect for her to practice some spells. Leila experienced a strong desire to please Tess.

"Okay. I am going to exercise some magic, but I can only grant one wish and I am going to let the good fortune of yours, taking care of it. Is that okay?"

Without fully understand Leila's intentions, the children exchanged glances and silently agreed."

Gracefully, Leila moved her arms into the air. Her eyes rapidly engendered a tenacious green color and she fetched from the air; a red pouch. With the same gesture, she created a piece of paper and a reed pen. As the paper floated in the air, she controlled the pen and wrote the children's names on the paper. Then, without touching the paper, she tore apart each name, folded, and tossed the piece of paper into the red pouch. Securely, she grabbed the pouch with her right hand.

Eyeing the children, she explained, "I wrote your names on these pieces of paper. Now, I'll pick one name."

Solemnly, Leila opened the pouch and using her left hand, pulled out a name. Contemplating the children, she proceeded, "The name that is written here will be the child, to *whom*, I will grant a wish. One child and one wish.

The children looked at each other. Their faces mounted into a quirk expectation. Leila unfolded the piece of paper and read, "… Tess." Then… happily repeated, "Miss Tess Viglianco."

Promptly, Tess jumped happily. "Yes…, yes…. I won!"

What the children didn't know was that Leila wrote the name of Tess four times. She wanted to grant a wish to Tess and on that moment nothing could make her change her decision.

David, Lucas, and Olivia gazed at Tess, a lucky ten-year-old girl. Tess found a coin on the street, and now she was in the position to request something. *Let's see what a smart ten-year-old girl would ask.*

While Tess returned her attention to her wish, Leila drew from the air, a thick book; The Bá-Onadi guide for magicians. All the laws of magic were written on it.

"Okay Tess, tell me your wish," replied Leila.

At that instant, an invisible witch appeared next to Tess and whispered something in her ear. The witch said, "Tess, you like dinosaurs. Ask for one." Tess didn't notice a witch had spoken to her as she followed the whisper thinking it was her thoughts.

"I want a dinosaur."

Strangely, Leila underwent into a bizarre impel. She stayed there holding the book with her two hands, her eyes staring at the pages which flipped, and flipped, as fast as possible until abruptly it stopped. Bravely, Leila uttered three words, "SCALRE…! KODASTA…! NIUVA…!"

Magically, a tall dragon appeared in the woods, next to them. Leila recovered from her eerie state, feeling extremely confused. She looked at the children and asked, "What happened?"

"You don't know?" asked Tess.

"No."

"Leila, this is not a dinosaur," said David Dreepel. "It is a dragon."

"Yes. I can see it's a dragon. Where did it come from?"

The dragon began to puff fire out of its mouth, walked away from the children, crossed the invisible grotto and strolled toward the city. The dragon knew where to go and what to do.

"Children, please, tell me what happened?" asked Leila, holding her thick magic book against her chest and following the dragon.

"Forget about what happened," added Olivia. "This dragon is puffing fire from its mouth and it is heading toward the city. If you do not do something, the city of Bonahunta will be on fire."

Walking fast after the dragon, Lucas said, "Leila, I think this happened because some unnatural forces possessed you. A strong power took charge of what you began to do. I felt it."

"Oh, my God! I need to do something."

"And whatever you plan to do, you must do it now," stated Olivia.

Leila and the children stopped walking. Leila glazed around and found a big rock. She ran to it. Leila placed the Bá-Onadi Book on top of the rock and opened it. The children grouped around her to help. They all began to read it.

David Dreepel had the ability to read one thousand words per minute. And he just did that. "QUARELLA," he said. "You have been removed from doing magic by the QUARELLA CURSE. This is what happened. You didn't perform any magic. Another magician did it for you."

"Oh! No…. QUARELLA? This is serious," uttered Leila. "If what you say is true, I'll have no power to stop this dragon and probably I will never become a magician."

"Wait a minute!" said Olivia. "What is this QUARELLA ?"

"Olivia, QUARELLA CURSE, means powerful misfortune," explained Leila. "The worst maledictions that one magician can exercise to another magician. A terrible ordeal."

"Why does David Dreepel know how to read that fast?" asked Lucas in a very intriguing way.

"I don't know," responded David."

The Dragon entered the main street of Bonahunta, puffing fire from its mouth, ready to create chaos. Fire spread all over the street and began to burn the trees and the tents that held merchandise to be sold at the fair. People began to run out of the streets to seek refuge elsewhere. They ran scared without knowing what to do.

"Leila, do something," cried Lucas. "This dragon is going to kill people."

While the dragon advanced, setting fire on the city, Leila, and the children remained checking the book of magic to see what could be done."

David Dreepel was flipping pages, reading fast to find a solution. Leila, tried to read fast too, but she could only roll her fingers over the pages.

Leila," said David Dreepel, "Here. Look at this tittle: THE QUARELLA CURSE."

"Please Leila, do something," pleaded Tess, very scared.

"I can't Tess. I am trapped."

"No, you're not, Leila," said David. He read what he found written under the QUARELLA CURSE.

"Look at this part. Every magician that falls into the QUARELA CURSE, has a few seconds of grace to be used before completely losing any power. The number of seconds is determined by the moon under which the QUARELLA CURSE was executed."

The children remained silent. They did not understand the connotation of David words. It was too complicated.

"Okay David," said Olivia, "Explain it better. Bonahunta is under the third moon. What that means?"

"That means, Leila has three seconds to use her power before she completely loses it."

"Then do something fast," added Tess. "The soldiers from the king will come and kill the dragon. I don't want to see it happening."

"Tess, what is more important? The people of Bonahunta, or the dragon?" inquired Olivia.

"Yes," added Lucas. "If you do not have a better thing to say, then; please…, say nothing. And don't forget that all this is happening because of you. You and your stupid dinosaur's fantasy."

Tess began to cry.

"See Lucas, you made her cry."

"Olivia, she needs to grow up."

David Dreepel had something in mind and quickly, he spoke. "Let's not fight. We need to be focused if we want to help Leila."

"Okay," said the children.

"Leila, you must use these three seconds you have in your favor," said David."

"No, David, I can't save the City of Bonahunta in three seconds."

"Listen Leila, if you do not use these *grace seconds of power* granted to you, magic itself will lose them. It will be three seconds of power, for nothing. You will probably remain trapped in the QUARELLA CURSE for the rest of your life. Do you want this?"

"No."

"Good, because I have a plan."

David eyed the children to see if they all were listening to him. Calmly he said, "Leila, you will use your three seconds of grace to give to me the *supremacy* to give away power. Do you remember what you did with Olivia at the beach in Nordache?"

"Yes."

"So, let's do that, again."

"David, you do not understand magic. I can only give you one minute of power."

"It's fine. There are lots of things that can be done in a minute, trust me."

"David, with this supremacy you also will not be able to give to someone more than a minute of power. And again, nothing will be done. *Gift Power* David, only last for one minute. We can't help this city in one minute."

"No, but I have an idea that might work."

"Okay, explain it better," said Leila.

"With the power you give to me, I will do exactly what you did in Nordache. I will give one minute of power to Lucas, one minute to Olivia, and one minute to Tess. And when I finish giving them the power, I still am going to have a few seconds, left."

Olivia looked at David and said, "Of course…. If you do that, we can have three full minutes of power to use."

"That's right," replied David. "That means: We will have 240 seconds in our favor to play with magic."

Leila began to see what David had in mind. Quickly she said, "Go ahead David, I think I know what you're planning to do, but explain it farther."

"Okay. I will give to Olivia the power to control fire, Lucas will control the rain, Tess will control the wind, and I am going to use the rest of my power to shrink the dragon."

An enormous silence wrapped them. Their minds engaged in something novel. The art of doing magic, mixed with the glimmer of their imagination.

"Marvelous idea," said Leila. "Let's do this now and let's hope for the best."

Leila and the children ran to the city, to the main street. The dragon was there blowing fire all over the city and scared people without mercy.

In the middle of the street Leila and the children stopped. Then, Leila once again, lighted her eyes with tenacious green, and said the magic words. "ALCATEZY…! TELAVERTY…! CARTIERY…!"

Immediately David Dreepel grasped the power and as he planned, used it as quickly as possible. Repeating Leila's words he passed the power to Lucas, Olivia, and Tess.

The children stretched their arms in the air as if they were genuine magicians. At that moment, their eyes held a tenacious look. They confidently, moved their lips and uttered a command. Instantly over the city of Bonahunta, the flames began to diminished, rain fell from the sky and a wind blew away the flames from the trees.

The residents of Bonahunta had never experienced such a vision. They watched the wonder in disbelieve. Some of them viewed it from adjacent little streets and others from behind the debris because they feared the dragon. Then, they witnessed the reduction of size, of the dragon. David Dreepel made it the size of a German Shepperd and secured it in a leash.

With 240 seconds in their favor, these four children saved the city of Bonahunta. The residents saw what they never imagined seeing. Fire, rain, wind, and a dragon reducing size; miraculously, performing at the same time. They saw what they will never forget.

It was magic from the heart.

CHAPTER
6

AFTER SAVING THE CITY of Bonahunta, Leila and the children enjoyed a moment of peace. They felt extremely happy to finally see the calm, once again, on the streets of the city. As the people slowly began returning to the main street, Leila, the children, and the small dragon, walked toward the city entrance to return to the Astafe Castle. They walked freely, captivated with the secrets of power and enjoying the mysticism behind magic.

"David, you had a wonderful idea," commented Leila. "Thank you for such help."

"Indeed David," added Olivia, "We have to admit that your ability to read fast brought us to the final stage of our decisions to save this city. That was impressive!"

"Yes," stated Tess. "Very impressive!"

Lucas quietly observed David. Something about David always intrigued him. "David, how did you learn all these things that you do?" he boldly asked.

David gazed at Lucas thoughtfully.

"No... don't say anything," added Lucas, "Because I know the answer: *I don't know*. Right?"

Smiling, David answered. "Yes. And I am not lying. *I don't know*."

A huge noise disturbed their peace and it came from behind them. It was the king's soldiers. They arrived quickly, riding beautiful horses and in a steady fast manner, surrounded them.

Speedily, one of the soldiers ordered to capture them. In a blink of an eye, they all were brought to the ground, had their hands tied behind the back of their bodies and the dragon trapped into a thick net.

Leila exchanged looks with the children, totally confused. *What is going on?* The soldiers of the King James Lamarcus threw them into a dirt wagon and took them to the Bacellar Castle.

At the castle, the soldiers conducted them to a huge room that had some oval stairs and a lovely stage. Sitting on the stage were King James Lamarcus, his wife Claudia, his lords and knights.

Leila, and the children stood at the bottom of the stairs. They still had their hands tied behind the back of their bodies. King James Lamarcus stood up and quietly, observed them. He was a tall man, thirty-seven years old, with light brown hair covering his shoulder, vivid eyes, and a pleasant beard, neatly trimmed. His wife was also a tall woman, relatively young and very beautiful.

"Who are you and what are you doing here in my city?" asked the king.

"Leila Maglaja, Your Majesty, we are not here to stay. We are traveling."

"You did not answer my question. What are you doing here in my city?"

"We're waiting for Mr. Nicolas Toscapela. He sent us here."

"Ah! You're in trouble, young lady, because Mr. Toscapela is a fake personage in all my books. He jumps from place to place and claimed to be the author of many things. He never proved anything to me. He has no authority in my province, so he shouldn't have sent you here."

"Yes, Your Majesty."

"Where do you stay?"

"We have our own castle. It is near the city, in Campos Vezulio. We will take it with us when we leave."

"You brought a castle here and will take it with you?"

"Yes, Your Majesty."

"How?"

"Magic."

The king became furious. He turned around and with a fist, hit the long table that was there, in the upper part of the stage. Then looking to his lords and knights, King James Lamarcus said, "How come, you… my lords and knights couldn't prevent it?"

"Your Majesty, please," started Leila.

"No, young lady. No magic in my province. Whoever exercises magic here; dies. And today will not be different."

Leila and the children exchanged terrified looks for they understood that this would probably be, the last day of their lives. Definitely, they will die, because the king was furious.

Some seconds ran through and during that time, the king stared at Leila. He wisely controlled his anger. "Young Lady, do you know that I have a son who is supposed to be eleven-years old and is condemned to be a child forever, because of magic? His name is Willian. A scorpion bit my son eight years ago, he was three. He never grew after that. He does not open his eyes or walk. He is a sleeping child. And the witch who did that disappeared. Now, you arrive in my city in an enchanted castle, bringing with you four children, a pathetic dragon, and utter the word MAGIC in my court?"

"Your Majesty, I am sorry," said Leila.

"Sorry?" The king turned to his lords and knights, and said his last words. "You all tell her that I am sorry, too. In my province, magic is condemned. In my province, magicians die. We will hang them today in the Passala Square, exactly like we have done with other magicians."

A huge silence filled the room. Some of the King James' lords did not like the idea of killing children. In fact, this never happened in Bonahunta. Claudia, the king's wife felt petrified. She knew how powerful magic can be and killing children can create another evil curse for the province.

There were five dynasties in My Jupiter Planet, the *Lastenians, the Cotejeeps, Garganás, Fabreus, and Rusharci.* They all spoke English and some other language. The Province of Normabell belonged to the Lastenian dynasty, and aside from English, they spoke Lastenia. The word *Passala*, meant *peace* in Lastenia. So, the real name of the square where King James Lamarcus planned to hung Leila and the children, was *Peace Square.*

Because of what happened with his son, King James Benarde Lamarcus, succeeded in keeping magicians out of his province for almost seven years. He accomplished it by hanging or burning any magician that appeared in town.

During the first year lots of magicians lost their lives in the Province of Normabell, and when the news about the king's new rules spread throughout the province, magicians stopped coming to Bonahunta.

In the course of six years no magician had visited the city, and if someone did, the king never acknowledged it. So, Leila and the children exercised magic in the wrong city. And apparently, the king would have no hesitation or fear, to go on following his rules.

To the residents of Bonahunta, killing magicians had never been news. However, today, aside from the hostile surprises that wobbled the peace of the city—the presence of the dragon; another bizarre event was about to happen.

In a few hours, Bonahunta would stage the cruel act of killing young people because of magic. And like always, no one had any power to stop what was about to happen.

As the words of King James Lamarcus floated inside the Bacellar Castle, his lords and knights remained silent with one question in mind. *Will the king have the courage to do what he just said?*

Bonahunta, had the utmost benediction any god could give away and the harsh curses any dark magician could spell. The Otela Moon was a powerful moon and its power carried the vestige of great surprises.

Sitting there in the upper stage, facing Leila and the children, the court of King James Lamarcus forgot that compassion galvanizes the heart. Neither the king, nor his lords could predict anything under the Otela Moon, because what could be predicted goes against the sway of this moon.

King James Lamarcus may believe that by killing magicians he will protect his province; nevertheless, at the end of his cruelties, he could encounter awful revelations. The reality dwelled like a ghost in the air or behind the fog of so many mysticisms.

Truly speaking yes, *magic...* in many ways could be dangerous; *surprises...* all the time revelations; and *power...* definitely, potent. Exactly, under this atypical trilogy lingered the Otela Moon.

What will be next to the City of Bonahunta?

CHAPTER
7

THE KING FINISHED HIS order and prepared to leave the room. He was infuriated and showed his dissatisfaction to his lords and knights.

The king took three steps to leave and stopped. He looked at Leila one last time. "You not only violated my rules young lady—using magic in my province—but you also brought a dragon which destroyed part of my city and scared my people. Nobody died, but people got hurt and tents caught fire. How dare you?"

"Your Majesty, *bruque, ginar par lunera?* said David Dreepel. In Lastenia it meant: Please, may I speak?

"Oh! Do you speak Lastenia?" asked King James Lamarcus.

"A little bit. Enough to communicate," responded David.

"And why do you know this language?

Lucas, Olivia, and Tess, exchanged looks. In their minds they knew what David would say. *I don't know.*

"I don't know, Your Majesty," answered David. Exactly as his friends predicted.

"If you don't know why do you speak Lastenia, what can you possibly have to say, that will interest me?"

"I do have something you will like to hear."

"Okay. You can speak," stated King James Lamarcus.

David Dreepel turned around and looked at his friends. Then he took three steps forward and returned his attention to King James.

"I am David Dreepel, and I am responsible for all that happened in your city today. Please hang me. Let my friends go. We're not real magicians. We don't know how this dragon really appeared in the woods. It seemed that we all fell under a dreadful spell. Everything was a mistake. Please don't kill them."

"Why should I accept your request? I am the king. I am going to kill you all. I don't do magic. My power is real. Aside from that, I have nothing to lose."

"Yes, you do, Your Majesty," replied David."

"I beg your pardon?"

"You do have something to lose if you kill Leila Maglaja."

"Okay. Go on, tell me," said King Lamarcus on the verge of losing his patience.

"Leila is from Lili Sandra, where the Red Scorpion that can cure your son, has disappeared. If you keep her alive, she will find the scorpion for you. *Par dolshe.*" *Par dolshe* meant: I swear.

King James Lamarcus held his words to himself. Now he studied his options. Nothing mattered more to him than seeing his son free from that spell.

"How do you know about the Red Scorpion?" asked the king.

DAVID DREEPEL

"You have sent great magicians and skilled hunters all over the Province of Bonavery looking for the red scorpion. People talk."

"Yes, replied the king. "People *cabari*." *Cabari* in Lastenia meant: talk.

"Tu mar shercy," responded David. In Lastenia, it meant: All the time.

Claudia Lamarcus, the queen, left her chair and approached her husband. She uttered in his ear what she had in mind. "James, listen to this young man," said the queen, "Spare Leila and the children. Follow your heart. I know you. You'll never have the courage to kill four children."

King Lamarcus eyed his wife. She constantly found a way to stay connected with her good instincts and regularly, introduce perpetual impact in his vital decisions.

"She did magic in my city, Claudia" added the king.

"Yes. But she knows every square inch of Lili Sandra. Think about that. Before, we never had anybody from Lili Sandra hunting for the Red Scorpion. People from Lili Sandra grew afraid of it. This quest terrified them and I don't know why. She could be the hunter we need and the magician that will uncover the dark side of this crossing."

The king silently, examined his wife wishes. She desired to see her son cured as much as him. During these terrible eight years, nobody could find the Red Scorpion. The king had employed the weirdest sorcerers he could find and had hired the utmost skilled hunters the province possessed, and nothing. The red scorpion was nowhere to be found.

From the upper stage, the king spoke to David. "I don't believe that a young lady, named Leila Maglaja, from Lili Sandra—out of the blue—will solve the mystery of the Red Scorpion. This is absurd but, the opportunity to see the results of such an idiocy charms my curiosity. In fact, the illogical would be kill Leila without knowing how silly this whole matter can be."

The king glanced at his lords to see if they agreed about what had been said. Some of them answered by holding a simple smile on their lips.

"Okay, David Dreepel," King James stated, "I accept your proposition. I will kill only you. Today, you'll be hung by my charge."

After that, the king turned to his soldiers and ordered, "Take care of the afternoon activity. David Dreepel will be hanging today, at 4:30 and I want the people of Bonahunta present at the Passala Square to witness the execution."

The king looked at Leila one last time. He told her his last wishes. "You will be prisoner of this castle, until you prove to me that you are capable to find the Red Scorpion. Do you understand?"

"Yes, Your Majesty."

As soon as King James Lamarcus uttered his last words, he turned to exit the room.

"Your Majesty," called Leila.

The king again stopped and quietly looked at Leila.

"Keeping me and the children in prison is not very smart," she explained, "Because in prison, I can't hunt for the Red Scorpion. In prison, I can't prove anything. The Red Scorpion does not live forever. Actually, it lives only twenty-five years. If your son was supposed to be eleven-years old, you already lost eight years since the spell. The Red Scorpion can survive by eating one insect per year and can sleep the entire year. When it sleeps it doesn't increase his poison and without the poison, we cannot lift the curse. The scorpion is not living outside, like the other animals. Somebody has it. According to what I already said you can see it will take more common sense to find and trap the Red Scorpion, than anything else."

"Common sense? What a pathetic conversation," said the king.

"No. A fierce knowledge, Your Majesty."

"How do you know so much about scorpions? You are too young."

"I am twenty-two.

"Like I said, 'Too young'."

"Your Majesty, I have learned common sense when I was still a child. Perhaps that is why my mind is sometimes… sharp."

"Where do you want to go with this conversation, young lady?"

"If I prove to you that I am smart enough to go after the Red Scorpion, would you let the children…me…and the dragon leave today?"

"I don't know. I don't trust witches. You will use magic to prove to me that you're smart."

"No. I will not. I am going to prove to you that I am capable to do what I propose. I can find the Red Scorpion for you. I can help you lift the spell which is harming your son. This is different."

"How different?"

"Would you let me prove it here, in front of you, your wife, and your lords and knights?"

Again, Claudia Lamarcus, the queen, approached the king. And again… she whispered in his ear. "Allow her to do what she wants. I like her confidence. She's young and wise."

The king knew he must please his wife, because what Leila had said about the Red Scorpion surprised them. Leila knew facts about the animal, they never heard about. Perhaps, the queen's intuition will bring good results.

Confidently, the king ordered everyone to stay in the room and he also returned to his seat to watch what Leila Maglaja could possibly do to convince his court she was smart.

Leila approached one of the soldiers that brought them to the Bacellar Castle and asked him to untie her hands. From the stage the king moved his head, allowing the soldier to do what Leila had asked.

After being released, Leila climbed the stairs and arrived on the upper stage. Humbly, she walked and stopped near the king.

"Your, Majesty, please, may I have your ring?"

"My ring?"

"Yes."

Queen Claudia, eyed her husband ensuring he would do what Leila requested. Following that, Leila asked the queen for one of her long gloves. With the ring and the gloves in hand, Leila walked toward the big table that was at the stage. At the table, she lifted the ring in the air, so everybody could see it. Next, she lifted the queen's glove to make sure everyone was watching. Calmly, Leila tossed the ring inside the glove.

"I am Leila Maglaja, and I am going to proof to this court that I can remove the king's ring out of the queen's gloves, without touching the gloves. And Your Majesty, I am going to do that without using any magic."

Leila paused for a second and silently, glanced at her audience.

The quietness of the room enlarged the space between Leila and the people around the court.

"Your Majesty, King James Lamarcus, do I have your word that I can leave with the children and the dragon today, if I do what I have proposed?"

The king thoughtfully, eyed his wife. Queen Claudia moved her head affirming that, *yes*. He should agree. The king looked at Leila and answered, "Yes. You have my word."

Leila folded the glove and placed it on the center of the table. Then, she asked the king in what he believed. The king said that he believed in God Eller, which is the god of My Jupiter.

Leila, humbly, knelt down in front of the table. She brought her head down to the floor and closed her eyes as if she was praying. She let the whole court of King James Lamarcus think she was pleading to God Eller.

A few seconds later, she opened her eyes and stood up. Imposingly, she looked at everyone. At the moment their faces held a tenacious wonder.

"Your Majesty," she said, "Please, chose one of your lords or knights to come to the table and check the queen's glove."

The King ordered one of his knights to go and do what Leila had asked. The chosen knight approached the table, grabbed the queen gloves, and inserted his hand in it. Instantly, his lips moved to deliver a soft smile. He held the ring and pulled it out of the gloves.

"Your Majesty, look!" said the knight, "She didn't do anything. Here is the ring." The knight lifted it in the air, so everybody could see the king's ring.

"Your Majesty," added Leila, "I just did what I had proposed. I brought the ring out without touching the queen's gloves and without using magic."

At that instant, everybody realized what Leila just did. She fooled them all.

"Young lady," said the king infuriated. He stood up and added, "You disrespected me, my lords and my knights, and used God Eller to trick my court."

"No, Your Majesty. I didn't use your god. What happened here has nothing to do with God Eller. I only asked you in what you believe because I have to connect you with some faith, otherwise, you would not allow one of your knights to come and check the queen's glove. I had to make you believe that I was using some power. In that case, the power of your god. But as you all know, there is no power involved in what I just did. No power of god and no power of magic. Simply astuteness."

"No. You tricked me. To the prison you go."

The queen… again… whispered in the king's ear, and this time, they exited to another room. "James, you will honor your word, because this young lady did what she said she would do. Yes, she tricked us all, however; she acted genuinely. The last time you did not honor your word, we had one year of plague in this city. I don't want to see something like that happening all over again."

Sadly, the king eyed his wife. It was a long glare, "If I keep doing everything you wish, I am going to lose authority and respect."

"No. You will not. Let them go. Send a soldier to watch them at all times. Order them to stay in town until Mr. Nicolas Toscapela comes. Then we meet with him."

"Claudia, Mr. Nicolas Toscapela, has no jurisdiction in my province. He is the most mysterious person I have ever met. He claimed to be a lot of things and nothing at the same time. He traveled the whole planet in furtive ways and visits all the king's courts as if he were a sort of god. I don't what to meet with him."

"He is *queconiche,*" said the queen. *Queconiche* in Lastenia meant perverso.

"Yes, queconiche," replied the king.

"So, because of such a characteristic, it is better to have him as a friend instead of an enemy. Think about it," added the queen.

The king closed his eyes in reverence of what had been said. Quietly, he evaluated the situation. He hated this kind of negotiation, when he had to antagonize his own decisions. His mind surfaced the edges of his head and when, once again, he opened his eyes, only frustration flashed out of them. He decided to free Leila, the children, and the dragon. He would wait for Mr. Nicolas Toscapela.

The king returned to the stage where his lords and knights remained waiting. He approached Leila, and said, "Young lady… at his time you will have what you wish. You can leave with the children and the dragon. You're free to go to your magic castle; however, you must remain there until Mr. Nicolas Toscapela arrives. Meanwhile, two of my soldiers will be guarding the castle. Don't try anything foolish because I hate myself when I lose patience and I can promise you, that if this happen; *you*—probably—will hate me more."

"Yes, Your Majesty. Thank you."

After that, the soldiers untied the children and guided them outside the Bacellar Castle. After they got the dragon, they all walked together to the Astafe Castle. At the Passala Square they saw some of the king's soldiers securing the place where David Dreepel would be hanged. There were lots of activities, already going on.

"Leila, we have to save David," said Olivia.

"I don't know how. I lost my power in the woods, remember? There is nothing that I can do."

"Call Mr. Nicolas Toscapela," added Lucas.

"I can't. I don't have the power to communicate with him. Now, we're at our own destiny. And we need to be together to survive."

"Leila, I don't care about what you say. We must save David," replied Tess.

"How, Tess? Tell me how?"

"With magic, with God Eller, or Mr. Toscapela, but David cannot die."

"I have saved us and nobody thanked me for that. Only saving *David* matters right now, right?"

Together the children looked at Leila. She was right, they never thanked her. "Thank you, Leila," they uttered in union.

After that Olivia spoke, she kindly said, "Leila, in front of King Lamarcus' court, you acted like a real magician. With your wise mind, you did save us from being prisoners. I will never forget that."

Lucas also said something, "Yes, thank you for acting so cleverly. You were amazing."

"You're welcome," responded Leila. "Now, let's face the new reality. We are in a big problem. There are two soldiers outside watching us. And we must start thinking how we will start hunting for the Red Scorpion. The king will never forget that I promised to find it."

DAVID DREEPEL

"As I understood," added Olivia, "The scorpion is in Lili Sandra. How will we get there?"

"Forget about Lili Sandra," added Tess. "Now, we need to save David. We must try."

"In about forty minutes, he will be executed," added Lucas. "We need to decide what to do. Tess is right. We will never forgive ourselves if we turn our back on him. Let's use our imagination."

Leila and the children separated from each other so their minds would be free to work. Lucas, Olivia and Leila remained inside the castle, but Tess walked through the back of it and sat in the garden where earlier, they had lunch. She had her mind focus in this mission—save David Dreepel.

She glanced around and saw the bridge they had crossed and she remembered the Rastaga Woods and all that happened there. The enigmatic force of it again, played with her mind. "Of course, the Rastaga Woods. There—I will find help," she said out loud.

Tess, looked around to ensure no one was looking and ran through the bridge, crossed it, and furtively walked into the woods. She believed that only magic could save David and she wished to find a sorcerer to help her.

Tess walked into the woods and before advancing inside it, she called for help. A little bit scared, she looked up and spoke. "Hello...! Somebody, please come and help. At 4:30 in the afternoon King James Lamarcus will hang my friend David Dreepel. Please help me save him."

As her voice traveled through the woods, a woman appeared between the trees. She had half of her face covered with a white cloak, only her eyes were visible. She was not very old, had long

65

blonde hair and wore a long blue, silk gown.

The woman looked at Tess. She said nothing.

Nervously, Tess examined the stranger.

"Who are you?" the lady finally asked.

"Tess Viglianco. My friend David Dreepel will be hanging today in the Passala Square, please help me save him.

"You are too young to be walking alone in these woods. Aren't you afraid?"

"I am. But I need to save my friend. King James Lamarcus is going to hang him."

The woman walked slowly around Tess and gingerly studied her. Suddenly, she stopped. Calmly, she took a lovely Purple Talisman she had around her neck and placed it on Tess neck.

"Take it with you", said the woman. "It will allow us to communicate. When I arrived in these woods, I slept for eighteen months. Almost two years. And I dreamt a lot. In one of my dreams, a fairy came and gave to me this Talisman. She told me that one day, a girl will come to these woods and she instructed me to give my Talisman to the girl. She explained to me that this would be the beginning of my communication with the outside world."

"Wow...! I am happy that I came," replied Tess.

"Me, too. It took so long for someone to come that I thought the fairy was only a product of my imagination. For a long time, I believed, no one will ever come to these woods."

"Why do you live here?" asked Tess.

"Oh! Some bad magicians are responsible for it. I don't know why. Forget about me. You do not have time to waste."

"Okay," perhaps, everything is happening for a reason," responded

Tess respectfully.

"Certainly."

"Now. Listen to me. I need your help to save my friend. Would you help me?"

"I don't need to help you," said the kind lady. "But I am going to tell you a secret. Do you know that you have the power to control the wind?"

"Do I? All the time?"

"Yes. You cannot use it for foolishness, but you can use it for a good purpose. And today, during the execution, if you create a little gust of wind, everything in the ambience will change and your friend will escape."

"Really. How?"

"Magic."

"Can I do magic?"

"Yes. Go. Trust me."

"Who are you?"

"I am Queen Naelia."

"From where?"

"I don't know. I only remember that I am Queen Naelia, and prisoner of these woods. I am not a magician, however, under the third moon, I can see a little bit of the future. Your friend is not going to die. Go to the square and bring some wind into the land. That's all. Don't tell anybody what I told you about your power. They don't want you to know that you have it all the time."

"Who doesn't want for me to know that?"

"People. Besides that, you're a child. No one will trust you."

Tess eyed the queen suspiciously.

"Go," said the queen, "If you don't leave now, you'll not make to the square on time."

Tess ran out of the woods, with only one wish in her heart; save David Dreepel.

Queen Naelia watched the girl darting out of the woods as if she just learned how to run and was eager to practice it. Queen Naelia brought to her lips her best smiled in eight years. The fairy said she would meet a girl under the third moon, so her connection with the outside word would be established. She thought it would never happen, for children never came to those woods. Queen Naelia inhaled in, gently. Thousands of thoughts visited her mind. *Perhaps... this is the girl the fairy predicted. Tess Viglianco.... Her chosen savior.*

CHAPTER
8

THE MINUTE THE NEWS about the king's pending activity reached out, the residents of Bonahunta instigated an interesting conversation. According to them, if the Otela Moon is the surprised moon; another peculiar manifestation was about to happen. They sensed the eerie aspect of it dangling in the air.

The residents of Bonahunta stopped their activities, which was cleaning the debris from the tents and streets, to go to the Passala Square to witness the show King James Lamarcus planned for the afternoon—an act of cruelty. No one knew what was going to happen with David Dreepel.

The king's soldiers appeared in groups, making sure everything would be ready for 4:30 p.m. Some of the king's workers created an upper deck to the center of the square and also brought a wooden box to place David Dreepel's dead body.

As the hours advanced, shorting the afternoon, around the residents of Bonahunta, rested the alarming expectation of all times.

What would happen? Will the king have courage to go on with such an atrocity? It will either be—the king's wishes or... magic?

Tess hastily bounced inside the Astafe Castle and found Leila, Lucas and Olivia, in the dining room. Their faces showed great distress, for they had been looking for her and couldn't find her anywhere. Aside from that, they looked extremely agitated because the time they had at hand, to help David, was shortening by seconds. Nothing really relevant came to their minds. They felt lost, discouraged, and powerless. When Tess rushed in, they were on the verge of giving up.

"I know how to save David," yelled Tess as soon as she saw them.

"Where have you been?" asked Olivia.

"It doesn't matter where I was. The good news is that I can save David."

"How?"

"Let's go to the square. I need to be there."

Leila and the other three children did not understand, but decided to follow Tess. They couldn't afford to lose time, so all the questions would have to wait. In a fast fashion, they walked to the square. The two soldiers, King James sent to watch them, also followed them.

At the square, they encountered the peculiar atmosphere Bonahunta always had, when somebody would die by the king's order. David Dreepel would be just another precarious human being, a miserable young boy who will become part of the history of Bonahunta.

The amount of people in the Passala Square elevated the importance of the event. It was unbelievable how fast the citizens stopped their activities to witness the death of a person. Beyond a doubt, David Dreepel failed to be a famous person, but he would gain the attention of the whole city for being the youngest boy to have ever been hung.

At 4:25 p.m., King James Lamarcus, his wife Claudia, his lords and knights, arrived to witness the execution. Underneath the hanging poles, there was a black chair, so David could stand on it. At the exact time King James desired the execution, two soldiers arrived with David Dreepel. At that moment, only magic could save that boy and Tess happened to be the only one, who knew it by heart. She hoped she could do what she had in mind.

David climbed up onto the black chair and the hangman placed the rope around his neck. David Dreepel never thought a bad fortune like that would ever come his way. While the people of Bonahunta, quietly looked at David, King James stood up and said, "This is David Dreepel. Remember his name, *David Dreepel.* He claimed he is responsible for what happened here today. This silly dragon and the fire. He denied being a magician, but couldn't explain how the dragon appeared in the woods and walked through the city. You know the laws of my province regarding magic. No magic should ever be exercised in my city. Never. So, like the other magicians, he must die."

The king raised his hand and claimed. "Should David Dreepel die?"

The people answered, "Yes…!"

Again, the king claimed, "Should David Dreepel die?"

"Yes…!" responded the crowd.

The king turned his head to the hangman and ordered the

execution. The whole square mounted into heavenly silence. At the edge of the deck, between people, Tess Viglianco closed her eyes and wished for the wind to come.

Miraculously, a soft, stiff breezy began to cross the land. The wind went on lifting sand from the ground, filling peoples' eyes with dust and carrying away hats. Everybody moved their eyes away from David Dreepel. People were either protecting their eyes from the filthy air, or holding their hats over their heads. It took only a few seconds for the blast to travel through the Passala Square; however, when the blast vanished, David Dreepel was no longer present.

On top of the hanging pole, there was an innocent grasshopper. A grasshopper that no one even noticed. A grasshopper that jumped away as if it was never there.

"Where is he?" asked King James furiously.

No one could answer.

"Soldiers, look for him in the crowd. He couldn't have run far. Trap him and bring him back."

For the rest of the afternoon the soldiers hunted for David Dreepel. They checked everywhere, even at the Astafe Castle. David Dreepel, simply, disappeared.

At the Astafe Castle, the children gathered around the dining table. They had questions for Tess.

"Did you create the breeze?" asked Leila.

"No," answered Tess. "I only prayed to Eller."

"You're lying," added Olivia.

"I am not."

"You said you knew how to save David," stated Lucas.

"Yes, I did. That's why I prayed to Eller to bring a wind, so people would be distracted and David probably would have a chance to escape. My idea worked. And my prayers were powerful."

"I don't believe you, Tess," replied Olivia. "I am your sister. Do not forget that I know you more than you can imagine."

"None of us believe you," stated Lucas decisively.

"Why not...? Her idea worked, and your friend didn't die," said a calm, familiar voice belonging to a man who stealthily came in.

"Mr. Nicolas Toscapela?" replied Olivia and Leila at the same time.

"Hello children," he said. "Hello Leila."

Tess came closer and hugged him. "Mr. Toscapela! Oh, it is so good to see you again."

"Yes, Tess. I feel the same."

A brief silence filled the dining room. For a slight moment the children rejoiced over the surprise. Since the encounter in Gargatuela, they hadn't seen each other.

"Oh, look what I have on my shoulder," said Mr. Toscapela, "A lovely grasshopper. I found it at the entrance, on the steps of the castle.

Mr. Toscapela, brought his finger closer and the grasshopper climbed on it. Carefully, Mr. Toscapela set the grasshopper on the edge of the dining table.

Tess examined it curiously. "It is as beautiful as the one we saw in Tee-Tee Cala."

The children began to move closer to the table to observe the grasshopper. They all agreed it was indeed, as lovely as the one from Tee-Tee Cala.

"Children tell me about the dragon," said Mr. Toscapela,

intending to grasp their attention.

"He is outside," replied Olivia. "Come to see it."

They all left the house to see the dragon. Outside Olivia asked, "How do you know about the dragon? Leila lost her power, she can't communicate with you."

"Through a crystal ball, I saw the dragon setting fire on the city. That's why I came."

The children remained quiet, observing the ancient man. "Mr. Toscapela, are we going to see David Dreepel again?" asked Tess.

"Of course. He must be hiding somewhere, waiting for things to calm down.

"He almost died and to make things even worse, Leila now is in big trouble. She has to find the Red Scorpion."

"Everything will be fine," stated Mr. Toscapela.

They approached the little cage where the dragon had been trapped. "Look Mr. Toscapela", said Tess. "Isn't he a beautiful dragon?"

"Yes.... Indeed.... But his size is pathetic for a dragon. We must change it."

"Are you going to let us keep him?"

"I will, Tess. But let's change his size. What about a middle-sized dragon? Does everybody agree with it?"

"Yes," answered the children in harmony.

"Great!"

Mr. Toscapela opened the cage and freed the dragon. Then, he lifted his head, refreshed the color of his eyes and said, "TUATAN...! TRASMOTA...! ULITRAGA...!"

The little dragon, which was the size of a German shepherd,

curved his long neck all the way back, until his head easily touch the ground. In a dramatic way he stretched his body, wiggled, twirled, then enlarged his feet and wings. He changed into a charming middle size dragon, kindly and inoffensive.

The dragon cheerfully blinked his eyes and released a friendly puff out of his mouth, a soft little fire. He brought his face close to the children as if all the time he knew them.

"Now, he needs a name," said Mr. Toscapela.

The children immediately agreed.

"Hmm! What could be a good name for a friendly dragon?" commented Olivia.

As the children involved their minds into the subject, Mr. Toscapela added, "I have a good name for him, if you all agree with it."

The children eyed the ancient man with countless interest. Calmly, Mr. Toscapela spoke. "One time I traveled to a planet called Earth. I was doing my experiment with Surdrape Time Fold Passage. I arrived at the beach and I saw people dancing on the sand. They had a thing called radio, playing music, and a wooden stick in their hands. While two people held the ends of the stick, the others kept dancing and passing underneath it. Every time, they started a new line, they moved the stick closer to the sand. The dancers needed to curve more and more toward their back to pass underneath it, without touching the stick. The name of the song was Limbo Rock."

The children didn't say anything. They took a moment to picture the dancers in their minds. They saw people curving toward their back, exactly like the dragon did when he was changing size.

"I like Limbo Rock, Mr. Toscapela," affirmed Tess.

"Yes, it is very unusual," replied Lucas.

"I agree with Lucas," said Olivia. "I love the idea of having a dragon with the name of a song."

"What do you think Leila?" asked Tess.

"Limbo Rock, is perfect. A unique name for… a special dragon."

They secured the dragon with a long chain and returned to the house. Inside, a great surprised waited for them. David Dreepel was in the dining room, sitting at the table, eating a sandwich that Mrs. Clenilde prepared for him.

"David…!" yelled the children happily. They ran closer to hug him.

"Are you okay?" asked Leila concerned.

"I am fine, Leila. Very hungry, but fine."

"Mr. Toscapela is here," added Lucas.

"Hello, Mr. Toscapela," said David looking up.

"Hello David. Nice seeing you again."

David breathed in deeply. He grabbed the glass with water and drank some.

"Mr. Toscapela, I don't know if I feel the same about you. Seeing you again only implies I can quickly engage in the complexity of my existence, right? Nothing else."

"I understand your frustration," responded Mr. Toscapela. "The end of your life suddenly emerged in front of your face as a terrible joke. It is okay to feel scared."

Tess walked around the table, examining the edge of it and investigating the floor. "Hmm! Where's the grasshopper?" she asked.

Lucas turned and said, "I bet you it disappeared again. Like always."

Suddenly, loud voices coming from the entrance of the castle stopped their conversation. Without a warning a knight, authoritatively, began forcing his way into the castle. Mr. Inbacula had to urgently block him.

"No Sir. You wait here."

To avoid visitors advancing to the dining room and seeing David Dreepel, Mr. Toscapela immediately, asked the children to remain in the dining room. Meanwhile, he walked to the entrance of the castle.

"Hello," said the knight, assuming the ancient man was Mr. Toscapela. "I am—"

"Vermascu," finished Mr. Toscapela. "I know who you are. You're the most valued knight in the King James Lamarcus' court. I must be of great importance, for the king to send you to pick me up."

"Yes, Sir. He wants to see you, urgently."

Kindly, Mr. Toscapela showed the knight the way out and together, they climbed into the carriage the knight brought and left.

Inbacula returned to the dining room to inform Leila and the children what happened. After having their attention, he said, "Mr. Toscapela just left to see King James Lamarcus."

"Oh, this is not good," replied Olivia, instantly, "The king will hold him prisoner."

"No," said Leila. "Mr. Toscapela will never be a prisoner of any king. He can deal with King James without any problem. He will be fine."

At the Bacellar Castle, Mr. Toscapela was taken to a private room where King James and his wife Queen Claudia, were waiting for him. The Knight Vermascu and Mr. Toscapela entered the room and humbly, Mr. Toscapela bowed saying, "Your Majesty."

"Mr. Nicolas Toscapela…," uttered the king, "Let's move to the table, to sit down for an honest conversation. You have been on my mind for too long."

"I may say the same, Your Majesty. I have been thinking *a lot* about you, lately."

At the table, the king said, "Mr. Toscapela, I need to know why you sent that young witch to my city. She appeared here with an enchanted castle, four children, and a pathetic dragon. The dragon set fire to my city, she fooled me in front my lords and knights, and David Dreepel used magic to disappear in the moment I was going to execute him."

Contemplating the king with rash thoughts in mind, Mr. Toscapela explained, "Your Majesty, first, we need to clarify things. For example; Leila is not a witch, the dragon is not pathetic, and David is not a magician. They arrived here for a specific reason and we all will leave tomorrow morning."

"What specific reason?" asked the king.

"I can't tell you."

"I am your king."

"No. I bowed to you in respect, but you're not my king. You are the king of the Province of Normabell. And for your information, the Province of Normabell exists, only because I am a man of great vision. That's all."

"You're not God, Nicolas."

"Neither are you, King James. Slow down your rage for it could complicate the fruition of the events. Leila will find the Red Scorpion for you."

"What about, David Dreepel?"

"Forgive him for the sake of your wife."

"What does my wife have to do with David Dreepel?"

"David is part of the quest to find the Red Scorpion. Leila can't do this without him. Having the prince cured would be the best thing this court will ever see. Lifting this enchantment will be good for everyone; specially your wife."

A long silence filled the room. Mr. Toscapela kept his eyes on Queen Claudia. He knew she would speak next.

"Mr. Toscapela, you talk about me as if I have secrets," added the queen.

"And I can talk about your secrets if you desire, Your Majesty."

"Are you disrespecting my wife?" snapped the king.

"No. But because of her, all of this is happening. Her aristocracy will be lost if her son dies."

The king eyed his wife. He remained speechless for an instant. "Is this true, Claudia. You married me to save your family name?"

"Yes, James. In the beginning that was the reason, but I fell in love with you. You changed my way of seeing this arrangement and now I also love my son."

"Your Majesty, be good with her. She's a good woman," added Mr. Nicolas Toscapela.

"You don't tell me what to do."

Standing to depart, Mr. Toscapela added, "No. You're right."

Thoughtfully, the king stared at Mr. Toscapela. He felt

uncomfortable in his presence. Mr. Toscapela always knew what to say.

"If your Majesty does not have a reason to retain me here, please, I'd rather leave. The air inside this room is turning thick and you have been insolent. So...truavec." In Lastenia language, *truavec* meant goodbye.

"I never liked you. And I never will," added King James. "You always speak about everything and nothing in parallel's podiums of connotations. To understand *you* is NOT TO HATE YOU; and TO NOT HATE YOU, is to be engaged in the bizarre course of your existence—which floats between shadows."

"Impeccable description about what is– NOT TO HATE ME and what is TO HATE ME. I like the way you see it, but don't you ever forget that—WHAT FLOATS—between shadows, coexists exactly to empower you… as a king."

"See…. Again…. You in front of me, with your bizarre way of talking. *Truavec!* Get out of my castle."

CHAPTER
9

NIGHT STROKED THE SKY of Bonahunta and nothing out of the ordinary happened. In the Astafe Castle, during dinner, Mr. Nicolas Toscapela informed Leila and the children that on the next day they would be leaving to Lili Sandra. Leila must appear in front the administrators of Loyporsha Magic School because of the incident at the Rastaga Woods.

She should have never taken the children to those woods. The innocent mistake may cost her the fulfilment of her dreams. Easily, she could be casting out of the magic school—she may never become a magician.

On the next day, after breakfast, they prepared to leave. Carefully, Mr. Inbacula brought the dragon inside the castle. Following that, Mr. Toscapela and Leila stepped out of it.

Mr. Toscapela raised his head and flashed out of his eyes, inflexible orange rays. Intentionally, he reduced the size of the castle, like Leila did before. He converted it into a souvenir size.

Then, silently, Leila picked it up, tossed it inside her dress pocket, looked around, and waited.

"Ready, Leila?" Mr. Toscapela asked.

"Yes, Sir."

Mr. Nicolas Toscapela, extended his cane, drew a line on the ground. The line turned orange and mysteriously, lifted in the air, folded in half, and in slow motion seesawed a couple of times; unfolded, and returned to the ground. As expected, Mr. Nicolas Toscapela said the magic words.

"DRIVABA...! ANAPOLENTRA...! MARGOREL...!" Confidently, Leila and Mr. Nicolas Toscapela crossed it, and vanished.

In Lili Sandra, Mr. Toscapela placed the Astafe Castle outside of the city, at the bottom of three gorgeous mountains, the Newzuma Valley; a valley full of birds, flowers, gorgeous trees, and an exquisite waterfall. From the valley, Leila and the children could walk to the city. Lili Sandra, also known as: The Gift City, held the best magic school of the Province of Bonavery.

The children strolled out of the castle, less surprised than the last time. They began to get use to the idea that whoever was in charge of their journey, would not let them know more than what they should. According to their latest discovery, getting out of the Astafe Castle in a different place could be consequence of *superb magic*, or simple the reward of a *unique routine*. They must keep going to understand their existence.

Lili Sandra entered their lives just to set the trail they must embrace to fulfill the next expedition. They all knew the upcoming pursue would keep them busy. The chase of the Red Scorpion will probably be a tenacious search and it must start soon. Behind this surprising quest, lingered the continuation of their lives, the core of their beliefs and the thrill of their expectations. In this frantic path of mystery, magic will be changing the past into the future and the future into the past. The children had no idea *how* and *when* the end would come.

For the mystery—the life of a prince rested behind a dreadful curse. For the magic—Leila, a young woman strived for the gift of making magic. Then for the journey—four children collapsed into a complex labyrinth of fictional incantation. Should the city of Lili Sandra, welcome the animation or should the animation welcome the city? The answers, like always, dangled far away concealed by the power of imagination.

On the morning they landed in Lili Sandra, Mr. Toscapela and the children accompanied Leila to the Magic school. Leila's misfortune suddenly turned out to be the priority in Mr. Toscapela's agenda. Nothing would happen until Leila's affairs were taking care of.

In fact, two reasons forged his priority. One had to do with Loyporcha Magic School decision. If Leila was expelled from the school, there would be no need to lift the QUARELLA CURSE. If she couldn't become a magician, it won't matter about living under the spell. She would never be able to do magic, anyway. On the other hand, if the school, for some reason, granted her another chance, then she needed to lift the QUARELLA CURSE quickly, before the time expired.

When they arrived at the school for Leila's hearing, every member of the Loyporcha Magic School Board of Administration, had been already present at the upper part of the marvelous library, waiting for them.

Before, Mr. Toscapela came to Bonahunta, he stopped at Lili Sandra and spoke with the administrators of Loyporcha Magic School, because he knew of what had happened at Rastaga Woods. He saw Leila's encounter in a crystal ball, and, in every way, he was responsible for Leila's training.

All the members of the board of administration must ware Ceburda Cloaks when at school teaching or conducting any type of drudgery. The cloaks were black on the outside and colorful on the inside. Usually, they appeared in *black* and *green*, *black* and *yellow*, *black* and *blue*, *black* and *purple*, or *black* and *orange*. The rank of the member created the color of the Ceburda. Magician with high ranking and seniors' status wore black and purple or black and orange Ceburdas.

Another entity that characterized the rank of magicians was the color of the light that zoomed out of their eyes when performing any magic. In the laws of magic, students and beginning magicians could only yield green lights.

The city of Lili Sandra was located in the Province of Bonavery, which was ruled by King Cesar Montanara. The Montanara family belonged to the Cotejeeps Dynasty, the strongest Dynasty in the country. When Mr. Nicolas Toscapela and the children entered the Loyporsha Magic School, one of Cesar Montanara's soldiers escorted them to the majestic school library. The largest library in the Province of Bonavery.

Leila's mother, Marcela Festalma Maglaja, was present. She wore the black and blue Ceburda, which was the last color before the two highest ones. As soon as she saw Leila, she walked toward her.

Anxiously, Marcela hugged her daughter. "Leila, my dear!" she uttered. "I am so sorry you're facing this tribulation. Trust our judgment. You're not the first student facing such a misfortune. You're young and this was your first mistake. The professors always have *such a factor* under consideration. Please, hope for the best."

"Thank you, mother. Let the fundamental force of magic decide. I know I made a mistake."

After that, Leila moved to the upper part of the library and sat at the gigantic rectangular table. She occupied the middle of the table and nine professors wearing their impeccable Ceburdas occupied the seats around her.

Professor Breno Coorbell spoke first. "Leila Maglaja, it is hard to believe that you are here facing such an ordeal. My dear… my dear… you…. One of my best students. What happened?"

"Professor Coorbell, I don't know. I cannot understand why I missed the dangerous facts of Rastaga Woods. I read the Bá-Onadi book three times. You know me. I have been always careful with my studies. In that case, I either read it and forget or some spell erased it from my mind. I have no other explanation."

A brief silence traveled through the library. The children and Mr. Nicolas Toscapela watched the nine professors checking the books scattered over the table. They did everything ceremonially and in slow motion, as if even the noise of flipping pages of books, would disturb their concentration.

The following professor to speak was Professor Virgilio Marchielle. He stood up and said, "My dear Leila, how come you dropped your care? You, such an outstanding young student. Your intelligence exploring illusion and your skills understanding the laws of magic had always been a gift. I would never expect seeing you in a situation like that. I always visualized you, triumphant in the center of magician's chambers, acting like your mother and father."

"Professor Marchielle, like you, I also saw my future like you just described. During this whole mission, I don't think I have dropped my care. No, Sir. I never did it. However, I have dropped my fear. I never thought one magician would use dark magic to harm an associate, like they did to me. Now, I can see my fault."

"Ah...! This low-spirit of magic... tricked you."

"Yes, Sir. I failed to see this darkness.

"Oh dear...! You're not the first one missing the power of low-spirit. Many magicians have sunk into this deep well. I would do everything in my power to give you another chance, but we have inflexible laws and we must follow them. I hope we will do what is right for both, *you—*and *magic.*"

"Thank you, professor."

At the end of the deliberation, the nine professors talked to each other using a low tone of voice. They showed one another, laws written inside the books they had at hand and wrote their votes on sheets of papers. Professor Breno Coorbell examined each paper. Suddenly, his face turned sad. They couldn't save Leila.

Professor Coorbell stood up and informed Leila what the board of directors have decided. "Leila, even though you're an extraordinary student, this school has decided to expel you. You placed four children in dangerous endeavors and brought an abnormal turmoil to the city of Bonahunta. The Loyporsha Magic

School of Lili Sandra can't ignore the seriousness of these affairs. I am so sorry my dear."

Leila closed her eyes in disbelieve. She would never be a magician. For her—magic was over. A long dry silence filled the library as if even the books on the shelves would have shed some tears for Leila, if they would have eyes.

"No… please… let me speak," said Olivia, standing abruptly, interrupting the quietness of the library and fearing nothing.

The nine professors oddly, eyed Olivia.

"I am Olivia Viglianco, I'd like to speak on Leila's behalf. What the school is doing with her is not fair. Leila saved our lives. King James would have killed us. It was my friend David and Leila, who stopped him. Leila didn't take us to the Rastaga Woods we went their alone, Leila came to protect us."

Mocking a strange face, Professor Breno Coorbell, immediately asked, "Is that correct, Leila."

Leila knew it was not correct, but look who jumped into the stage to help her—Olivia Viglianco. Who would imagine that? The girl—who had problems trusting her.

"Well…. Sir—."

"Professor Coorbell, please let me speak for Leila," asked Olivia. "I know she is very nervous, because being a magician had been her only dream."

"Okay, Olivia. You may continue. Tell me in detail what happened."

"We entered the Rastaga woods by ourselves. I swear. If Leila was with us, we didn't see her. She most likely was invisible."

"What?" asked Professor Coorbell.

"Yes. She was invisible," repeated Olivia. "Ask my friends. None of us saw her." Olivia turned and spoke to David, Lucas and Tess. "Did you see Leila, when we entered the woods?"

"No," they immediately answered.

"Inside the Rastaga woods," proceeded Olivia, "Tess...my sister...asked Leila to do magic. Leila said no. She explained to my sister that she could not play with magic. Then, mysteriously, the Bá-Onadi book appeared in Leila's hand, as if its appearance was part of a small ritual. Leila seemed possessed by some power. When my sister saw that, she didn't waste a second. She went ahead and asked for a dinosaur. Can you imagine that? A dinosaur...?"

The professors exchanged gazes, but said nothing. Olivia, advanced with her revelation. "Before Leila could say anything, the pages of the book began to flip in Leila's hands. They flipped, fast and faster, until they snappishly stopped. Leila's eyes stared over one page, brought a green light from her eyes, uttered three magic words, and then—the dragon appeared."

"All this happened in the Rastaga Woods?" asked Professor Marchielle.

"Yes, Sir" responded Olivia.

"So, Leila was invisible when you entered the woods, but she became visible inside of it?" commented Professor Coorbell.

Olivia took a moment to think. She had to control her lies. She looked down fearing about what to say next.

"You see Professor Coorbell, after we walked inside the invisible grottos, the Crist–"

"The Cristonela Grotto," added Professor Coorbell.

"Yes, the Cristonela Grotto. Leila became visible again."

"It's unbelievable, the things that can happen in the Rastaga Woods, right?" added Professor Marchielle.

"Indeed, Sir. Unbelievable," replied Olivia

"And what did the dragon do?" asked one of the professors.

"The dragon crossed the Cristonela Grotto, exited the Rastaga Woods, and walked straight to the city. David Dreepel, who can read a thousand words per minute, began to read the Bá-Onadi book. And quickly, found out that Leila had been taken by dark magic—the one called QUARELLA CURSE. As you can see, none of this was Leila's fault."

"It is truly abnormal what happens in these woods. As it had been written in old books—*the power of dark magic never fails to surprise us,*" commented Professor Marchielle.

"David Dreepel?" uttered Professor Coorbell.

David stood up and said, "Yes, Sir."

"The son of Magno Dreepel?

"Correct."

"Your father and I went to school together. He is a good friend of mine. He worked many years for Loyporcha Magic School doing excavations in different part of the country. Even though he constantly traveled for his explorations, he always returned to the school to share his work with us. After all that happened with King James' son, your father had to abandon us. He left eight years ago. We all missed him. When was the last time you saw him?"

"I have never seen him, Sir."

"Oh…! I understand. He probably stays away to protect you."

"I believe so."

"We know he is doing an important job to protect the integrity of magic. He's involved in a top-secret mission. Be proud of him."

"I am, Sir."

Professor Coorbell, returned his attention to Olivia. "Please young lady, tell me what happened when you discovered that Leila was under the QUARELLA CURSE."

Olivia began telling what happened and stopped, because David interrupted her. Humbly he said, "Professor Coorbell, please, let me explain this part because I was the one who unfolded the mystery of the QUARELLA CURSE."

"Okay... go ahead."

"Because I can read fast, I discovered that under the QUARELLA CURSE any magician would have one second of grace period, and because the Otela Moon, is the third moon and was over Bonahunta, Leila would have three seconds."

"That's right," said Professor Marchielle, "We call this, Steady Pendula."

"Yes," affirmed David. "After that discovery, Leila came up with a brilliant idea. She gave me the power of giving away power. I immediately gave one minute of power to each one of my friends. During 240 seconds, we dominated the fire, produced rain and wind, and I controlled the dragon. The people of Bonahunta, looked at this magic, thinking it was a bizarre phenomenon. All this was Leila's perception to save the city of Bonahunta."

"Incredible!" added the professors in harmony with their eyes studying Leila.

At that instant, Leila eyed David Dreepel. She couldn't believe he gave her the credit for his idea. Afterward, Professor Coorbell spoke again. "Leila, you used your three seconds of Steady Pendula to create

240 seconds of magic. Outstanding! Absolutely, marvelous!"

"Oh!" said Lucas, "There is more." He raised from his chair, "May I?"

"Yes. Please," responded the professors.

"I am Lucas Lambert, and I am also traveling under Leila's care. You should see what she did at the Bacellar Castle. Intelligently, she confronted King James Lamarcus and fearlessly saved us from being prisoners in the Bacellar Castle. And all was done without using magic, because she was still under the QUARELLA CURSE spell."

"Prisoners?"

"Yes, Sir."

"King James Lamarcus held you prisoners?"

"Yes."

Professor Coorbell shook his head and commented, "Of course, because of the dragon and magic."

"That's right. To save Bonahunta, we performed magic in his province."

A slight silence ran through. Then Marcela Festalma Maglaja, the mother of Leila, spoke to Tess. Since the beginning of the reading, she had been watching Tess Viglianco. Calmly she said, "Miss Tess, I want to hear something from you. I believe you also have something to share. Yes."

Tess stood up and spoke. "Yes, ma'am. I do."

"Please. We're listening."

"First, promise me that what I'm going to say will be used to help Leila."

Marcela Maglaja gazed at the professors. They all moved their heads in agreement.

Tess took the floor. Kindly she began. "What I'm going to say may shock you, because it shocked me. There is a lot of strange things going on in the Rastaga Woods. People are held prisoner there."

"What?" shouted Professor Coorbell. "It can't be true."

"It's true. I spoke with one of the prisoners, Queen Naelia."

Two professors immediately raised from their chairs in disbelieve. Tess walked forward, climbed the stairs, arrived at the upper part of the library and approached Professor Coorbell.

"I can prove, I spoke with her. She gave me this Talisman." Tess brought it out of her chemise.

As soon as Professor Coorbell held the Talisman in his hand, all the other professors walked closer to see it. "What? The Purple Talisman?"

"Yes, the Purple Talisman, which symbolizes the strength of the Rusharci Dynasty," explained Professor Coorbell. "It disappeared from the Suacileu Tabernacle in the Calvendra Forest, Province of Cordavia eight years ago."

"That's why no one could ever find it. The Talisman had been held by Queen Naelia in the Rastaga Woods," added Leila's mother.

"Miss Tess," said Professor Coorbell, "Thank you for placing the Talisman in our hands. Unfortunately, we must return it to the Suacileu Tabernacle."

"I understand, sir." responded Tess. She quietly returned to her seat at the lower part of the library.

Without any farther explanation, Professor Coorbell lifted his head, brought orange color out of his eyes, and fetched from the air a lovely purple velvet jewelry box. Calmly, he placed the box over the table and secured the Talisman inside it.

Next, a huge silence filled the majestic library. The professors began whispering words to each other, re-evaluating their decisions about Leila Maglaja being expelled from the magic school. Now, according to them, Leila never lost control of anything. On the contrary, she used her power wisely to protect the children and the city of Bonahunta. Even though she knew she was under the QUARELLA CURSE, she acted fearlessly to save lives.

Again, they wrote words on sheets of paper and consulted laws written on thick books. For some time, no words disturbed the solid silence among them. Some of them walked around the table and murmured something in the ears of another professor. Apparently, they realized that keeping Leila out of magic would hurt *magic more* than Leila. And for the sake of sorcery, they must make the right decision.

Professor Coorbell stood up and spoke. Confidently he said, "Leila Festalma Maglaja, *we*, the members of this board, have decided to grant you a second chance. The Loyporsha Magic School of Lili Sandra will accept you for the study of magic. This hearing is over and you're dismissed. Young lady, you're free to go."

"Thank you, sir. Thank you so much."

As the professors prepared themselves to leave the library, Leila climbed down from the upper part of the library and reunited with Mr. Toscapela, and the children. Happily, they hugged each other and sat again. For some time they remained wordlessly observing the magnificent shelves full of imposing books. The children enjoyed the moment like no other. They had experienced contentment, gratitude, and proudness. They realized they would never forget such a day. They not only had saved Leila, but they had also recovered the right to go on with their journey.

At the end of these suitable seconds, they all left the school and walked to the Newzuma Valley, to the Astafe Castle.

"Children, thank you for helping me," said Leila, as soon as they entered the castle. "I don't know what would have been of my life, if I couldn't keep my studies."

Olivia decided to ask Mr. Toscapela the question of the year. Rebelliously, she said, "Mr. Toscapela, why didn't you do anything to help Leila? If I didn't jump up to speak, she wouldn't have had a second chance."

"I would have helped," he explained. "I would have done it differently, but I am glad that all of you could handle the situation without me."

Lots of questions furtively occupied their minds. Novel doubts disturbed their peace and prohibited them to articulate new words. They didn't believe in what Mr. Toscapela had said. He seemed to have no interest, what so ever, to help Leila. More likely was that he waited to see what they—the children—could possibly do.

Following this worthless conversation with Mr. Toscapela, they had lunch at the lovely dining room of the castle. Leila was happy and the children joyfully embraced that amusement as well. Following lunch, Mr. Toscapela stood up to deliver the saddest news they could ever imagine to hear on a day like that.

"Children, I am leaving Lili Sandra today. And I will be away for a long time. I don't even know if I ever will be coming back. Mr. Inbacula holds under his guard, a valuable book in case you feel lost. He also has all the instructions in how to use the book. In this book you will find answers to your troubles and will find guidelines in how to travel around, while looking for the Red Scorpion."

The children tried to verbalize their views and their worries about the matter, but were interrupted.

"Don't say anything children, because at this moment not even I, with my power, can't change my intention. Please accept the path of my destiny. David Dreepel must keep alive his journey and he will need help. Go together and conquer as one, for the end will tell it all. The outcomes are bigger than what you have in mind."

The children endured the sad news inquiring nothing for they felt Mr. Toscapela would not listen. They embraced the new reality with sadness and hoped to acquire the strength they needed to fight the next contest. Slowly, they innocently sunk into the enactment of another idiotic thriller.

After saying good-bye, Mr. Toscapela walked out of the Astafe Castle, and gazed around. Then, with his cane, traced a line on the ground, fired lights from his eyes and calmly said the three magic words. With tears in his eyes, he crossed the line. Swiftly… he disappeared.

Mr. Nicolas Toscapela, arrived in the city of Miami, State of Florida, Country United States, Continent North America, Planet Earth, Milky Way Galaxy, year 1985.

Leila and the children remained in Lili Sandra, in the year 1654 dealing with Medieval problems. They had no clue to where Mr. Nicolas Toscapela went. However, among them stayed one piece of magic holding the power which would reveal the secret of his life.

Limbo Rock—the dragon

BOOK TWO

The Power of the Aliel Girl

CHAPTER
10

"WE'RE AWARE OF THE manner of his departure Leila," said David Dreepel. "Mr. Nicolas Toscapela was crying."

"No. He was not."

"Yes, I saw the tears in his eyes."

"Hard to believe," added Leila. "A man with so many sources will not weep. I think you saw light reflections over his eyes and thought it was tears."

"All right Leila, if you don't want to believe, then don't believe."

"David," uttered Leila, "We all will miss him. We all will ask questions until he comes back. We all will wait patiently because now, Lili Sandra is our home."

"Why do you say that?"

"Well, if we leave here, we lose the Astafe Castle. It cannot be shrunken anymore and it cannot be transported anymore. From now on, this will be forever part of Lili Sandra."

"Another law of magic, right?"

"Right, David. Some interludes hold limitations and this is one of the cases."

As all of them returned inside the castle, Mr. Inbacula and Mrs. Clenilde went to the back of it to feed the dragon. Three middle size stables edged the back of the property and since no horses came with the castle, the dragon lived in one of the stables.

As soon as Leila finished speaking with David, her mother, Marcela Maglaja, walked into the castle carrying, with her, a big bag full of books.

"Mother!" called Leila, "I am glad you came, because we should talk. I have lots of questions and the children seem scared about the reality that Mr. Nicolas Toscapela once again, has departed."

"Obliviously," she said, "Also, I am not happy with it. I didn't want to see him going away. That's why I didn't come for lunch; however, I am planning to stay for dinner."

"Great," replied Leila.

"So, you knew he was leaving?" commented Tess.

"Yes, he told me at the school, before the hearing."

"Why did he desert us?" inquired Lucas.

"His way might be different from ours," answered Mrs. Maglaja.

"Suppose we agree with you. Now, what?" replied Olivia.

"What... what?" asked Mrs. Maglaja.

"What should we do?" added Olivia.

"Prepare for the next calling. Did you forget that Leila must find the Red Scorpion?"

The children remained quiet. They didn't forget, but they felt abandoned. Their minds couldn't think of anything else but the departure of that ancient man who always came from *nowhere* and leaves to *somewhere*.

Leila and her mother invited the children to the dining room where they could sit and talk. She took the books out of her bag and carefully placed them on the table.

"Children, thank you for speaking at the hearing on behalf of my daughter. I will never forget that. And Tess, you have no idea what you did today. Bringing back the Purple Talisman, created an incredible chain of new events. Now, the Loyporsha Magic School will be able to return it to the Suacileu Tabernacle and when the truth about Queen Naelia spreads out, a serious investigation concerning Rastaga Woods will take place."

"Mother, what do you think, snipped up that made me miss the information about the Rastaga Woods?"

Mrs. Marcela Maglaja, looked at her daughter and said, "When I was sitting at the table during the hearing, I observed Tess Viglianco. I discovered that she has a beautiful aura; an aura of positive energy and infinite innocence; two traits that easily attract light and darkness. Realistically, you were the target, but Tess became the supreme connection."

"Really...? How...?"

"From the upper stage in the school library, I saw her in a mirror," explained Mrs. Maglaja. "She found a coin on the street, picked it up and bought you a flower. She asked you to put the flower in your hair."

Leila and the children listened alertly. Their minds traveled back in time to the streets of Bonahunta. How did Mrs. Maglaja know that? Incredible...!

Leila's mother proceeded unfolding the strange episode of the life they had encountered.

"The lady selling the flower was a dark witch. That flower, Leila, was supposed to end up in your hair and it did. The flower carried the spell that made you forget everything you have read about the Rastaga Woods."

"Oh! This became my imminent trouble," uttered Leila.

Tess immediately left her chair. She ran to Leila crying. She hugged her. "I'm sorry, Leila, please forgive me. I didn't know."

Leila held Tess back and looked into her eyes. "Tess, this was not your fault. The witch had chosen you because of your appearance. Your aura reflected free spirit and humble forces. You had no way to avoid such dark doings."

Leila's words allowed Tess to feel a little bit better, but she hated the idea that everything went awful wrong, because of her. She quietly returned to her chair.

After she sat down, Lucas commented, "And Tess, I thought you were lucky because you found that coin. I guess I was wrong, right?"

Tess said nothing. She felt miserable.

"I witnessed all of it through a mirror when we were at the hearing," said Leila's mother. "That's why I challenged Tess to speak. I wanted to see what she would say to help you. And, Tess, I'm glad I followed my instincts, because you not only helped to save my daughter, but also lessened the mystery around the disappearance of the Purple Talisman. Now, Queen Naelia can also return home, because we will take her from those woods."

David hurriedly stood up intending to say what he had in mind. "Mrs. Maglaja, we all want to help save Queen Naelia? Please tell us what we have to do."

"No David, this is impossible. You have to help Leila find the Red Scorpion. And before Leila starts this quest, she has to lift the QUARELLA CURSE. She can't go searching for the Red Scorpion without her magic power."

Mrs. Maglaja, you're absolutely right," affirmed Olivia. "Leila needs to gain her power back and we're all ready to support her on it."

A long silence traveled through the dining room. Apparently, all that they wanted to say vanished quickly, because they seemed to be already for action in the coming pursuit.

"Mrs. Maglaja," David finally spoke, "Since you know more about magical endeavors, guide us in this course. Please, where should we start?"

"That's why I came, David" she answered. "From now on, the Astafe Castle will be part of Lili Sandra. It cannot be use to travel as it was previously. No one can enlarge or shrink it as before. Mr. Nicolas Toscapela asked me to assist Leila, Mr. Inbacula, and Mrs. Clenilde decorating it."

"So, we will be living in Lili Sandra?" asked Lucas.

"For some time, yes."

"Will Leila be living here with us?"

"Yes."

"Great…!" said Olivia, gladly.

"As soon as possible," added Mrs. Maglaja, "I'll bring new books to the library. Mr. Toscapela said this library needs lots of books and he asked me to take care of it."

They exchanged looks probably imagining the library full of books and David Dreepel reading them as fast as he will be grabbing them from the shelves. One thousand words per minute.

"Mrs. Maglaja, tell us what needs to be done to lift the QUARELLA CURSE. I feel that we must work on it as soon as possible."

"Yes, Olivia, you're right on this. We shouldn't waste time. Let's sit closer and please pay attention to it, because lifting a curse is serious business. Leila will have only one chance to do this. If she does not accomplish the task, there will not be another opportunity."

The children moved to the chairs close to Leila and her mother. They felt scared for Leila. They seemed eager to know the details of the upcoming affair and couldn't hide their worries. Nothing in magic was easy and spells from one magician to another was even worse.

Mrs. Marcela Maglaja took a few seconds to observe the faces of the children. They gave her the impression of being on the verge of flying away with whatever instructions she might give them. Through the expressions sealed in their eyes, Mrs. Maglaja realized how much they loved Leila.

"Leila must seize the Ghost Orchid which is a beautiful white flower that grows just once a year next to a waterfall. Only Leila can pick it from the ground and when separated from the ground, the flower will live only two hours."

"Wow…" exclaimed Tess. "This will not be easy."

"No," replied Mrs. Maglaja. "Unfortunately, to escape from the bad spells magic transports, some living thing must die. It is either a person, an animal, or in this case… a flower."

"And where we can find this flower?"

"Wait Olivia, I'm not there yet. Leila has to pick the flower from the ground, bring it home, boiled it to produce the *potion number five*, and drink it."

Leila eyed the children. Silently, she wiggled her head. *It... will... not... be... easy.*

Leila's mother continued with the information. "My daughter must bring water from the waterfall to boil the flower."

Now the children looked at each other and laughed. "Finally, something easy, informed Tess. We have a waterfall here in our backyard."

"No... Not this waterfall. The waterfall near the place we find the Ghost Orchid. The orchid doesn't bloom at the same province every year. The places change according to the moons. Today, before I left the school, I looked at it. Lili Sandra is under the influences of Verbena Moon so... one orchid is here in the Province of Bonavere. According to the book it blossomed three days ago, in Perdura Valley."

"All this is written in a book?" asked Olivia.

"Yes. The book of powerful flowers."

"You are saying that under the Verbena Moon one Ghost Orchid always blooms in the Chechela Waterfall?" asked Leila.

"That's right," said Mrs. Maglaja.

"Interesting! Very interesting!" replied Leila.

"If the Chechela Waterfall is located in this province it shouldn't be complicated to get to it, right?" asked David.

"Correct, but it will be difficult to get to the flower."

"Why?"

"The huge valley of Perdura is the foothold of the Poulesta Mountain Range which extends for more than sixteen miles. And exactly in the middle of it, runs the Chechela Waterfall. Truly speaking, the steep mountains are impossible to climb."

"And, of course, the flower blooms on the top of the mountain," repeated Olivia.

"Exactly there," responded Leila. "Next to the waterfall."

The moment shifted away without words. The children occupied their minds imagining the mountain range and the waterfall. *Chechela…? What a name for a waterfall.*

"The place holds a breathtaking panoramic view," added Leila's mother. "However, for what Leila needs to do only good faith can help. She must lift this curse with *potion number five* and all potions under *odd* numbers—terrify the magicians."

"Mother, I want to read about the details involving the Ghost Orchid before I start to do anything. It is important to acknowledge every attribute surrounding the existence of this flower if I want to succeed in the quest of it. Aside from that, I must be in control of this venture with mind and heart, because if I fail, it will not matter that Loyporsha Magic School had given me another chance. Under the QUARELA CURSE, I can't pursue magic.

"Leila, my dear, you'll succeed lifting this curse. I believe in your skills."

"Perhaps only my skills will not be enough. Think about it. I have to do everything by myself. I can't use magic and I can't enjoy the help of any magician. Perhaps, what this witch has taken from me will never be recovered. My power to do magic became a tenacious fight inside the brutal and cruel anathema… that magic can offer."

"Yes, Leila. I know how you feel. Long ago, the QUARELA CURSE gained the reputation of being the dangerous sorcery affiliated with the dark side of magic. The power of it scared even the best magicians; however you have a clear spirit that can be as powerful as dark magic. Please believe in it."

David Dreepel grabbed one of the books that was on the table. Silently he read the title. *DETAILS OF THE QUARELLA CURSE.* David opened the book and began to flip the pages. Mrs. Marcela Maglaja, Leila and the other children, quietly eyed David, as if they knew he would soon deliver some important information. And he did.

"Here, it says that after Leila picks the Ghost Orchid, the flower will survive only two hours. Leila needs to return and dance under the rain holding the flower in her hand. She must dance for an entire minute. Following that, she should boil the flower and drink the potion."

Olivia mocked her face to express her frustration. She brought out what instinctively disturbed her thoughts. "What happens if it's not raining?"

Tess and Lucas dropped their lower lips. Quietly, they exchanged looks. *If it didn't rain, she loses the flower.* Such reality bitterly disturbed their thoughts.

While their thoughts embraced the sad truth, Mrs. Maglaja and Leila crossed their arms thinking. They took a moment to analyze the problem in all dimensions. This will indeed be the tricky part. Water must fall from the sky.

"How can I solve this problem without using magic?" inquired Leila. "The flower will die in two hours. From where am I going to get my rainy day?"

"Well Leila, perhaps faith. Don't be discouraged. Not yet," said her mother.

This new reality left them dispirited. Each one remained silent connected with their theories.

"Why… if—."

"If what?" shouted David.

"If Lucas brings the rain?" replied Tess with toughness wrapping the tone of her voice.

Tess' words brought some hope to their hearts and they enjoyed it. A unique calm rubbed out their worries and allowed a sincere stillness to crash down.

Moving her head right to left and looking at everyone, Tess added, "He's not a magician. He will not violate any rule. Correct?"

"Correct," affirmed Leila.

Another silence ran through them all.

"Okay," said Lucas. "If I am not a magician how come I will bring the rain, Tess?"

"Well… when I spoke with Queen Naelia, in the Rastaga Woods, she told me that I…all the time…have the power to create and control the wind. I cannot play with it, but I can use it for a good reason. I'm wondering, if the same happens with all of us. You can create and control the rain, Olivia can create and control the fire, and David can shrink and enlarge things."

Lucas gazed around with strange thoughts troubling his mind. He laughed. "Do you really think I can make it rain anytime I want?"

"No, Lucas. Only for a good cause," explained Tess."

"And do you think that lifting the QUARELLA CURSE will be sorted as a *good cause?*"

"I do," replied Olivia and David in agreement."

Now, the children turned their heads to Mrs. Maglaja and Leila. They waited to see what mother and daughter would say about such a bizarre revelation.

"What do you think mother? Could it be true? I mean, what Tess just disclosed?"

"Yes, Leila. Having power can simply be an act of belief. When David passed to them one minute of power to save Bonahunta, it might have inflicted their minds deeply enough to be forever part of their minds as everlasting faith. Never forget, that surprises always refine the outcome of any situation."

"But, how?"

Mrs. Maglaja stood up, looked at the children and smiled. She felt happy that she had met them. They were intelligent and genuine. After concentrating on what she would say, she began.

"What I'm going to tell you is one of the greatest secrets of magic. It is a liability which no magician could ever control, we can only understand it. When a—gift power—has been used with the vigor of your soul, a vast amount of passion generates the energy involved in it. If during the process some of these beams of energy break down, the force of it stays forever inside your mind. And like Tess just said, for a good cause, it can be re-used."

"The Terlara Secret, right?" replied Leila.

Immediately, David grabbed another book from the table—the Book of Spells. He opened it and passed the pages quickly. In the middle of the book he read, "The Terlara Secret had been accepted by ancient magicians as a *gift*, not a magic spell. It's in fact, the strength of souls in union with noble hearts. Legend says that every insect that generates light of its on, can pass it away, and the most common are the grasshoppers."

"Grasshoppers?" shouted Lucas.

"Yes," responded David.

"We saw one in Nordache," added Tess.

"Then… in Bonahunta," stated Olivia.

"That's right. Mr. Nicolas Toscapela brought one into the castle," added Lucas.

Mrs. Maglaja and Leila seemed lost in time. Quietly, they exchanged looks that carried thousands of thoughts. Souls and hearts as mind energy. These children naively twisted the conversation as if the subject matter belonged to their precarious existence like everything they had been engaged.

Mrs. Maglaja and Leila ran out of words. They crashed into infinite abyss of oddness, a pristine figment of awareness, a new kind of mythology. Therefore… what intrigued them more was the insect.

Why… suddenly… this… talking… about …. Grasshoppers?

CHAPTER
11

THE SOLUTION FOR LEILA'S problems had come with two divine attributes some children had the privilege of possessing; one was *piercing instinct* and the other *boundless virtue*.

The spontaneous manner David Dreepel always acted, had motivated Leila to move on making decisions without fearing the consequences. David had brought to any problem, some precise results. He knew by instinct what intuition stored for him as a piece of triumph.

Then, on the other side of the coin, emerged Tess Viglianco, who shaped the outcome of many events by displaying an impeccable innocence. She held daring expertise, that exposed astound revelations.

Because of the Book of Spells, David disclosed the Terlara Secret, which was the strength of heart and soul; probably... just probably... attached to some grasshopper legend. Nevertheless, the whole subject matter had begun, because of Tess. She, with her special innocence and free spirit, dared to mention Lucas' ability to control rain. Definitely, the rain Leila would need to dance with the flower.

After all, it was David's *piercing instinct* and Tess's *boundless virtue* that began overlapping the furtive mystery surrounding the capture of the Ghost Orchid.

Indeed, they uncovered a great reality inside a flattered fantasy. Now, in order to continue with the utmost decision of helping Leila, David said. "I think we should count on it, that Lucas would be able to help with the rain. What do you think about that Leila?"

"I don't have another choice do I?"

"No, my dear. You don't," replied her mother. "Believe in the ability of this boy. Lucas might, with the power of his mind, fix the rainy dilemma."

"I agree," snapped Olivia. "Everything is possible if the cause is good. Every brain hides its own capability. Remember, Tess saved David by controlling the wind."

"I brought in a soft breeze, Olivia. It was not a forceful wind."

"Whatever, Tess. This could be done with the power of magic or with the power of mind and you did it with the power of your mind. And do you know what fabricated the good result? The desire you had to save David. In other words, the feelings in your heart and soul."

"I believed in what Queen Naelia told me, that I… all the time… have this power."

The speculative conversation between Olivia and her sister influenced Leila and David to agree on the subject. They decided to trust in Lucas and hope for the best.

"Now," added David, "We need to solve the transportation problem. How will Leila get to the Perdura Valley and how will she climb the Poulesta Mountain Range?"

"No magician can transport her or help her to elevate to the top of the mountain," explained Leila's mother. "We magicians can't interfere in it. Our hands are tied."

"Yes. No magic," replied Leila.

The children left the dining table and walked to different corners of the room. Only Leila and her mother remained at the table. They opened some books and alertly began to look at their contents. They hoped to find a solution for this problem before they lost the flower. They believed that a word or a picture inside these books would uncover something they needed to see. And it did.

Fifteen minutes later, from the corner of the room, again... Tess turned and shouted, "The dragon! Limbo Rock!"

"The dragon what?" asked Olivia.

The dragon can take Leila to the top of this Paoleta Mountain."

"It's not Paoleta, Tess," stated Lucas. "Poulesta"

"Okay Lucas... Pou... les...ta—Mountain."

"How... Tess?"

"Flying. Look here. In this picture a dragon is flying."

Urgently, all the children moved close to Tess and silently stared at the book page that was open. They saw a picture of a flying dragon. For some time no words traveled through the dining room, only a sharp quietness pierced the seconds.

Tess let them hold the book and from the middle of the room, she observed their astonishment. They all seemed to be crashed into the same reverent interlude. Then to carry away the awful shock her discovery brought in, she added, "Mrs. Maglaja please tell them dragons… fly."

Olivia laughed, shaking her head, then boldly said, "Tess, have you ever seen Limbo Rock flying?"

"No, but it doesn't mean he can't do it."

"This dragon fell into the pathetic category of dragons," added Lucas. "It's true, he is your lovely pet, but do not forget he was supposed to be a dinosaur."

"Lucas… I hate you. You–"

"Enough, children," shouted Leila. "We are not here to fight and please help me not to waste any time. What Tess has found makes a lot of sense. Think about it. Dragons… fly. If a dragon could be my transportation, why not, Limbo Rock? We never saw him flying, but… on the other hand, we never asked why?"

After being silent for a moment, Olivia spoke. "Perhaps he never flew because we kept him secured by a chain."

"Just a minute, Leila. I don't want to lose him," stated Tess. "If we free him, he might fly away and never comes back. No. He is my dragon. And it will be living where I live."

"Tess, this dragon doesn't fly," replied David.

"How do you know that?"

"I just read it right now."

"Okay, read it again."

"A dragon which is product of magic is created under the Leedrofic Adaptation Spell. These kinds of animals learn things by communication, only."

"Okay. Limbo Rock is a product of magic. So, we need to talk to

114

him," replied Tess.

"That's absolutely right," added Mrs. Maglaja.

"Ah! Now, I begin to understand," said Olivia with a bright smile on her lips. "He is an animal that never learned his skills?"

"Kind of. And that's the problem we have to solve," explained Leila. "David, please start reading about dragons because now, I am convinced that Limbo Rock is my best option."

In the wake of this new opportunity the children once again, walked to the corner of the dining room and silently embarked on this new wide imagination and they pictured Limbo Rock flying. Willingly, they began to use their minds to make it happen.

"Dragons… fly. They have long necks, long tails, big wings and they fly." Tess repeated out loud.

Then, she drifted away analyzing the problem they had at hand. She started thinking that life without magic was not nice. They must help Leila; however, with their ordinary skills they couldn't do much.

"Maybe we should just pray," suggested Olivia confidently, making sure everybody listened.

"No," uttered David. "I think we have another way to solve it." With all eyes following him, he approached Leila.

"Did you find something, David?"

"No. Not yet. But I remembered something that might help."

"What?"

"Mr. Inbacula."

"Mr. Inbacula, what…?"

"He might store the solution for this problem."

"Where?"

"In the book Mr. Nicolas Toscapela left with him?"

After hearing such revelation the children walked closer. "I remember him talking about the book," said Olivia.

"What kind of book is it?" asked Tess.

"I don't know. I think it gives instructions. For some reason I think there are important things written in it and some of the revelations have to do with the dragon."

"Mr. Nicolas Toscapela always surprised us," commented Leila.

"He said the book could help us in our traveling needs," added David. "Please, let's check on it."

"Of course, but what are you looking for?"

"I don't know for sure. Perhaps in the book we can find a way to make the dragon fly; some guidelines. Why would Mr. Toscapela allow us to keep the dragon if he would never fly? And Mr. Toscapela knew that we might need transportation to go after the Red Scorpion."

"Yes," shouted Olivia and Tess almost at the same time. "David is right. We must look for answers in this book." Then Tess grabbed Leila's hands and pleaded. "Please Leila, call Mr. Inbacula."

"Okay. I'm going to get him."

Leila guided herself to the kitchen and talked to Mr. Inbacula. In less than a minute Leila and Mr. Inbacula returned to the dining room. Mr. Inbacula had a book in his hand. It was a middle size book, blue cover, titleless and not very thick; about two hundred pages maximum.

Mr. Inbacula had spent most of his life as the castle's caretaker. He was born in the Cordavia Province in the year 1595, and was fifty-nine years old. His black face only showed kindness and he seemed to be very intelligent. He spoke three languages, English, Lastenia, and Racyque. Leila pulled a chair and Mr. Inbacula took a seat.

At that moment everybody inside the dining room had their eyes on him. The precise moment of knowing how helpful an *untitled* book could be, just arrived.

"Mr. Inbacula," said Leila "We need to find out how to get to Perdura Valley and arrived at the top of Poulesta Mountain Range, without using magic. I need to lift a terrible magic curse and I can only do that with the Ghost Orchid. Please, let's check the book to find out if something that was written in it, can help. We wish to find out if the dragon can fly."

Inbacula moved his head affirmatively, indicating he understood. Then he turned and spoke with David.

"Master Dreepel," said Inbacula, "Master Toscapela instructed me to only open the book with you. You need to be next to me."

David gazed around to see what comment would come from the others. There was none. David moved closer to Inbacula.

After exchanging glances, Inbacula stayed put and opened the book. Nothing was written on the front page. Inbacula attentively explored it. Then, he began to flip the pages cursorily. Nothing was written down to be read. Worried, Inbacula lifted his face and stared at David.

The old man and David Dreepel exchanged the longest contemplation any person could ever have. It seemed that one knew what was going on and the other didn't. A lapse of time had to pass by, to fix the sudden disturbance that crashed between them.

"Master Dreepel," spoke Inbacula, "Could you read something?"

"Yes."

"What did you read?"

Kindly David said, "Mr. Inbacula, please close the book and slowly open it once again, on the first page."

Quietly, Inbacula followed the directions.

When the first page was opened, David read out loud. "GO TO PAGE 33."

Humbly, Mr. Inbacula, followed the instruction and opened the book to page 33.

On page 33, there was a message and they both could read it. Inbacula read it out loud. "Dear, Inbacula, go to your room, close the door and talk to Analia."

"Who is Analia?" Everybody asked in conjunction.

"Analia is my daughter. She died long ago. She was only twelve years old."

"Oh no!" uttered Tess. "He has to talk to a ghost?"

"No Tess, *spirit,*" rephrased Mrs. Maglaja. "We call it a spirit."

"Why, Mr. Inbacula's daughter?" asked Lucas.

"I bet you, it is because she holds the secret of it. There are spells hidden somewhere and for some reason, this girl became part of this enchantment," said Olivia confidently, as if from long ago, she had taken a course on spells and spirits.

Leila and David observed Inbacula, silently. They felt strange about the request and decided to give him some time. The mystery around the petition probably confused him more, than it confused the others. And aside from that, he should be the one wanting to talk to his deceased daughter. He should be the one believing that something good will come out of it.

"Master David," finally Inbacula said, "I'm going to my room to communicate with my daughter. Please, wait for me here."

While waiting, David kept himself busy reading the books Mrs. Marcela Maglaja had brought.

In the room, after closing the door, Inbacula called the spirit of his daughter.

"Analia…" he waited. Nothing. "Analia…" he waited. Still nothing. "Analia…" he waited.

Slowly, a figure of a twelve-year old girl, wearing a white dress, the same dress she was buried with, appeared in the corner of the room.

"Dad…" she uttered, using the power of her mind. All the time she spoke without moving her lips.

"Yes… Analia, I am glad you came."

"Me, too. What do you need, Dad?"

"I'm working with a young woman named Leila Maglaja. She is taking care of four children. They have a dragon they call, Limbo Rock. They need to know if Limbo Rock can fly."

The transparent silhouette of Analia, turned her face toward the right. She smiled.

"Yes, Dad. The dragon can fly. However, to see this happening he must drink *potion number three*. Please get paper and pen and right down the recipe. This is the potion that will make the dragon stimulate his skills."

Inbacula opened a small drawer, took out a piece of paper and a reed pen. As Analia communicated with him, he wrote down the ingredients to create *potion number three*. When she finished, she said, "Good-bye Dad. And good luck."

Mr. Inbacula remained quiet watching his daughter Analia vanishing in the corner of the room. Her spirit faded away charmingly, the same way she came in. Her spirit seemed peaceful, filled with bright and completely joyful. She carried with her a stealthy acuity.

When her image completely disappeared, Inbacula brought to the room a delightful smiled. He felt glad he saw her one more time. Then calmly, he opened the drawer in his dresser and placed his reed pen in it. "The dragon can fly," his voice expressed his happiness.

Inbacula De Boizati Percata, strolled out of his bedroom knowing his daughter had become part of a magnificent crossing and that her life will be forever remembered. She didn't die; not in spirit.

On this peaceful afternoon when Inbacula, once again walked into the dining room, Leila, the children, and Mrs. Marcela Maglaja, immediately gathered around him. Their eyes deliberately asked the same question.

"Yes, Master Dreepel," said Inbacula. "Limbo Rock can fly. But we have to help him. We need to cook a *potion number three* and he must drink it. I have the recipe."

Inbacula passed the recipe to David Dreepel and he began to read it out loud.

"Ingredients: Three pounds of Ginger, Three Tongues of Parrot and three pairs of Eagle Wings."

The room was quiet as they listened and he continued. "Directions: Boil the ingredient for three hours. Let it rest for three hours then pour it into three bowls. Serve it to the dragon at three o'clock."

Every eye in the room was on him as he had more information. "Make sure the dragon drinks it all. Be careful because everything needs to be done in terms of three."

CHAPTER
12

NEXT MORNING, WHILE THE birds happily flew around the castle singing their songs, Mrs. Marcela Maglaja also marched in. She found Leila and the children at the table having breakfast.

"Good morning Leila. Good morning dear children… Mr. Inbacula…and Mrs. Clenilde! Oh, today EVERYTHING will be ALL and ALL will be EVERYTHING. This is another way to give urgency to our neediness. Leila my dear, as soon as possible, we will be cooking this magic *potion number three*. We shouldn't waste any time doing this. The instant you finish breakfast we all must go shopping at Alyfurna Creation."

"What is Alyfurna Creation?" asked David.

"It's a store which belongs to Loyporcha Magic School, a place where you can find all kinds of ingredients, dried stuff and animal parts to make potions."

Quickly, Tess jumped from her seat. Eagerly she wanted to say something and assuredly she did. "Mrs. Maglaja, I disagree to kill animals to make magic potions. I can't participate in it."

Mrs. Maglaja smiled a soft, genuine smile and let Leila speak for her.

"We will not kill animals, Tess," said Leila. "The Loyporcha Magic School has hunters out in the wildness all year long, picking dead animals. We only use animals that died by natural causes."

"Oh!" exclaimed the children, happily and in union. Their minds seemed to be troubled since yesterday with this matter.

Following Leila's words, Mrs. Maglaja spoke. "Children, learn something about magic. Only dark magic kills animals to make potions or trap a spell. Respecting the animals has always been an intrinsic sub-ordinance revolving laws of magic. Good magicians respect it even before having their credentials."

The children felt incredibly pleased with the news. On one hand they treasured the enigmatic principles of magic and on the other hand, they loved the dwells of animals. Thus, the information they had acquired today about magic, simply eliminated any conflict they might encounter in the future.

Olivia also spoke. She spent the whole night thinking. Yesterday, after dinner she brought to mind something unlikable. She wanted to talk to Mrs. Maglaja to clear it up, however, everybody was tired and she ended up not saying anything. But she would today.

From her seat she started, "Mrs. Maglaja, yesterday you said Leila cannot use magic to lift this QUARELLA CURSE, right?"

"Yes. I said that. And it's true. Very true."

"Isn't Limbo Rock magic?"

"Yes, Olivia. The dragon is a product of magic. An enchantment called *Leedrofic Adaptation,* but he had not been created to help

Leila lift the QUARELLA CURSE. The dragon had come to life for reasons that we still don't know. The potion number three will simply stimulate the skills he already possessed. For some reason these skills, until now, remained dormant. Truly speaking… the dragon had been crafted at the instant Leila collapsed under this curse."

"That's true. I witnessed it," shouted Tess.

Lucas quickly said, "Of course you witnessed it, Tess. The dragon had taken the place of your dinosaur. Never forget that."

"Lucas and Tess, please," cried Leila, "Let's avoid comments that are not helpful." Then, hurriedly she turned her attention to Olivia. Kindly she explained, "Olivia, I know it's difficult to understand the procedures of magic, but in time you will find the way. According to the rules; I can't bring into this search any magician to aid me during my battles but, I am allowed to use anything already in existence, around me."

"Yes, but I read that even though you can't use a magician in the course of the quest, at the very end, you will need one. You do know that, right?" asked David.

"Yes, David. The Bá-Onadi book of magic says the three words capable to lift the curse, require to be verbalized immediately after I drink the boiled Ghost Orchid. And only a senior magician with black and orange Ceburda could do that. In other words, at that moment, only a magician would be able to read the three magic words."

"Apparently," added Lucas. "After drinking the flower, Leila's brain will grant these words to the senior magician. I read it in the Bá-Onadi book."

"That's right. These words have been, all the time, hidden in my brain."

"Okay," added Mrs. Maglaja. "I find such a conversation very interesting, nevertheless, the clock never stops and we have work to do. Let's be ready to go to Alyfurna Creation. Eagle wings are very rare. If someone gets them before us…, oh my, oh my! I don't know where to go to find them."

In a blink of an eye, the children acknowledged the seriousness of the situation and switched their attention to the pending work laid ahead of them.

"Mrs. Maglaja, you're absolutely right. We must hurry to get these ingredients," declared Olivia. "I'll be ready in a minute."

Everybody finished their breakfast and ran upstairs to their room, changed garments and hurried down to the entrance of the castle, as quick as possible. The children were dressed in lovely medieval clothes and colorful hats.

Eager to see this Alyfurna Creation store, they followed Leila and her mother as if they were leaving on a great vacation. David and Lucas walked next to each other and Lucas took the moment to talk to David. He had questions bothering his mind since the day before.

"David, why did Mr. Inbacula call you Master Dreepel?"

"Oh, Lucas! Why do you always have these weird questions? You know my answer."

"Yes, I do. Like always… *I don't know*, right?"

"Right, Lucas. There are millions of secrets about my existence troubling me as much as they trouble you, Olivia and Tess. For example, my father. I have never met him. Tell me what happened about your childhood. I met you in Nordache, remember? After the two years traveling with Leila, nothing comes to my mind. Do you remember this time? Do you recall the events? Do you miss anything?"

"I don't even remember my parents, David."

"See... we promenade inside a complex journey without knowing our past and without a hint of our future. Now, we will be engaging in this mission which consists in helping Leila lift the QUARELLA CURSE and after that, we must grip the strange hunting of the Red Scorpion. We must find this animal or the King of Normabell will throw us in jail. Have you thought about that?"

"I have David. And at least, for a change, this is a piece of the future we can contemplate; being in jail."

"Indeed, Lucas. Not a pleasant piece of future, however, less mysterious."

At the 776567 Novaselma Street, Leila and Mrs. Maglaja stopped, turned around and waited for the children. Nearly, behind them were Olivia and Tess, and then Lucas and David.

"Children," said Leila, "The Alyfurna Creation store belongs to Loyporcha Magic School. The store was opened four years after the school's inauguration. It was 217 years ago."

Tess tried to create that amount of time in her head. "Wow...!"

After passing the school, they entered the Alyfurna Creation. The store seemed older than 217 years. Inside, dark large windows decorated the walls, and tick miasma covered the space in between the displayed wooden tables. A horrible stench arose from the walls as if at every five minutes, the candles attached to the candelabrums released a dreadful odor into the ambience.

126

Mrs. Mathilda Serafina approached them the minute she saw Mrs. Marcela Maglaja. Then holding a festive smile she saluted.

"Professor Maglaja, what a pleasant surprise seeing you again. How's everything at the school?"

"Good, Mathilda. Very good."

"How is my son doing?"

"Intelligent young man. Hugo will pass my class with high qualifications. His memories…impress me."

"Oh, that boy! He's my everything."

"Be proud."

Mrs. Mathilda Serafina, brought out a joyful expression. "How can I help you, Professor?"

"Hmm…here."

Mrs. Maglaja turned to her daughter and said, "Leila please show Mrs. Mathilda the recipe."

Cordially, Leila saluted Mrs. Mathilda and promptly, introduced the children to her. Following that, Leila obeyed her mother and passed the recipe to Mrs. Mathilda. For a short moment, Mrs. Mathilda only had eyes for the ingredients in the recipe. "Eagle wings…?" she exclaimed intriguingly and out loud.

"Don't tell me you don't have it," replied Mrs. Maglaja.

"No, Professor. I have them and they are very fresh. They have been drying only for a year. I have them in the back…. Come."

They all followed Mrs. Mathilda. The children seemed plainly interested in seeing the eagle wings. Silently, they walked behind the adults.

Mrs. Mathilda passed three large rooms packed with tools to be use when exercising special-forces and substances to make magic potions and shelves full of books holding fundamental elements of physics, enchanted properties, and quantum mechanics of power.

At the end of the third room, Mrs. Mathilda entered a small square chamber. The walls were hidden by a green filthy color plus a whacked low brown ceiling covered by spider webs.

Mrs. Mathilda approached one of the walls, confidently placed her right hand against it, as if she was pushing it back. The wall rolled over... and over... and went farther... and farther... and farther... as if it would never stop going toward infinity.

Mrs. Mathilda walked in and they all paced with her. While advancing, she sometimes stopped, grabbed herbs or animals' legs, brought it to her face and happily smelled them.

"Oh, I have fresh things here professor. Please smell this rabbit ear...hmm...! Enchanting...!"

After walking for almost five minutes inside this tunnel, they all stopped. Mrs. Mathilda squashed herself between two long wooden tables.

"Here they are. Eight of them. Eagle wings. Mr. Solíz brought it to me last year, after the fire in Pervessa Forest in the Province of Monavira."

Mrs. Maglaja got closer and began to select the three pairs of eagle wings she would buy. She lifted then in the air and smelled them. "Indeed Mathilda, very fresh. Now... the parrot tongues."

"Here", responded Mrs. Mathilda, walking quickly around other tables. "Parrot tongues from Tee-Tee Cala Island. Hurricane Ovalta killed them last year. The hurricane happened under the Odila moon. I don't trust that moon. Only tragedy when that moon is around."

DAVID DREEPEL

The children heard Mrs. Mathilda. Olivia jumped quickly, "Did you hear that David? Hurricane in Tee-Tee Cala Island. Isn't that the island where we met? Leila picked us up at the beach in Tee-Tee Cala, remember, in 1985?"

"Yes. From there we went to Gargatuela," commented Lucas.

"So... they're talking about a place that we have been living—333 years in the future?" added David.

"Oh...no!" cried Tess. "Stop that conversation. I don't want to think about that lovely grasshopper we saw at the beach. Don't tell me that one day it could die because of hurricanes."

"Oh...Tess, why do you have to always talk about things that do not make sense." commented Olivia. "Why bring that grasshopper into this conversation? A grasshopper which belonged to a future that we probably will never see again. Imagine... 333 years in the future."

"I love animals Olivia, and some grasshoppers from the future probably, will end up here like the parrots. Or do you think that magic spells do not use them?"

Lucas who walked a little bit farther just turned. "Of course magic uses grasshoppers. Here they are, as dry as... they are green."

They advanced closer and stopped in front the huge table filled with dry dead grasshoppers. While contemplating them, David's stomach began to roar like he was going to throw up. He was pale, felt weak and couldn't speak.

"Leila, please help!" called Olivia. "I think David is going to throw up."

Immediately, Mrs. Mathilda jumped over and fetched a piece

of cloth from her apron. As soon as she passed it to David, he vomited on it.

"What happened?" asked Mrs. Mathilda, watching Olivia in the eyes.

"I don't know. Could it be he couldn't handle the smell? I mean the smell of dead grasshoppers?"

"Mmm… perhaps he is sensitive to it. Some people are sensitive even to lady bugs."

"Mother, go ahead and finish buying the things we will need. I'm taking the children outside. Please do it fast, because we have a lot to do before the end of the day."

"Okay, Leila. Go on and watch the children."

Leila had done what she had in mind. Without delay she took the children outside and together they waited for her mother. A few minutes later, Mrs. Maglaja arrived next to them carrying two leather bags full of the ingredients. They immediately returned to the Astafe Castle with one purpose in mind. It was time to initiate the cooking of potion number three.

As soon as they arrived at the castle, they speedily grouped around the kitchen table which occupied half of the kitchen and had two enormous benches at both sides. Mr. Inbacula brought a big pot to the wood stove and Mrs. Clenilde began to fill it with clean water. Leila and the children took the books they left scattered on the dining room and willingly, began to look for everything related with the *potion number three* and QUARELLA CURSE.

"We must read as much as possible about what we are going to do," stated Leila. "Let's go over the recipe Mr. Inbacula gave us and carefully read the instructions. We also must look for facts related with the lifting of the QUARELLA CURSE. Obviously, we will find something we didn't yet read. It is always like that... believe me... no matter what."

On another table, close to the stove, Leila and her mother initiated the ritual of taking the ingredients out of the leather bags Mr. Maglaja carried with her.

They solemnly, brought out the items one by one as if they had cost lots of *guilts* and had belonged to an art museum. *Guilts* was the money used in My Jupiter. Carefully, they placed the ingredients on top of the small table. While the two ladies thoughtfully observed them, Olivia spoke.

"Leila, no.... We cannot start cooking today."

"Why not, Olivia?"

"Check the recipe. Everything needs to be done in terms of *three*. Cooking for *three* hours. Let it cool off for *three* hours, serve it in *three* bowls and feed it to the dragon at *three* o'clock."

Leila and the children grouped together in the middle of the kitchen, to read the recipe once again.

"What time is it now, Mr. Inbacula?" asked Olivia.

"12:30 p.m."

"See, Leila. We have to start cooking around 9:00 am, so at 12:00 p.m. the cooking time will be over. Then we will have another three hours to cool it off, time enough to have it ready to feed the dragon at 3:00 p.m."

"Wow... Olivia... good observation," said Leila.

"I didn't know you're good with numbers," added David.

"There are lots of things about me that you don't know, David Dreepel."

"You're absolutely right. We can't do this today," replied Leila.

Lucas, who was also reading the recipe and instructions, quickly jumped in. "The instruction doesn't say in what 3:00 o'clock we should feed the dragon. It could be AM or PM. That means we can start cooking at 9:00 p.m., today if we want."

"Yes… Lucas, you're right," said Mrs. Maglaja. "But then we will need to feed the dragon at 3:00 am. Don't you think it will be too dark and inconvenient?"

"Yes, ma'am. Definitely, too dark."

They all agreed to postpone the cooking for the next day, because even feeding the dragon at such an early hour would be tricky. The dragon might not feel like eating at such an hour.

Leila slowly returned the ingredients to the bags and the children began organizing the books, in order to take them out of the kitchen.

"Leila," said Mrs. Mablaja, "I'm leaving. It's getting late and I have to teach a class at the Loyporcha Magic School in the evening. I must go home to prepare it. You are in good hands. These children possess sharp minds and fervent strength to go on helping you. I'll come back tomorrow."

"Fine, mother. And thank you."

As Mrs. Maglaja turned to leave, David spoke. He had a book in his hands. "Leila, we must be carefully to not waste time because there is a state of limitation to lift the curse. If three Ghost Orchid blossom and died since the curse was put into action, the curse will stay forever."

Leila exposed an upsetting face and shouted at her mother. "Mother! How is this possible? Did you know that?"

"No," answered Mrs. Maglaja, walking closer to David.

David continued reading. He believed the information he found should be brought to their attention.

"Leila, your mother said that this year, two flowers already blossomed in different provinces. That means... if you missed the one in Perdura Valley, you will not be able to lift this curse."

Leila stared at her mother enraged. It seemed that suddenly, she decided to blame her mother for what had happened with her at the Rastaga Woods.

"Why is this happening to me, mother? You know something that I do not, right? Please, in the name of our relationship... tell me."

The children never saw Leila in that state of anger and worse than that, they would never expect it like that—in a snap of a finger—and with her mother?

"Leila I'm not hide anything from you. Like I said before. You... were a target."

"Please, keep going. I am twenty-two-years-old. Why am I a target? All I have done until now was study to become a magician. I have been accepted at Loyporcha Magic School like everybody else, by passing the NURCUÁ, a test that every student has to take. Then, I decided to do my practice before graduation and accepted Mr. Nicolas Toscapela's offer to guide these children to David Dreepel's journey. If I'm a target... please tell me. Target of what?"

Tess, who had been quiet the whole afternoon, opened her eyes wildly. She sensed she was also a target, because they used her with the coin; 3 *guilts*, and the flower. She desired to hear all that Mrs. Maglaja had to say. She must know more about her being a target, too.

"Leila, I am your mother. How come I would mislead you in anything? Your commitment with magic should not blind you. You must understand magic has a *light* and *dark* side. You became a target because of jealousy."

"I am not yet a magician."

"Leila, how old were you the last time you saw your father?"

"Fourteen."

"Your father is among the best magicians this planet has ever gotten. The Draba Legion of Dark Magicians hate him. I am talking about this jealousy. He left Lili Sandra in the name of a big cause and to protect us. I believe he will come back when the time is right."

"Oh! That's why I became a target?"

Mrs. Marcela Maglaja walked toward the living room to leave the castle. She then stopped one last time. "Leila Maglaja, you're the only person who can bring your father back to Lili Sandra. And don't ask me why I know it; for I have no answer. I just know it."

Mrs. Maglaja exited the room, feeling miserable, knowing that her daughter had to find her way between *light* and *dark* magic.

While a rough silence infiltrated the room, Leila eyed David Dreepel with a forceful look. Their eyes stared firmly without blinking.

"You... David.... You know something. I feel it."

"I do. But I'm receiving this information now. And I think that's happening to calm you."

"Then, speak."

"You're the soul girl. Twenty-two years ago, in 1632 the Aliel Comet stroked the blue sky of Lili Sandra. On that day, only one child was born in Lili Sandra. That child was a girl and that girl was you. Because of it your mind holds secrets that, not even you know. It will take another hundred years for the comet Aliel to return, meanwhile, you will be the soul of this legend. The Aliel Legend. You will be gradually, revealing every secret that has been incrusted in your mind at the right time and to the right people. Only you control that. You were named after the comet."

"How?"

"Well…, spell ALIEL back words."

"LEILA?"

CHAPTER
13

ON THE NEXT DAY, early in the morning, Leila began the preparations to finally cook the *potion number three*. The potion, they all believed would awaken the dormant skills of the dragon. Mrs. Maglaja and the children reunited in the kitchen of the Astafe Castle to assist her accomplishing the task.

Exactly, like the day before, Leila carefully began taking the ingredients out of the leather bag. She believed so much in this potion that she wanted to wisely, take care of every detail involved in the cooking of it. Leila wished for the dragon to take her to Perdura Valley and to the top of the mountain. Without a doubt, Limbo Rock would be the miracle she needed.

Mrs. Clenilde proceeded with the function of boiling the water and Mr. Inbacula attentively, managed the time. In order to have the recipe ready for 3:00 p.m., Leila had to insert the ingredients into the boiling water no later than 9:00 am. Any mistake could delay the whole process, not talking about the risk of losing the ingredients.

And as planned, when the time was right, Leila performed the action of, one by one, introducing the elements into the boiling water. She did it ceremonially, with the children nearby watching the deed like students do in potion-cooking classes.

Mrs. Clenilde kept herself next to the stove constantly, stirring the water and making sure all the ingredients poached well. When Leila finally assured everything had been taking care as it should, she called her mother and the children to the dining room.

"Mother," she said, "Do you think that if everything works well with the dragon, I can go to pick the Ghost Orchid today?"

After a moment of reflection, her mother responded, "I think you shouldn't go to Perdura Valley in the afternoon. If you really want my opinion, I say no. Go tomorrow morning."

"Oh, I am losing time. Every day that passes, it's one day less in the life of the flower. I must control this situation, before the dark side of this tribulation triumphs."

"If we succeed making the dragon fly, you should make plans for tomorrow. It will be dangerous flying over the valley when it's getting dark. Picking the flower and collecting the water from the waterfall, in the dark, will be risky. You do not want to jeopardize the mission, Leila. Listen to me. Make plans for tomorrow morning."

Silently, Leila swallowed her frustration. She recognized she could not pick the flower in the dark. She also could not feed the dragon before three o'clock. Her mother won. It would be tomorrow.

Now, with her conclusion in mind, Leila went to have a meeting with the children. She had to communicate with them before departing to the valley. The children needed to begin preparing themselves for the next journey; the hunt for the Red Scorpion.

When Leila left the kitchen, she sent the children to the dining room and there they remained, sitting at the dining table, waiting for her.

Leila finished the conversation with her mother and turned around to go meet with the children. As soon as she moved forward, she hesitated. She took a moment to express her regrets about the way she spoke to her mother the day before.

"Mother, I'm sorry about yesterday, I lost my temper and hammered on you without reason. My frustration blinded me. Please forgive me. I'll be carefully from now on."

"Apology accepted. I know you do not have time to talk about lots of things and I do understand."

"Mother, do you know that in the history of Lili Sandra there was a day that only one girl was born in this city?"

"Yes. And that girl was you."

"Do you know that I was named after the comet, Aliel?"

"Yes. Aliel written back words is, LEILA."

"Why you never told me that?"

"Fear. This must remain a secret because of the Draba Legion of Dark Magicians. How do you know that?"

"David Dreepel told me."

"And the children heard that?"

"Yes."

"Leila, please talk to them. Only a few people should know you're the soul of the Aliel Legend. For one hundred years the dark side of magic will be doing the impossible to find this girl. The secrets guarded in your mind at any moment can place your life in danger."

"Don't worry, I'll talk to them."

"Leila, how did David know that?"

"He told me he was receiving the information as he was revealing it to me."

"Why?"

"He believed it happened… to calm me."

"Hmm, this young boy…. Another secret attached to Lili Sandra, right?"

From the time the children had the first encounter with Leila in Nordache, she had been the most important person in their lives. She had been the figure protecting them and guiding them through the struggles they had endured. Nevertheless, her mother was right. David Dreepel was another mystery. Not even he knew the enigma of his life.

Since two of the massive problems challenging them engaged in the stage of the last fruition, Leila decided to move on with the impending hunting venture they had ahead and uncover the mystery of the Red Scorpion. She had to find it before King James Lamarcus got tired of waiting and captured them. If they returned to Bonahunta without the scorpion, they would have no chance. They will be hanged.

At the dining table, Leila sat and talked. "Children, let's focused on our next mission and find the Red Scorpion. It's time to start reading about it. I count on your help, as always and if necessary, mother can bring more books. I remember what Tess told me on the morning we arrived here. On that day, I did not give it any attention. I was very worried about my hearing at the Loyporcha Magic School, and I simply ignored what she had said. However, after knowing she had the Purple Talisman, I changed my mind and gave it my full attention. Then facing Tess she asked, "Do you remember that dream, Tess?"

"I do, Leila."

Leila quickly, explained it to David, Lucas and Olivia. "Tess had a dream about where we should start looking for the Red Scorpion. I believe the power of the Purple Talisman allowed this vision."

"The yellow house, right?" shouted Tess.

"Yes, the yellow house."

For the next forty minutes, Leila and the children looked for books relating to scorpions and they carefully studied the map of Lili Sandra. They remained in the dining room until Mr. Inbacula walked in announcing the cooking time ended.

Leila said thank you to Mr. Inbacula and they all returned to the kitchen to check on the potion. The cooked ingredients disappeared, as if they were never present and the water turned clear as crystal.

"Incredible!" uttered Olivia and David Dreepel instantly.

"This is how magic potions work," added Leila, "The ingredients degenerate in all capacity."

"Why does a dragon need to drink eagle wings?" asked Tess.

Mrs. Marcela Maglaja explained, "The eagle holds ultimate power to fly high. The parrot, possess the greatest ability to talk, and ginger offers pure substances. These three constituents sentinel the spell in charge of the enchantment. It liberates the skills of the dragon."

"In magic children," added Leila, "Each animal transports the truthfulness of its configuration. For example, the dragons subsist as *transfixed* animals. Dragons never change. If a dragon is good, it will die being good. If a dragon is bad, it will die being bad. They belong to the six great potency of magic: *love* and *hate; brightness* and *darkness; mysticism* and *diabolism.* Love and hate—belong to the dragon's heart. Brightness and darkness—belong to the dragon's mind. And mysticism and diabolism—belong to the dragon's soul."

"I definitely need to read more about dragons to understand Limbo Rock better," commented Tess.

"Long time ago," explained Leila, "Here, in My Jupiter; under this concept began the legion of dragons. There are two legions: The KORDENTES and TESARTIZ. Love, brightness, and mysticism form the legions of KORDENTES. Hate, darkness and diabolism, the legion of TESARTIZ.

At three o'clock, they all went outside to finalize the foray with the *potion number three*, which consisted in feed the dragon and see what would happen.

Mr. Inbacula brought the dragon to the back terrace. Limbo Rock had his left foot attached to a heavy chain and Mr. Inbacula walked next to him holding the chain all the time.

When Mr. Inbacula arrived with the dragon, the three bowls were filled with *potion number three*. As the dragon approached the bowls, his nose twitched indicating he inhaled the smell of it. After being placed in front of the bowls, Limbo Rock began to drink from the dish in the middle, then he moved to the right one, and last… the one in the left.

Everybody remained quiet just watching. Their hearts in suspense and fingers crossed. They eagerly wished to see something happening, soon. The moment froze their entire existence.

First the dragon rested over the terrace stone as if he was going to sleep. He even closed his eyes. Leila and the children stayed observing. A wave of frustration breezed their minds.

For two minutes nothing happened. These were the longest two minutes they had to endure without any action. Then instantly Limbo Rock stood up. He vigorously yielded his wings and charmingly lifted them up and brought them down. Dramatically, he stretched them extensively, puffed a little fire out of his mouth, swayed the wings freely, and began to fly.

Carefully, Mr. Inbacula gave him more chain and for a couple of times he flew in a circle, until he landed in front of Leila and the children. He had an amazing happy face.

Tess Viglianco stepped closer. She arrived in front his face. "Limbo Rock... you can fly."

The dragon moved his neck also showing his joy and indicating he understood her.

"Now, that you can fly, can you take Leila to Perdura Valley?"

The dragon moved his head affirmatively and articulated few words. "Yes, Tess. I can."

Tess turned around in astonishment, "He spoke. The dragon spoke. Did you hear him?"

"Oh no... Tess again.... Now, she is the only one who can hear the dragon," commented Lucas tediously. "But... why not...? This is her dragon."

"I also could hear the dragon," said Mr. Inbacula.

Leila walked closer. "Really, Mr. Inbacula?"

"Yes, Miss Leila."

"That's extraordinary. We have two people who can hear the dragon." Leila clapped her hands happily.

"What did the dragon say?" asked Olivia.

Mr. Inbacula let Tess answer the question. She quickly said, "Yes. He can take you to the Perdura Valley."

Following that, Leila spoke. "Tess, tell Limbo Rock that we will be living tomorrow, early in the morning."

"Yes," answered the dragon. Then he politely explained, "Tess, tell Leila that even though she can't hear me, I can hear her. And tomorrow you also need to come to Perdura Valley, because you're my ally. Without you I will have no communication with her."

The dragon articulated clearly, moving his mouth as if he was a real person speaking. His voice carried an enchantment beyond explanation; a musical allure conveyed by a kind male beast.

Tess told Leila all that was said and they set the time for the next day around 9:30 in the morning.

Limbo Rock was a pretty dragon. His shiny green color spread all over his body as if he lived under the moon light all the time. His body displayed tranquility as if he just came out of a dragon's cave after sleeping for years. His two legs could, at any time, lift him up, making him taller than any person. One charming tale stretched far from his body with a little arrow shape at the edge; indicating the end of it. On his face, two lovely eyes carried away a profound, penetrating look. His mouth was big enough for the size of his body and at any moment exposed sharp bright teeth that showed no danger at all. The sound of his voice delivered kindness for those who could hear his words. He indeed belonged to the KORDENTES legion of dragons.

"I can't understand why Tess always… ends up ahead of us," snapped Lucas. "Now, aside of finding coins on the street, she is going to fly with Leila on her stupid dragon."

Suddenly, the dragon stretched his neck, creating a ring of fire around Lucas and in slow motion lifted him and the ring of fire, up in the air. Limbo Rock kept Lucas flouting inside the ring of fire for some seconds. Everybody covered their mouth in disbelieve. *The dragon does magic?* Lucas seemed terrified.

Tess begged the dragon to bring Lucas down. Quietly, the dragon obeyed. He slowly placed Lucas on the ground safely and stopped the fire. Then… the dragon spoke.

"Tess…, tell Lucas, that I may be a stupid dragon, but it's better than to be like him, a foolish prince."

"Prince?" replied Tess.

"Yes," said the dragon. "Tell him that I want an apology."

Without understanding what the dragon implied about… *foolish prince*, Tess replied his words to Lucas and added, "Lucas, he wants an apology."

"I…am…sorry, Limbo Rock. It will never happen again," said Lucas.

The dragon smiled. He friendly shook his head.

After that, Inbacula began to take the dragon back to the stables. They walked quietly, side by side, until the dragon, kindly said, "Inbacula, now that I fly, speak, and do magic, you don't have to keep me at the stables and in chains. Like you, I also know my duties with Miss Leila and the children. I want to live in the back, at the bottom of the mountain, next to the water fall. There is a small cave there. It's the perfect place for a dragon at my size.

Inbacula stopped walking. He seriously eyed the dragon, winked, and smiled, "How do you know there is a cave there?"

"Did you already forget I do magic? My mind can travel distances that your mind can't possibly imagine."

Mr. Inbacula now wobbled his head. He gazed at the dragon intuitively and he grasped the concept.

"Mr. Limbo Rock" added Inbacula. "Wish, granted, however, promise me you'll send a ring of fire to the castle when you need me."

"I'll come to the terrace for my meals. I want to see the children every day, if possible. Did you see the face of that child when I scared him to death?"

"I did."

"He will never disrespect me again."

"Is he really… a prince?"

"Oh yes! As much as I'm a dragon."

CHAPTER
14

AS IT TURNED OUT, the following morning squeezed in gently. It was a reward for what they had accomplished on the day before. The dragon can fly. Leila and Tess looked renewed, energetic, prepared, and buoyant. Only one event shall occupy their minds from now on; going to pick the Ghost Orchid before dark.

Outside the Astafe Castle the dragon, Mr. Inbacula and the children, had been waiting for the great moment. The moment, Leila and Tess would depart to Perdura Valley, flying on a dragon. As always, their expectation had framed their emotional state of mind. On one hand, they caught the excitement of the magic involved in it and on the other hand, they feared the dangers of the forthcoming episode.

David Dreepel approached Leila and passed to her the canteen she must have in order to collect the water from the water fall.

"Leila, please do not forget to collect the water."

"Thank you, David. I will keep it in mind."

"Leila, please… take good care of Tess. She's only ten years old. I don't know how safe it is to fly on a dragon."

The dragon heard what David Dreepel said. He turned his head to Tess.

"Tess, tell David to not worry because not you, nor Leila, will ever fall when flying with me. My magic will be holding you. Not even the hats you are wearing can drop."

Tess quickly repeated what the dragon said. Olivia sighed with relief when she heard it. Tess also dropped her fear. From the very beginning Tess wanted to help Leila lift the curse, however, the sudden reality of flying with Leila, on a dragon, scared her more than she could imagine.

After making sure she had everything she needed, Leila decided it was time to leave. The dragon lay down on the ground, Tess jumped on him and immediately Leila did the same. As the dragon instructed, Tess would ride in front and Leila behind her.

When the dragon opened his wings and began to lift himself in the air, the children waved to Tess and Leila. They now erased from their minds any distress. For an instant they disregarded entirely all that was not illusion.

Assuredly, the dragon flew over Lili Sandra, near the clouds and no one saw them. They were all the time concealed. They traveled for forty minutes then they saw the valley.

While crossing Perdura valley, Leila and Tess looked down and around to enjoy the beauty of it. The green trees close to the mountains looked so clean they appeared to have been washed a minute ago. The flowers held such shining colors that not even the darkness of night would have the power to affect their immaculate aspect. All kinds of birds filled the ambience either flying from tree to tree, or moving around over the spectacular green-green grass. The pungent silence traveled away in conjunction with the meek waterfall noise.

Limbo Rock landed precisely next to the Ghost Orchid. Leila and Tess climbed down and silently looked at the flower. They could never find words to describe the splendor of it. The leaves and steam of the flower held two shades of green and the petals displayed the clearest, shiny, white, ever imagined.

"Oh, I wish I didn't have to pick it from the ground. This is the most beautiful flower my eyes ever saw."

"Leila, we need the flower. The enchantment of it may force you to drift away from the real purpose of being here," added Tess. "Please, pick the flower."

"Yes. I must concentrate on what I came to do." Decisively, she kneeled down, opened the leather bag she brought, took out of it a little knife, cut the flower and tenderly placed it inside the bag. Next, Leila grabbed the canteen she had wrapped around her waist, walked closer to the waterfall and carefully filled the canteen. She performed it believing in the power the water possessed. The water carried the vigor to galvanize the darkness of the curse.

Following that, Leila told the dragon she was ready to fly back. They left the valley and before noon they landed once again at the back terrace of the Astafe Castle.

Mrs. Maglaja, David, Olivia, and Lucas, rushed outside to receive them. By looking at Limbo Rock's face, they silently agreed that it was worth a voyage, the details… of course… later on. Mr. Inbacula came to speak with the dragon. He brought with him a bucket of water which he held up for the dragon to drink.

"Go ahead Inbacula, ask," said the dragon.

"No. I know she got what she needed. Thank you."

"Assamola," responded the dragon. *Assamola* minted *you're welcomed* in Racyque language.

"Mr. Limbo Rock, no one speaks Racyque in the Province of Bonavery," explained Inbacula.

"I know. But I do."

The dragon turned and left for his cave at the far end of the valley. The fact that several details must be taking care off in order to lift the curse, triggered a new type of concentration around Leila and the children. They knew a difficult task lay ahead and of course, their role in this tribulation was not yet over. Such reality elevated their concern to a next level of meditation. Today will be the day they will put the QUARELA CURSE away forever.

In the sequel of this darkness wrong doing, the second step was to bring down the rain. Leila must dance one minute under the rain holding the white orchid. In truth, what she had to do was very simple, nevertheless, the rain does not come and go like natural spills. Without the rain she couldn't move on to free herself. Will Leila be really lucky to advance breaking the cycle of this dark magic? Will Lucas Lambert be seriously capable of bringing water from the sky?

David Dreepel, kept reading to see if he could find how to create a rain without using magic or how to use magic without using a magician. No magician could create the rain for Leila, but any person could use whatever force was available to bring the rain.

"Lucas, you do not have to say any magic words," said Tess. "When I helped David, I just looked firmly at the ambience and thought about the wind."

"I don't think I can do that," stated Lucas. "From the bottom of my heart, I wish I could do something to help, but it will not work."

"Stop this nonsense," shouted David. "Grab your heart and soul, and your desire to help Leila. Let God Eller, or the Kordentes Legion of Dragons, or fairy tales do the rest. With a simple desire in her heart, Tess brought the breeze which save my life. You can do the same. So, reorganize the desires of your heart, step outside and bring the rain."

Leila and her mother were in the kitchen also revising some books. They desperately, wished to find an alternative for the rain in case Lucas failed to use his gift.

Mrs. Maglaja felt frustrated and said, "Leila, talk to Lucas and convince him to give it a try. He's your best option."

A deep silence ran through and increased the blankness of Leila's thoughts. She looked to the flower on top of the table, considering how sad it would be if she loses it after having made the trip to the valley. She meditated upon the difficult mission she had at hand.

As Leila confined with the sadness she experienced, for she did know what to do next, the children ran in delightfully. They noisily flocked around the kitchen table.

"Leila, grab the flower and let's go outside. I'm going to help you," said Lucas. "I have a strong desire in my heart to do that. Perhaps, in it… lives the power I would need."

Leila hugged Lucas wordlessly. Then she picked up the flower. They all went to the back terrace of the castle. For a few seconds,

Lucas held the hands of David, Olivia and Tess. "Please, let's hope for the best."

Lucas walked away and stopped in front Leila. She was wearing a long white dress, the same one she wore to go to the valley to pick the Ghost Orchid. Her hair fell abundantly over her shoulders. Lucas opened his eyes wildly, looked around and contemplated the sky. He did as Tess said. He only wished for the rain to fall down.

Their thoughts carried the weight of the magic they were about to witness. Their eyes looked up in total distress, agony and expectation, tied them together. They paused for some wonder. They waited until swiftly a frail noise gradually began to fill the air. It was the noise of water falling from above. Incredible…! Lucas brought rain to the Newzuma Valley.

Leila immersed gratefully into the rapture of this rain. Mutely, she celebrated the moment, thanked the sky above her head, moved left and right, turned around, dancing and danced with her flower. The rain lasted for a minute. All that Leila needed. Following that, they all returned to the kitchen to boil the Ghost Orchid.

Obviously, Mrs. Clenilde had the water from the waterfall in a middle size pot, boiling. Leila approached the stove and submerged the flower in the hot water. Magically the flower dissolved entirely, as if it was made of sugar and the water became thicker, very similar to milk. The adults and the children submerged into the enchantment of it. In many ways, the outcome of this endeavor intensified their beliefs.

As the pot was set aside for the potion to cool off, Leila asked, "Mother, where is Professor Breno Coorbell? Without him I cannot finish it?"

"I'm here, my dear, Leila" answered the professor walking franticly next to Inbacula, who opened the front door for him. Professor Coorbell carried a joyful smile on his lips and confidently put on his black and orange beautiful Ceburda.

"I am ready for this unusual ordeal. Once in my life I did it and it was long, long ago, but I recall everything from that day."

From this point on, Professor Coorbell took control of the activities. First he approached the table where the pot with the potion was placed and looked at it. He leaned over and observed it closely.

"Oh yes, it has stemmolas. Perfect."

"What is stemmolas, professor," asked Olivia.

"It is the veins of the stems of the flower. Come here, look. Do you see these tiny green hairs over the milk water?"

"Yes, I do."

"This is the stemmolas. It means the flower was healthy. Very healthy."

Professor Coorbell grabbed a mug and poured some of the potion in it. He walked to the center of the kitchen and said, "Leila, please stand here and drink all of it. Do this in front of me. I need to see the words that will come out of your mind. Do not move or turn until I say we are done. Do you understand?"

"Yes."

Leila placed herself in the middle of the kitchen and in front Professor Coorbell, she began to drink the milk of the Ghost Orchid. Mrs. Maglaja, Mr. Inbacula, Mrs. Clenilde and the children, remained close to each other observing the activity.

When Leila finished drinking the potion, her eyes closed and her head started spinning fast around her neck. It turned faster, and faster... until it abruptly stopped. Lots of alphabet letters floated from her head. They were white and they swung in the air as if they belonged to a ritual dance. As they calmly seesawing for few minutes, they rearranged themselves and the first word formed in the air for Professor Breno Coorbell to read it.

The professor read out loud, "LARPRICONE...! Then came the other words, "BREATIZELMA...! DURABOYANTE...! TARFIARA...! DRIVADORZA...!"

As soon as the professor finished reading the fifth word, the letters of the alphabet mixed and transformed into a beautiful white orchid. The orchid swirled around Leila until its petals disconnected from the stem and fell down. While on the floor, the petals converted into beautiful doves which instantly, flew throughout the kitchen and then out the window. When the doves were no longer in the kitchen, Leila opened her eyes.

"Great Leila!" uttered the professor. "You're released from this horrible curse. Everything, went perfectly well."

Leila hugged the professor, then her mother, and the children.

"Now, do some magic," said the professor, "I want to make sure your power is back."

Leila looked at the children and said, "Children come with me to the dining room."

Not only the children, but all the adults followed her. In the majestic dining room, Leila pulled out some chairs to create space around the dining table. Then she said, "Tess had a dream about a yellow house as the place to start looking for the Red Scorpion. Let's see how many yellow houses we have in Lili Sandra."

Glancing around, Leila retrieved from the air a map of the city of Lili Sandra. Without touching the map, she unfolded it and slowly placed it over the dining table. All yellow houses appeared on the map and the streets names flashed in and out. Leila jumped to express her happiness and grabbed David Dreepel and danced with him.

"Yes, I have my power back."

Again, she approached Professor Coorbell and happily said, "Junara." In Lastenia it meant *thank you*.

Finally, the QUARELLA CURSE was lifted and Leila would be able to keep her studies and one day becoming a magician. Now, hunting for the Red Scorpion will be her next challenge; however, there were lots of things she didn't know. For example; her greatest encounter was not the Red Scorpion, but finding her real purpose inside the Aliel Legend. Obviously, she carried secrets that she didn't even dare to imagine.

For the people, she always will be… LEILA. But for the sake of magic, she was already born… as ALIEL.

CHAPTER
15

ON THE NEXT DAY, without any delay, Leila and the children walked toward the center of Lili Sandra and rented a carriage for the whole day. Leila used the same young man her mother always did business with, Cairo Tartavel.

"Cairo," said Leila, "Good morning."

"Good morning Miss Leila. How can I help you?"

"I need you for the entire day. Will it be possible?"

"Of course."

"Good," added Leila. "I will be hunting for some yellow houses. The first one is on Polka Gardena Street. The house number is 7543."

In less than a minute, they were all inside the carriage traveling across the city to find Polka Gardena Street. This was the North part of the city and the children saw a landscape they had never seen before.

At the Polka Gardena, Cairo Tartavel stopped in front a lovely small yellow house at the corner of the street. Leila and the children got out of the carriage and Leila knocked on the front door. Immediately, a young lady opened it and talked to them.

"Yes," she said, "May I help you?"

"Hello, I am Leila Maglaja and they are my companions. We are looking for a Red Scorpion and according to the information we have, it is here in Lili Sandra hidden in a yellow house. Have you seen it or heard about it?"

The young lady answered quickly. "No!"

"Thank you."

"You're welcome."

Leila and the children climbed into the carriage and left. They went to Casta Chinsal Street, about ten blocks away and an old man who answered the door, also never heard about the Red Scorpion. They thanked the man and left. They did not stop looking. After that, Cairo Tartavel took them to another five streets and none of the yellow houses they visited had surprised them with any good news.

Leila and the children felt disappointed because nothing positive had come about and of course, Lucas began thinking that Tess's dreams about the yellow house happened to be as wrong as her wish at the Rastaga Woods.

While turning the carriage to leave, Cairo spoke. Kindly he said, "Miss Leila, instead of going to Basta Kerena Street, let's go to Pedrad Vestida. People say that weird magicians lived on that street. Do you have that street on your list?"

"Leila glanced at her list. "Yes, I do."

"Great… we're going there."

"But Cairo, we're close to Basta Kerena. Let's go there first."

"Miss Leila, the yellow house you're looking for is in Pedra Vestida. Trust me."

Leila decided to trust in Cairo's instincts.

They traveled west and twenty minutes later, arrived at Pedra Vestida Street. It was a short street filled with ugly dirty houses and at the very end of it there was a miserable small, yellow house. As soon as Leila saw the house, she felt happy. Intuition told her… that was the house.

Excited, she and the children got out of the carriage and walked toward the miserable yellow house. "Children," she said, "Be carefully because we don't know what we might find inside it. I feel our search ends here, but I cannot guarantee what will be next."

Leila glanced at the children, breathed in deeply and knocked on the door. A short, skinny, old lady answered the door. As soon as she saw Leila and the children, she pressed the door firmly attempting to close it. Quickly, Leila placed her foot in front the door and stopped the action. With the help of the children, Leila forced herself in. Once inside, the old lady moved back with indignation flashing out of her eyes.

"Leila Maglaja…! Get out of my house or you will regret you have come."

"Jacira Caponette…"started Leila, "Who would expect that? You babysitting the scorpion? Where is the Red Scorpion?"

Instead of an answer, Jacira Caponette brought a yellow color to her eyes, raised her right arm and quickly lifted Leila into the air. Jacira Caponette had acquired the second rank of magicians. She could flash yellow light from her eyes when executing magic power.

Ravenously, with all her power, she sent Leila against the wall. After she bounced against the wall, Leila fell on the floor unconscious.

Olivia and Lucas ran toward Leila to see what they could do to help. The old woman eyed them with the intention of doing with them the same she did to Leila.

"Do something David," said Tess. "Go on, use your power! Shrink her!"

"No! I don't think I can do that."

"David, shrink her! Do exactly what you did with the dragon."

"She has power. This will not work with her."

"You have power in your heart and soul and you're not despicable. The good always overpowers the evil."

David saw the old lady elevating her arm to harm Olivia and Lucas. He firmly looked at her and imagined her petite. *Why not make her smaller that a German Shepperd? Yes.... In the size of a cat?* As he finished his thoughts, in the size of a cat... she became.

The next few seconds, the old lady glanced at David, trying to bring yellow light to her eyes to do some magic, but it did not work. David grabbed her and sat her in her rocking chair in the dining room. Silently, she realized that by being small, she couldn't harm them anymore.

Leila opened her eyes and saw Olivia and Lucas next to her.

"Where is she?" asked Leila.

"She is in her rocking chair harmlessly. In the size of a cat," said David Dreepel.

"Wow.... Were you able to shrink her? Did your power work?"

"Yes, Leila. It did."

With the help of the children, Leila set on the floor. She had pain in her back because of what Jacira Caponette did to her. David and Lucas helped her to move and sit in a chair.

"Are you okay, Leila?" asked David.

"Yes, my back hurts, a little bit, but nothing that I can't handle. Perhaps I should have some water."

Steadfastly, Tess and Olivia ran to the kitchen to get the water. David and Lucas stayed in the living room with Leila. Tess returned with the glass of water and Leila immediately drank it. After drinking some water, she felt better and attentively eyed the children. "Thank you," she said.

Calmly Leila stood on her feet and stretched her back. While doing that, she noticed that Olivia was not with them. Scared she asked, "Where is Olivia?"

The children looked around and realized that Leila was right, Olivia was not with them. Worriedly, they started walking through the other rooms of the house, looking for Olivia. As they advanced toward the kitchen, they met with Olivia.

"Leila, come to see what I found," said Olivia, "In the basement. There is a man in chains down there."

Leila and the children descended the stairs and saw a skinny man, hair all over his shoulder and face, sitting on the floor and his feet attached to a heavy chain. It was obvious, he was blind.

"Please, help me to get out of here. This witch has had me like this for four years."

"Why?" asked Leila.

"Because I found the Red Scorpion."

"Is it here? Where is the scorpion?"

"Oh... now I don't know. She took it out of this house two

months ago. She probably knew you were coming."

"No, she didn't know, but it doesn't matter because without the Red Scorpion, we don't have anything to do here."

"No. Wait... I don't know where the Red Scorpion is, but I know who can find it for you."

"Okay. Who?" asked Leila.

"Marco... Prado... Cashemire."

"And who is Marco... Prado... Cashemire?"

"My brother. He is brilliant. Another great magician and scientist this planet has the privilege to possess. He writes about spells and gravitation. He knew by memory 745 spell words and has special powers to create Chrystal Balls."

"Where is he?"

"He lives in the basement of Loyporcha Magic School. He secretly works for the school."

"And who are you? asked Leila.

"I am King Duayne Prado Cashemire."

"Oh, you're the husband of Queen Naelia, right?"

"Yes. Jardel Vinclaro Caponette killed her."

"No," shouted Tess. "Queen Naelia is alive. I spoke with her."

"What?"

"Yes. I have spoken with her. Now, I understand why I had the dream about the yellow house. The Purple Talisman held these mysteries together."

"Who are you?" the king asked.

"I... am—"

"Come on children," interrupted Leila, "Let's help the king and together leave this place. It is dangerous to remain here. Jacira will come back. Remember, in a minute she will recover her size and will attack again."

"Jacira Caponette keeps the key to my chains in the pocket of her dress," informed the king.

"Oh no," exclaimed David. I shrank Jacira, so the key is no longer the same size."

"Don't worry," added Leila, "I can break this chain."

Leila brought green light to her eyes, extended her arms and broke the chain. Following that, they exited the yellow house and returned to the Astafe Castle. At the castle, Leila looked for Inbacula. When she found him, she said, "Inbacula, please take care of—"

"Oh…! King Duayne Prado Cashemire?"

"Yes. Who are you?"

"Inbacula."

"God Eller, have mercy. Inbacula, what are you doing here in Lili Sandra?"

"I am here serving Miss Leila."

"What a pleasure knowing this."

"Are you blind?"

"Yes, Inbacula."

"I am sorry, Your Majesty. However, it's good to know you're alive. I thought you were dead."

"Lots of people believed this is the case. I think the whole Province of Jarmayra believe I am dead."

Leila spoke again. "Inbacula, I'm glad you and King Cashemire know each other. Please take him upstairs and prepare a bath for him and help him to cut his hair if he wants to do that. Ask Mrs. Clenilde to prepare the best room available for him."

"Yes, Miss Leila."

Now, Leila and the children returned outside and asked Cairo to take them to Loyporcha Magic School. They must talk to Marco Prado Cashemire before Jardel Vinclaro Caponette had a chance to talk to his mother.

At the school, Leila looked for her mother. She found her inside a classroom, teaching an afternoon class. Leila asked the children to wait in the hallway. She entered the classroom and whispered on her mother's ear.

"I just found King Duayne Prado Cashemire. I need your help."

Leila's mother brought an astounded expression to her face. Following that, she spoke with the students and explained to them, she must end the class because of an emergency. Without delay, the students closed their books and prepared to exit the classroom. While Mrs. Maglaja was grabbing her coat to do the same, Leila asked, "Do you know Marco Prado Cashemire?"

"Yes, I do. He's the brother of King Duayne Cashemire."

"Do you know where he is?"

"No. For a long time no one knew anything about him."

"Well, according to King Duayne, Marco Prado lives and works in the school basement."

"What?"

"Just like I said, I think only a few people know it."

Wondering how true it might be, Leila and her mother walked straight to the school library to see if they could speak with Professor Breno Coorbell. Leila needed to check on the accuracy of it. They went straight to the library because usually, in the afternoon, Professor Coorbell spent time there, reading.

As soon as they entered the school library they saw him sitting in the corner of the room close to a huge window. Leila, her mother and the children approached him.

"Good afternoon Professor Coorbell," said Mrs. Marcela Maglaja.

"Good afternoon," responded the professor, lifting his head surprisingly. He eyed them suspiciously. Normally, no one dared to disturb him when he was reading.

"Professor Coorbell, I am sorry we're bothering you, but it is an important matter," explained Mrs. Maglaja.

Closing his book and concerned about what could be the issue, he added, "Alright. What happened?"

"Leila and the children just found King Duayne Prado Cashemire here in Lili Sandra. He had been a prisoner of Jacira Caponette."

"King Duayne Cashemire is alive?"

"Yes."

"Oh… this matter needs my full attention. Let's go."

"One moment Professor Coorbell," said Leila, "Before you decide what to do, I need to know something. King Cashemire told me his brother Marco Prado Cashemire, secretly lives in the basement of this school. If this is true, I must go to see him. According to the king, he is the only person capable to help me find where Jacira Caponette took the Red Scorpion."

Professor Coobell, who was already standing to go see King Cashemire, quietly sat down. "I can't help you with this matter,

Leila. Secret is secret, and we… sixth magicians… agreed to never disclose it."

"Does the school keep him prisoner?"

"No. He wanted to exit from society to protect the Aliel Legend. He dedicated his life studying the power of the Purple and Red Talisman. He's brilliant. He said that only the Aliel girl could save him from the Draba Legion of Dark Magicians."

"How?"

"Helping him to solve the mystery of the Talismans. The Talismans needs to be unified and return to the Suacileu Tabernacle."

"Professor Coorbell, who told you that?"

"He did. Marco Prado."

Leila studied the professor for few minutes. Then she said, "I am the Aliel girl professor, so I must see him. No one has more secrets for him than I do. You see? I need him and he needs me."

"You're the Aliel girl?"

"Yes."

"How did you find out about that?" the professor asked.

"I did," responded David Dreepel, "For many years only her mother and father knew it. Now I, Lucas, Olivia, Tess, and you… know it, too. And it should remain a secret."

Thoughtfully, Professor Coorbell focused his attention to David. He felt uneasy that David Dreepel suddenly knew such top-secret information.

"Who has trusted you with such a restricted secret?"

"I don't know. I'm David Dreepel. And my existence is a classified topic even to myself. Today, I know that Leila is the Aliel girl. And tomorrow… she might find who David Dreepel really is, because I don't know anything about my existence."

"Well… I know your father," said the professor, "But the perplexing journey of yours, has secrets that I prefer to not know for my safety and yours."

"It is hard to believe that you don't know where David Dreepel's father is," said Leila, "But like you have said, 'To avoid dangerous endeavors, let's take one step at a time'."

"That's right Leila. And remember, the Aliel legend keeps intact the magic of My Jupiter. Be proud that you're part of it."

"I am. And now back to my business… *one step at a time*" said Leila. "My next step today is to see Marco Prado Cashemire."

"I have to check with the other professors, Leila. I cannot take you to see this man without consulting the other magicians. I will be accused of breaking an agreement."

Leila looked around disappointed. She had to see Marco Prado today. Something inside her head said this is the moment.

"Professor Coorbell, nobody else can know I am the Aliel girl. So, you can't disclose this conversation we just had to the professors. The solution for our problems can be simple; you and my mother take the children back to the Astafe Castle and I go to the basement to meet Marco Prado Cashemire. Show me the way to the basement, I can do this furtively. You know nothing. You were at the Astafe Castle speaking with King Duayne Cashemire."

Professor Coorbell glanced at Mrs. Maglaja and then at the children. He inhaled deeply. He hated the idea of not helping them. Aside from that, it was true that Leila and Marco Prado needed each other to keep the journey's fruition.

"Okay Leila. I feel great that you're the Aliel girl. This revelation makes me very happy. And just because of it, I will do what you wish."

Then, he asked her to follow him. He took her to another corner of the library, far from Mrs. Maglaja and the children. When he was ensured no one was listening, he said, "Go to the far end of the school, the north side of it. On the left corner, there is an entrance to a small chapel. Behind the altar, there is a wall that slides toward the right and exposes the secret passage to the basement. I never told you that. Okay?"

"Okay. Thank you."

Leila turned around to return to where her mother and the children remained waiting, when, Professor Coorbell quickly held her hand. "Leila, promised me that when you find out who David Dreepel is, you will tell me before you tell anybody else?"

"Do you want this deal with Leila or the Aliel girl?" Leila asked.

"Why such a question?"

"Well, because one has the control of her thoughts and the other… only secrets."

"Explain it better," added the professor.

"The Aliel girl can tell you secrets you may not believe. For example, tomorrow she can tell you that David Dreepel is a grasshopper. Would you believe that?"

"Of course not."

"See, she can be as baffling as that."

Leila left and Professor Coorbell closed his eyes in reflection. He breathed in peacefully and silently repeated, David Dreepel…? Grasshopper…?

He laughed at Leila's sense of humor.

CHAPTER
16

ONE OF THE BEST words to modestly say when secrets are involved must be the first one that appears quickly inside our minds. And as ironic as it might be, the real meaning of this word should be irrelevant. A grasshopper, in that case, for Leila, became the whisper, an animal, a secret or perhaps only articulation. However; for some time the riddle will be disturbing Professor Breno Coorbell's intellect.

As soon as Leila left the library, she ran to the north side of the school and found the entrance to the small chapel. She climbed the altar steps and looked for the wall behind it. Following Professor Coorbell's instructions, she opened the passage and descended to the basement. Calmly, she advanced inside it. The lower ground floor was half dark, half bright, and the smell of herbs and potions steadily, impregnated the air.

For a moment, Leila strolled around observing the high shelves full of books and the long tables scattered at the center of the room.

The tables were packed with black caldrons of different sizes and all kinds of magic essences surfaced the spaces between the caldrons.

She moved warily, breathing gently, concerned about what could be next. Her mind held questions like: Is this man kind? Or a Monster? She knew nothing about him—Marco Pardo Cashemire.

"Hello dear," a lovely voice uttered. It came from one side of the library and from the top of a huge ladder. The man appeared to be about forty-two years old, had an widespread gray hair which extended comfortably throughout his shoulder, and at the moment; he wore a long brown tunic and held a massive purple book in his hand.

"Hello," responded Leila. Now looking up with an interesting expression on her face. "I am—"

"Aliel…," finished the man. "I know who you are. I have spent nine years of my life here waiting for you. No magician had ever studied the Aliel Legend with such a dedication as I did."

Moreno, the assistant and protector of Marco Prado came into the library from a small room located at the back of the basement. He ran to Leila, grabbed her arms and started to force her out of the basement. Moreno was the servant who brought to Marco Prado whatever he needed. Moreno even prepared his food.

"Master, I don't know how this young girl found the entrance to here?"

"Calm, Moreno. She's no danger. This is the girl I have been waiting for. She is Leila."

Moreno looked at Leila in disapproval. He felt guilt for not seeing her coming in.

"How did you find the passage?" asked Moreno, nosily. "Somebody told you about it, because in years no one saw me coming *in* or going *out.*"

"It was Professor Coorbell," answered Leila. "And he disclosed it to me because he knew this encounter between Marco Prado and I… would have to happen one day."

"See, Master. Someone told her about the passage."

"It's okay Moreno. Everything is fine."

"Yes, Master. Call me if you need me."

"I will."

Moreno silently walked away. When he disappeared through the small room in the back, Leila spoke, "Mr. Cashemire, I am sorry, I—"

"Don't worry, Leila. Moreno is like that. His job is to safeguard me and he feels proud with the way he does it."

At this point of their conversation, Marco Prado came down from the ladder. Now, standing next to Leila between the many tables he had scattered all over the basement he began to talk. Marco Prado still held the massive book in his hand.

"Why did you come today?" He asked in a gentle tone of voice. "Is this a result of the great evidences you have stored in your mind?"

"No," answered Leila. "I came because I have good news for you and because I need your expertise to help me find the Red Scorpion."

"Ah!…The Red Scorpion. Of course."

"You do know what happened with the son of King James Lamarcus, right?"

"Of course."

"I became involved in the search for the scorpion," explained Leila.

"Sometimes we can't avoid things like that to happen, right? The intrinsic maneuver of mysterious power. Tell me, what is, the good news you have for me."

"Your brother King Duayne Prado Cashemire, is alive. I found him today in Jacira's yellow house."

"Yellow.... This was the color of the house," said Marco Prado."

"Did you know she had him?"

"No. But I knew my brother was hunting for her and he never returned. After all these years, I thought he was dead."

"Fortunately, he's not. He's completely blind, but alive."

"Blind?"

"Yes."

"Oh… this is sad."

"Yes. Very sad," added Leila. "Why did your brother want to find her?'

"He knew she had the scorpion."

"How?"

"I told him."

Leila studied Marco Prado from the top of her eyes. "And how did you find out about that?"

"Through one of my crystal balls. I saw the Red Scorpion and discovered the plan Jardel Caponette and his mother, Jacira Caponette, had in mind."

"And why didn't you save the king's son?"

"I did. He is alive, not dead."

Leila eyed Marco Prado suspiciously.

"I could never see the color of the house, Leila. I always knew the scorpion held the supremacy of the curse and only with it, we could lift the spell. However, finding the scorpion and bringing it to the castle became a saga to every magician. I couldn't find the way to help catch it."

"But you told your brother, Jacira Caponette had it."

"Three years after the son of the king was harmed, my brother came to visit me. I told him the whole story and about the disappearance of the scorpion."

"Of course, your brother was in Nordache, and knew nothing about the curse."

"That's right," responded Marco Prado. "My brother was the King of Jarmayra Province. He lived in the Shelicart Castle in the city of Nordache. Caponette anarchists, entered the castle, killed my brother, kidnapped Queen Naelia and her two daughters."

"But King Cashemire didn't die," stated Leila.

"No. A noble servant saved his life and kept him hidden for two years. During this time, the people from Nordache believed that Jardel Caponette also killed Queen Naelia and her two daughters."

"When I was in school and was studying the Province of Jarmayra, my mother told me that sad story."

"On the year my brother came to visit me, I just had discovered, through one of my new crystal balls, named Kiulaya, that the scorpion was hiding here in Lili Sandra. My brother went to Bonahunta to see King James Lamarcus. He thought that by informing the king the scorpion was in Lili Sandra and promising, he would be hunting for it, he will gain a strong ally for the war to destroy Jardel Caponette. Millions of people had died in Nordache because of Jardel Caponette."

"I know that," said Leila. She was fully aware about the conflict.

"Although Jacira Caponette was the witch who entered the castle and caused the harm to the little boy, Jardel Caponette was the one who orchestrated everything," explained Marco Prado.

"Yes, but this is a powerful curse. Only a great magician would succeed in doing such harm."

"Indeed," added Marco Prado. "He had a magnificent magician helping him, plus the power of the Talismans."

"Ah… yes the Talismans," commented Leila. "Who was the magician helping him?"

"Orca Cinfera."

"I have heard of him. The Fantastic Cinfera, right?"

"Yes. Very clever," added Marco Prado. "This whole thing with the Red Scorpion really started eight years ago, in 1646. On this year, compelling battles between the most notorious provinces of My Jupiter gained significant importance. They were the Provinces of Bonavery, Jarmayra, and Normabell. The conflicts started because Jardel Vinclaro Caponette desired to unify the three provinces and crowned himself as the new king."

Of course, he wanted the power."

"Always, Leila" replied Marco Prado. "In these conflicts the main issue has always been the power. Everyone desires to be king, queen, prince, or princess. In fact these *wishes* became the disease of this planet."

"How did your brother find Jacira's whereabouts?"

Politely, Marco Prado invited Leila to sit down. He felt their conversation would go on for some time. After finding a nice spot between some of the tables, they sat down, and in a sweet tone of voice, he began to talk again.

"I have found in my crystal balls, that Jacira Caponette confined herself at Rastaga Woods. After the Red Scorpion curse, she moved to Lili Sandra with the scorpion, because Jardel Caponette feared King James would find the scorpion if it stayed in the Province of Normabell."

"Was she always in that yellow house?"

"I believe so. But I could never see the color yellow. The yellow appeared nebulous in my visions. I felt she lived close, however, I didn't know where."

"How do you think your brother found her?"

"He was living on the streets as homeless, investigating. This is what he said he would do because he had nothing else to lose."

"Do you know that Queen Naelia is alive? She lived as a prisoner in Rastaga Woods."

"Yes, I know that. Professors Coorbell told me. I have the Purple Talismans here in the library. He asked me to guard it until we return it to the Suacileu Tabernacle."

"Why did Caponette select the year 1646 to harm the son of the king?"

"Jealousy. He hates King Lamarcus because he married princess Claudia Salvati Rutnery. Claudia's father is the king of Cordavia Province, another land Jardel Caponette wishes to acquire. He wants the princess for himself. He believes in the union of these provinces to enhance the trade between the cities. Jardel Caponette needs to have the most notorious provinces of My Jupiter under the jurisdiction of one king. And of course, *he*…as the king."

"Now I understand why the conflicts. His first ambition was the union of Bonavery, Jarmayra, and Normabell. Then by marriage the Province of Cordavia."

"Exactly, like that," stated Marco Prado. "Aside from that, he holds lots of resentments against Loyporcha Magic School. The school recognized your father, Vachal Maglaja and Magno Dreepel, as the most magnificent magicians, and brilliant scientists this planet ever met in the course of two decades. This credit destroyed Jardel Caponette's prudence and he became the best villain ever. Since his intelligence never crashed under any concept, he succeeded in harming thousands of people."

"Who do you think can stop him?"

"I don't know, Leila. He graduated from this school with high standards. He is as good as I am, and now, he has a great warlock from the old time, a high priest from the Draba Legion of Dark Magicians, Orca Cinfera at his side.

"Oh…no! Your brother said you're magnificent and I believe in him. Do not compare you with this old-time warlock."

"I am good, Leila, but I am more scientist than magician. I like to study, discover things, and create what wasn't yet in existence. I am more like Mr. Nicolas Toscapela. I prefer to be the inventor."

Leila smiled a soft smile. She liked Mr. Toscapela and missed him.

"How long have you been living here?"

"Perhaps, nine years."

"Where had you been living before coming to the school basement?"

"In Calvendra Forest. After the Purple and Red Talismans had been stolen from the Suacileu Tabernacle. I decided to investigate the incident. The professors of Loyporcha Magic School needed to know how it happened. They needed an explanation. For years only chosen magicians knew the location of Calvendra Forest and Mount Mascratti. So, how did Jardel Caponette discovered it? And how did he succeed getting inside the Suacileu Tabernacle?"

"Obviously, Orca Cinfera", added Leila.

"Yes. He and Caponette re-wrote these unsuitable new pathways for the history of My Jupiter. They not only stole the Talismans, but also became the fresh revolutionaries people never expected to see. Frantically, they went on harming the public and destroying whatever obstacles crossed their ways. Lately, no one sees them on the streets because all the magicians desired to see the Talismans back at the tabernacle. The magicians are hunting for them and they know it."

"I have the impression that you know where Caponette and Cinfera are."

"Yes. I discovered it after Professor Coorbell brought the Purple Talisman to me. Because of fear, they lived at the south side of the Rastaga Woods. The Talismans have their own NORNÚLA; which in Lastenia, means—DIVINITY. I think this *secret power* of the Talismans, forges the panic they are experiencing."

"Right now, they don't have the Talismans, right?"

"We know they have lost the purple one, because we have it, but we don't know where the red one is. Remember, magic works in strange ways. They can have it very well hidden that my crystal balls cannot show it. And if they have the Red Talisman, they are just waiting for the right time to strike again."

"Then what do you think? Do they—?

"I don't know Leila. I am only questioning; The Red Talisman. Do they have it?"

CHAPTER
17

LEILA THOUGHT THE RED Talisman would appear quicker than everyone expected. There was a feeling of confidentiality about this. The DIVINITY in *it* is the power of *it*. And the unknown... can also bring joyful surprises.

Leila believed in the power of magic and she would keep her faith alive, no matter what. Calmly she asked, "Marco Prado, do you know what happened with me and the children in Bonahunta?"

"I do, Leila."

"I am here because of that. I need to find the Red Scorpion, otherwise King James Lamarcus will kill us. Your brother told me, you might know where Jacira Caponette took it."

"The scorpion is in the Dezatela Desert in the Province of Jarmayra, 2,546 miles East of Nordache."

"What?"

"Don't worry. You will be there on time. The scorpion arrived there yesterday. It took Jacira's helpers, two months to get there.

These servants don't have a special form of transportation, they went by horses. They are lucky the desert is on the border of Province Jarmayra and Province Normabell, otherwise, it would have taken them almost a year to get there."

"How big is the desert?"

"Huge. But don't worry, Leila. Everything will be alright. In fact, it will take at least two weeks for the scorpion to acclimatize. There are lots of caves that have no entrance for people, only small animals. Get there as soon as possible, because if the scorpion gets into one of these cavities, it will be hard to capture it."

"And how fast do you think I can get there? It will take the same amount of time the Jacira's servants took or… perhaps more."

"No…. David Dreepel will take care of it. How he will do that, I don't know. Tell him to check the book Inbacula has."

"Why are you telling me that?"

"I saw him using the Surdrape Time Fold Passage. Such a vision makes me think that Mr. Toscapela had thought about this moment. You will end this journey with the children. Don't be afraid."

Leila breathed deeply and released the air in slow motion. "Thank you," she uttered. "Thank you so much, Mr. Cashemire. Your words lessened my fears."

"Marco Prado. I like to be called Marco Prado."

"I should say, *Your Majesty*, because you're a prince."

"Oh no Leila, this aristocratic titles are for my brother. Not me. I am Marco Prado."

"Okay, Marco Prado. Do you want to come to see your brother?"

"No. I can only leave the school when Jardel Caponette and Orca Cinfera would not be able to find me. I made a promise to never exposed myself until they were defeated by higher power. You and David Dreepel are building their miseries."

"I don't see it happening... but David Dreepel said I carry secrets that I don't even know. I didn't tell you any today, did I?"

"Not. But in another time…, you will."

Leila stood up to leave the basement when Marco Prado asked her to follow him. "Listen. Before you leave this basement, let me give you a code."

Marco Prado walked Leila to one of his crystal balls located on a table in the center of the room. Gently he swirled his right hand around the globe. Two words appeared inside the crystal ball. Calmly, Marco Prado said, "Leila, read and memorize these words. With these two words we will be able to communicate. OTORGATA…! VOLTAPARY…!

Leila repeated the words, memorized them, and left the basement, as furtively as she walked into it. Outside of the Loyporcha School she found Cairo waiting for her.

"Cairo?" she called. "Oh! It is great to find you here available."

"Oh! Miss Leila, after I took your mother, the children and Professor Coorbell to the Astafe Castle, your mother asked me to return and wait for you."

"Oh! Thank you."

At the Astafe Castle, Leila had a meeting with the children. She allowed her mother, Professor Coorbell and King Cashemire to be present.

"Thank you, Your Majesty King Cashemire for telling me about your brother. You're right. He is adorable and very kind. He said the Red Scorpion is in the Dezatela Desert. It arrived there yesterday.

We need to catch it before it enters into small caves. He also said to ask David Dreepel to check on the book Mr. Toscapela left with Inbacula. There we should find a way to get to the desert quickly."

When Leila returned to the castle, the time was a little bit after four o'clock. She didn't have lunch, so, Mrs. Clenilde prepared something for her to eat. While she was eating, David Dreepel and Mr. Inbacula began to examine the book.

Mr. Toscapela, left the book in the care of Inbacula; however, Inbacula was not allowed to open the book without David next to him. Some pages of the book Inbacula can read, and some... only David.

Again, the first page always indicated in what page to go. Since they need to find out how to get to Dezatela Desert as quickly as possible, the first page read, GO TO PAGE 132.

On page 132, David Dreepel read: David, remember when, in Gargatuela, I used Surdrape Time Fold Passage type of transportation to transport you and your companions to Nordache, Province of Jarayra, year 1985? I am going to give you the power to use it; however, there are rules. If you do not follow the rules exactly as they are written, the power of such an amazing form of transportation will be taken away from you.

First, you have to say the preamble which is the same I used in the Dunes of Gargatuela and it is written down in this book; followed by the three magic words you must utter. You have to memorize all of it. For this task, ask Inbacula to read page 77.

Second, with your finger, you will draw a straight line on the ground. The line will magically become orange and will be visible for all of you.

DAVID DREEPEL

Third, You, Leila, Oliver, Lucas and Tess have to hold hands. After uttering the three magic words, cross the line together.

Rule Number One:
Never use the time transportation for your own purpose. It needs to be related with an intrinsic episode of you journey; otherwise, you can end in a place and time that you would be trapped forever.

Rule Number Two:
Never give the information you have to anyone. Not even to Leila.

Rule Number Three:
The power I am giving you holds limitations. For example: You can only travel inside the year you are in, and inside the planet you are living. Never to another century, planet, or galaxy. Attempting to overthrow your limitations will cause your existence to vanish from the planet. At no time try it.

After reading page 132, David Dreepel said, "I understood the instructions; however I need to memorize what I have to say. According to the instructions, Mr. Inbacula needs to read page 77."

Immediately, Inbacula opened it to page 77 and he and David read: Inbacula, please let the book stay with David for five or six hours. He has to memorize something. After that, the book should be returned to your care.

Inbacula closed the Titleless Book, gave it to David and exited the dining room. Leila, who was waiting for David to finish checking the book said, "David, tell me. How are we going to go to the desert? And when can it be done?"

"Tomorrow, Leila. I need to memorize what Mr. Nicolas Toscapela called *preamble* and the three magic words I have to say. After that, we should be ready. He is giving me, I think for this occasion only, the power to use the Surdrape Time Fold Form of Transportation. I will be able to take us to the desert in two or three seconds. After we cross the line on the ground… we will have sand under our feet.

"Marvelous!" replied Olivia "Like always… Mr. Toscapela is the savior."

"Oh, I missed him," added Tess.

"Me too," finished Lucas. "And now, allowing David to use this form of transportation, we will be the quickest children on the planet."

"No… Lucas," explained David. "I cannot use it whenever I please. There are rules and limitations."

"Can we break the rules?"

"No, Lucas. Such an attempt may vanish us from existence."

Their conversation went on and on. Everybody felt happy with the news about the way they would get to the desert. Especially, now, that they would experience such a thrill with David Dreepel, as a commander-in-chief, it would be an unforgettable encounter.

Leila delighted in the fruition of this afternoon. Finding the scorpion's whereabouts seemed easier than lifting the QUARELLA CURSE. Without hesitation, she set the trip for the next day.

King Cashemire enjoyed his moment at the castle as well. After being a prisoner for four years he was able to take a warm and long bath and have his hair cut short. As expected, Leila invited her mother and Professor Coorbell to stay for dinner and they all spent the whole afternoon talking and making plans.

Suddenly, King Cashemire said, "Professor Coorbell, would you help me to free my wife from those woods? I mean… can you use magic to do that?"

Instead of Professor Coorbell answering, Leila did. Apparently, at the moment, she was ready to release some of the secrets the Aliel girl carried inside her mind.

"No, Your Majesty, not now. First we need to catch the Red Scorpion, go to see King James Lamarcus and lift the curse his son is under. According to the revelation I am receiving now, we cannot go to Rastaga Woods before we have the two Talismans in our possession."

"But we don't even know where this Talisman is," added the king. "The life of my wife is in danger."

"No. At this moment, Queen Naelia is not in danger. She is just a prisoner."

"How do you know that?" asked the king authoritatively and impatiently.

"I am receiving this information right know. I don't know how, but they are in my mind. Queen Naelia is not in danger."

"Your Majesty," added Professor Coorbell. "You must trust Leila, because she is special." Professor Coorbell took a moment of silence. Leila and her mother noticed Professor Coorbell would love to tell the king, Leila is the Aliel girl.

"No, Professor Coorbell," replied Mrs. Maglaja. "You will not do that. Too many people already know that and this can become a dreadful threat for my daughter."

"Know what?" inquired the king.

"A secret that involves the Aliel Legend," replied Mrs. Maglaja. "Please, Your Majesty, let's respect what my daughter brings to the table for the sake of the struggles that created lots of pains to our provinces, and that yet, aren't over. Look at you. You are here saved... because of my daughter."

"Oh! I am sorry Leila," said the king. "Thank you for rescuing me from that house. I will always be grateful to you and the children. However, understand my frustration. I have been a prisoner for four years in that small yellow house and now I am blind. I have lost my daughters, and my wife. Suddenly, I am free and I found out my wife is alive. How do you think I should feel? I am afraid that the only thing I have left will be gone, if I don't act quickly."

"It is okay, Your Majesty, I understand your frustration" added Leila. "Lately, I have experienced it a lot. However, I want you to trust me and grasp the magic of it. One Talisman is one. And the other... is the other."

"Well..." exclaimed the king, "I don't know, Leila. It took eight years to find the Purple Talisman. Imagine if takes another eight years to find the Red one. I am hopeless."

"Don't be. It will not take us eight years to find the Red Talisman. This Talisman is close. I can smell it."

"I hope you're right," said the king. "However; I think that going to the Rastaga Woods first and trap the Red Scorpion after, would be more reasonable. Save a human being, then rescue an animal. The only problem with that is magic, right? In magic; things work differently."

"Absolutely right, Your Majesty," added Leila. "In magic; we can't place the future behind the present, because magicians need the present to change the future. So, for the sake of magic, let's do first… what must be done first."

BOOK THREE

THE PURPLE-RED TALISMAN

CHAPTER
18

THE RED TALISMAN WAS close. Leila sensed its presence. She didn't know where she would find it, but her instincts would eventually guide her to the exact space it occupied. The problem around this search was the scorpion and she needed to find it first. And if she didn't act fast, she would lose it.

After breakfast, Leila and the children prepared to leave Lili Sandra to go to Dezatela Desert. Before leaving the house Inbacula gave her a small iron cage, so she would be able to secure the scorpion when she found it.

When positioned outside the Astafe Castle ready to depart, David exercised the preamble.

> "In the name of what I can control. The ability of having the power of imagination, esoteric code D.L.O.T.L. two seconds fragmentation and incorporation, space, time folder, the present, Dezatela Desert, Province of Jarmayra, year 1654."

David traced a line on the ground with his fingers. The line gained color. It turned orange and mysteriously lifted in the air, folded in half and in slow motion seesawed a couple of times. Following, the line extended once again and gradually returned to the ground.

They all remained on one side of it. Leila secured the iron, wooden cage with her left hand and used the other hand to bond with Olivia's hand. Then Olivia gripped David's hand. David took Tess's, and finally, Tess held Lucas's. They were all in line holding hands.

"Are we ready?" asked David.

"We are," responded Leila.

"Okay," replied David. I must say the magic words. "DRIVABA! DORDONEL! CONTANEWSMA!"

Together they jumped over the orange line and magically disappeared. Mrs. Maglaja, Inbacula, and Mrs. Clenilde stayed behind with a beyond belief look tainting their eyes.

"Incredible, right, Mrs. Maglaja?" commented Inbacula.

"Yes. Mr. Nicolas Toscapela and Magno Dreepel had succeeded in folding the time. I am wondering what could be next."

"Can you imagine if one day we all could use it? Travel would become an outstanding reality in My Jupiter."

"Absolutely, Inbacula. Absolutely. But the only thing we can do now is hope for that. I believe the future always comes with fortunate surprises."

"Indeed Mrs. Maglaja... indeed."

The Dezatela Desert displayed the most peculiar landscape on the planet. Aside from being huge, it shielded eccentric rock peaks, and enormous caves. When Leila and the children arrived there, a vigorous wind showed its presence in all directions. The sand in the form of long snakes elevated in the air, as if the whole desert suddenly decide to leave the ground to go up in the sky. Leila and the children had to crouch down, close together, next to a huge boulder, until the windstorm ceased.

Fortunately, this particular squall traveled incredibly fast and crossed the south side of the desert in less than ten minutes. Luckily, Leila and the children managed to survive this first strange encounter.

Afterwards, Leila and the children stood up, shaking their wears and swiping off the sand from their faces. Leila succeeded in protecting the cage and their medieval hats by securing them between their bodies. Spontaneously, they all glanced across to connect with the environment.

"Now what, Leila?" uttered Olivia.

"Well… we need to find the scorpion. According to Marco Prado it will be at the south side of the desert because it is part of the region border of the Province of Normabell. Exactly, where we came from."

"Sir Marco Prado believed the scorpion will be close to the border," added David.

"Marco Prado said the servants of Jacira would never enter deep into the desert to free the scorpion. It would be too dangerous for them. So, the desert is huge, but we arrived already on the south side of it and close to the border. Chances are the scorpion is close."

Vigilantly, David stared at a boulder close to them. "Oh! Look at this cave. It appears to be a man-made dome."

The boulder had a one hundred sixteen feet diameter, ninety feet high and the external part of it showed no irregularities.

"What did you say, David?" asked Lucas.

"This cave. Look at it. It's perfect. It looks like a man-made type of thing."

"This is not a cave, David. It's a boulder."

"No. It's a cave."

"David…, a cave has an opening and I don't see any in it."

"Oh, it has entrances. Look at the base of it. Many accesses."

"These little cracks…?" commented Lucas, "These are not gaps. They are just small breaks on the boulder."

"This is a cave, Lucas," affirmed David.

Assuredly, Lucas pointed to the boulder and said, "Leila please tell me what is this?"

Leila and the girls took a moment to contemplate the rock. Together they said, "It's a boulder."

"See, David. Behind these cracks there's nothing more than the rest of the rock."

"This is a cave," insisted David, now a little bit annoyed.

"Okay," said Leila, "David insists it's a cave so let's walk around and find out if there is an entrance to it"

"Okay," agreed Lucas. "However…, before going ahead with this exploration, I have an idea."

"What is it?" asked Olivia.

"Why didn't Leila use whatever magic she can to find out if the scorpion is around?"

"I like that," added David, "What can you do, Leila?"

Leila lifted her head slowly as if she already had something in mind. "I plan to scowl the surroundings and grasp whatever energy exercises its influence between these rocks. I may catch some consistent vibrations."

"Great!" added the children with excitement.

Leila set the cage on the ground next to the boulder. "Please, help me take care of it," she said. Then confidently, she lifted her right arm in the air, brought green lights out of her eyes and acutely glared at the ambience.

While she did that, the children remained close and quiet. Leila gently turned her head to the left, then prudently to the right. She walked forward, attentively turned around, knelt down, brought her face close to the ground and scanned the sand. Observantly, she held this pursuit for a couple of minutes, then she exited the green light from her eyes.

"I detected an odd vibration. The sound was gentle, like heart beats of a small animal. It could be the scorpion. We should stay here and explore the area. If what I sensed is indeed the beats of his heart, he is very close. We should begin to look behind and over the rocks."

"And caves," added David.

"Yes, David, but real caves," commented Lucas.

"Children... we are here on a mission. Deserts are not a friendly place to stay very long. Let's work," said Leila. "To find out if the Red Scorpion is in the vicinity, we should wisely examine the zone. However, let's keep ourselves close. Understood?"

They replied *yes,* and immediately, separated from each other and began moving around.

David, who believed the boulder, was indeed a cave, walked away by himself. After the windstorm, many sand hills formed between the middle sized rocks scattered over the sand. Leila and the children spent time in the vicinity of these sand hills hunting for the scorpion. They meticulously, searched the arid region, believing that in a moment's notice, they would find what they were looking for. Scorpions hide between rocks and they had many around them. Each one walked prudently examining all group of rocks nearby.

Nevertheless, nothing happened. Olivia and her sister Tess felt discouraged with the outcome. They suspended their search to meet with Leila and find out what to do next. They walked side by side, back to the boulder, where Leila left the small iron cage.

They advanced, sensing the harshness of the desert when abruptly, they stopped. Their eyes witnessed a marvelous commotion, an unexpected chase—the Red Scorpion was coming out of a crack on the bottom of the boulder. The scorpion moved fast and behind it there was a grasshopper. It seemed the scorpion feared the grasshopper and began to run away.

Olivia and Tess exchanged curious looks. "Is this the Red Scorpion we are looking for?"

"I think so," added Tess. "How many Red Scorpions do you think live on the planet?"

"I don't know," responded Olivia.

"Let's followed it," replied Tess.

The scorpion, speedily left the boulder and began to walk on the sand. Since the sand had lots of crests because of the windstorm, the scorpion couldn't have a fast pace. Olivia and Tess hurried after it.

"We need to stop this animal before it finds a place to hide," commented Tess.

"Yes, but how?" inquired Olivia.

"I don't know. We must think of something."

They hurried in pursuit of it with their eyes focused on the sand. They didn't know what to do. Olivia felt helpless. She ran in front of Tess; afraid she would lose it if they did not come up with some idea. The scorpion kept moving forward and soon it would find a group of rocks to hide under. Olivia became part of the commotion and kept her pace after it until she noticed she was running alone. She stopped and turned, looking for Tess. She found Tess standing there.

"Fire… Olivia,"

"What?"

Scorpions do not like fire. Bring a ring of fire around it and it will stop running."

"But—"

"But what, Olivia? Close your eyes and wish for a ring of fire around it and you will see a ring of fire… around… it. Trust me."

Olivia decided to obey. This was not a time to *believe* or not *believe*, *do* or *not do*, *create* or not *create*. She closed her eyes and imagined the ring of fire around the scorpion.

We can't explain the power of soul and heart connected in the same smooth orbit. In a second, a beautiful red flame appeared on the sand and the fire closed, magnificently, around the scorpion. The Red Scorpion stayed in the center of it motionless, exactly like Tess had predicted. The scorpion closed its eyes, as if his existence came to an end.

"You stay here. I am going to get Leila and the cage," said Tess.

She ran back to the boulder and found that Lucas had fallen from a rock and Leila was trying to help him sit down.

"Leila, we found the Red Scorpion. Please come with the cage. Olivia has it trap inside a ring of fire."

"What?"

"We found it! Please bring the cage."

Leila, in steady fast fashion left Lucas and ran to help Olivia and Tess. Between the three of them, the mission was finally, accomplished. They succeeded in trapping the scorpion in the cage.

At the aftermath of this tottering moment, everybody crowded near Lucas, who almost injured himself badly. They spent some time watching the Red Scorpion inside the little iron cage. Now, it had its eyes opened. They all agreed it was a beautiful scorpion.

"Oh! Did you get it?" asked David as he approached them.

The children turned around surprisingly.

"David?"

"I knew it was a cave."

"Yes. The scorpion came from underneath it," said Olivia. "Where were you when—"

"Olivia, I was behind this cave, looking for an entrance."

"Did you find one?" asked Tess with a piercing look.

"Many. I was right. This is a cave not a boulder. It is a huge and tall cave."

The longest silence that ever existed between them just went through and it became as deep as an abysm. Their minds held an intense astonishment. *Did David get inside this rock?* Olivia and Tess, who saw the grasshopper behind the scorpion, also had strange thoughts. *Where's the grasshopper?*

"David did you enter the cave?" asked Olivia willingly.

"No, Olivia."

"Then, how do you know it's tall?"

"We can see it from the outside, no?"

"Do you know that a grasshopper chased the scorpion out of the cave."

Oh… not again, this grasshopper story," said David.

"I noticed that when the grasshopper is around you are not; and when you are around the grasshopper is not."

"Tess—"

"No, David. Listen… I saw the grasshopper for the first time, in Nordache and when it disappeared, I found you sitting on the ground underneath the tree. Then when I brought the wind and saved your life, you disappeared again and a few minutes later, Mr. Nicolas Toscapela appeared at the Astafe Castle carrying a grasshopper on his shoulder. He sat the grasshopper on the table. We went out to see the dragon and when we came back, we found you at the table eating and the grasshopper was gone."

"Tess is telling the truth, David," added Olivia. "At the Alyfurna Creation Store, you threw up when you saw the dry dead grasshoppers. Now, we had it chasing the scorpion and you again were not present."

"You must be joking, right?" replied David.

"Not for an instant," said Olivia. "There are lots of secrets behind your existence. Perhaps you're not human and need to accept it."

David remained quiet. He felt sad about what Olivia just said. He didn't want to be Suborder Caelifera; however, he also could not explain his existence any better.

While struggling to understand what could possibly be the life of David Dreepel, a drastic change of the ambience captured their attention. The sky engaged into a nightmare insurgence. Colossal dark clouds emerged and covered the sun light. Then, as fast as the darkness sheltered the area, an avalanche of forceful lightening rushed through in strange fast motion.

"Children!... Look at this," said Leila. "The rain is coming in horrible fashion. David, please concentrate on what we have to do because we need to leave this place now."

"Yes Leila," he answered. "Let's get together and make it happen."

When they were holding hands and waiting for David's performance, Leila added, "David, we will not be going back to Lili Sandra. We will go to Bonahunta, to see King James Lamarcus."

"For this I have to change the place when I articulate the preamble.

"Yes," said Leila.

"Okay. In what province is Bonahunta?" asked David.

"Province of Normabell," answered Leila.

In less than a second, David performed his task and together, they jumped the line and arrived in Bonahunta, Province of Normabell.

They landed smoothly in front of the Bacellar Castle. It was 1:30 in the afternoon. Bonahunta offered no trouble. The sky was very blue and the streets very empty. It looked as if the people suddenly decided to take a break from their activities.

As Leila and the children began to climb the stairs to enter the Bacellar Castle, Leila felt a strange force inside her mind. Her brain suddenly talked to her. *Say the code words Marco Prado gave you.* Obediently, Leila moved her lips and uttered, "OTORGATA...! VALTAPARY...!"

Without any delay, Marco Prado began to have a communication with Leila. Through her thoughts he said, "Jardel Caponette and Orca Cinfera are inside the castle. They knew you would come and since they were close, at the Rastaga Woods, they arrived first. Everybody inside the castle is under a spell. They are sleeping. You need to be strong. Jardel Caponette and Orca Cinfera want the scorpion. Orca Cinfera had used three words to exercise the *enchantment* they needed to enter the Bacellar Castle safely— VALCA...! DOLIMACHA...! PELCA...! If you articulate VALCA...! DOLIMACHA...! PELCA...! backwards and at the right time, you may break the spell they plunked over the castle. Please, use your judgment about what could be the right time. Good luck."

Since Leila stopped her actions to hear Marco Prado, the children thought she changed her plan about going inside the castle. They remained next to her in observation. When, once again, she turned her attention to the children, they in conjunction asked, "Won't we go in?"

Leila told them about her communication with Marco Prado. Carefully, she and the children walked into the Bacellar Castle. They found Jardel Caponette and Orca Cinfera waiting for them, sitting behind the huge table where the king and his knights usually, dined together. King James Lamarcus along with some of his servants and knights lay on the floor in the hallway, sleeping.

Leila and the children approached Jardel Caponette and Orca Cinfera quietly and afraid of what could happen. Leila knew that having the scorpion with her, would give her some advantage. She might use it to control the situation for a start.

"Hello Leila Maglaja," said Jardel Caponette in a sharp tone of voice. "We finally get to know each other. How are you doing?"

She eyed him before responding. Then, bravely she spoke, "I am good. However, concerned about how much of a loser you and Mr. Orca Cinfera will be. I hate to harm great magicians."

"Cut the good speech. You know we don't need that."

"You may not, but I do," added Leila.

"Give me the scorpion. Nothing will save you and these foolish children."

David stepped forward and said, "Be careful Mr. Caponette, because there is a *first time* for everything and Leila can surprise you."

Quickly, Jardel Caponette lifted David in the air and sent him against one of the walls. Leila jumped closer and lifted Jardel Caponette from his chair and also threw him against the wall.

"Leila Maglaja," uttered Orca Cinfera, "Let's not waste more time. Put the cage on top of the table, slowly." Leila obeyed. "You will die today," explained Orca Cinfera. Then, he fetched a knife from the air and sent it straight to Leila. She saw it coming and steadfastly reproduced herself into fifteen Leilas as the knife just missed her.

"That was good, but not enough to save you, because this is the *right time* to destroy you and the children, once and forever. Nothing can change this moment. Nothing!"

"That's right. Say good-bye to Bonahunta," stated Caponette now back on his feet.

The words—*right time*—said by Orca Cinfera, made Leila remember what Marco Prado said. Marco Prado told her she must find out when it would be the right time. Leila decided that was now. And assuredly she lifted her arms, brought the green light out of her eyes and she said nothing.

In a blink of an eye, she and the children began to float up in the air, up and up, until their heads touched the high ceiling of the castle. Jardel Caponette kept them floating, moving their arms and legs as if they were spiders dangling from their webs. He wanted to talk before eliminating them.

"Your mother, Marcela Maglaja, will be the next one I will destroy, then your father. I don't know where he went, but eventually, his path will cross mine."

Leila tried to send him some of her power, but immediately Caponette deviated it by bringing out of his eyes an orange light that created hundreds of poisonous snakes which covered the floor, moving recklessly, one on top of the other, eager to eat whatever they found.

From the corner of the room, Jardel Caponette and Orca Cinfera laughed… in great commotion. They enjoyed the show with great excitement. A student of magic would never be able to stop them. Leila succeeded to lift the QUARELLA CURSE they plunked on her, but would never scape the power of the magic they could perform together.

"When I bring you down, these creatures will understand why they are here. They bite and kill," said Jardel Caponette.

During this fantastic undertaking for Caponette and Cinfera, some strong and hideous noise came from the entrance of the castle. The noise advanced toward the dining room where the bizarre activities were going on.

Jardel Caponette and Orca Cinfera, twisted their heads to the entrance of the room and saw what they would never expect at that moment. It was a surreal type of thing and something totally out of their wild expectations. It was a great blue tiger with two impressive long wings and fabulous shining green eyes. It was the APERAGLA Tiger. One of the most supreme animals ever created by Strauda Legion of Light Magicians. The tiger was a Patronage Spirit. It sustained its existence between human and quadruped. Some magicians lived their whole life without having the opportunity to see one.

Jardel Caponette, quickly dumped Leila and the children down to the floor over the snakes and attempted to run toward the dining table to grab the cage with the scorpion, to escape. They couldn't lift their feet off of the floor.

The tiger flashed a thick white light out of his eyes, organized the snakes into a huge ball, lifted it from the floor and magically sent it into the air and out the window.

Both, Caponette and Cinfera realized they must use their commands together in order to fight the tiger. Quickly, they flashed orange lights from their eyes and directed it to the tiger. The tiger overextended his body and roared against Caponette and Cinfera. Cleverly, flashing the white light from his eyes, the tiger raised them in the air and above the dining table. Purposely, pointed their heads toward the window, and one after another, speedily, hastened them into the sky.

Leila and the children watched everything, standing up against one of the walls of the room. When the tiger finished his amazing presentation, its body engaged into a shocking transformation. Charmingly, the tiger became a pleasant man; age 42, blond hair down to his shoulder, lovely green eyes, and superb smile.

"Dad?" said Leila.

Vachal Maglaja opened his arms and hugged her.

"My dear Leila… you have no idea how much I have missed you."

"Dad, why did you leave us? Where have you been?"

"Leila, we will meet again, soon, very soon. Now you have no time. You need to break the spell that is affecting the Bacellar Castle. Only you can do that. Then keep going with your mission and save the king's son. The scorpion is in danger. At midnight the Otela Moon will be gone. The new moon is called the Ophema Moon also known as the incandescent moon, and cruel spirit moon. Under it, dark spirits dance at night and harm the peace. You can't take chances."

Then, kindly he looked at the children and added, "Lucas, Olivia, and Tess, I am glad Leila has accepted this mission. Your existence establishes the peace of the great aristocracy of this planet. And David Dreepel, you are the redeemer of infinity journeys."

Leila's dad turned around, regained his form of tiger, lifted his wings and flew out of the castle through the window. Leila and the children ran to the castle window to watch him disappeared. The tiger crossed the sky and faded between the clouds. Its manifestation left behind lots of questions.

On the aftermath of the tiger, Lucas spoke first. He did it eyeing David from the top of his forehead. "David, tell me… why you have been chosen to be the redeemer?"

David, thought for an instant. Then like always answered, "I DON'T KNOW."

CHAPTER
19

INSIDE THE BACELLAR CASTLE King James, his servants and knights were still under the spell Jardel Caponette and Orca Cinfera used to get into the castle safely. They remained on the floor, in the hallway, sleeping.

"ACLAVE...! AHCAMILOD...! ACLEP...!" said Leila at the same time she flashed the intensive green light out of her eyes. These were the three magic words Marco Prado Cashemire told her to say reversely, in order to lift the spell. She hoped this was the right time to say them.

Slowly, King James Lamarcus and four of his knights who were lying on the floor in the hallway, close to the dining room, woke up. Their faces held an abnormal expression. They looked like animals in dangerous space and completely forget what had happened.

Though, King James Lamarcus rubbed his head with one of his hands, puzzling thoughts occupied his mind. Confused, he stared at Leila.

"You…? Again…? In my territory doing this magic of yours? Young lady, today I guarantee… you will have no good fortune on your side."

"Wait… Your Majesty…," said Leila. Quickly, she advanced toward the table and grabbed the little cage with the scorpion. Skillfully she lifted it. "Look what I have here…. The Red Scorpion."

King Lamarcus opened his eyes widely, conspicuously, as he breathed in deeply. With imperative attitude approached Leila, held the cage and steadily brought it close to his face, "It's indeed it… hmm? I have imagined it bigger, didn't you? Beautiful…!"

"Yes. Very spellbinding animal. In my opinion, one of a kind," added Leila.

"Without a doubt," replied the king.

"Please, King James, take us to your son. We should not waste time. At midnight we will have a new moon, the Ophema Moon. Chances are that novel energies will be swirling the sky and we shouldn't take any chances."

"Fine, young lady. Follow me," said the king.

Quietly, they walked to the south side of the castle, where the boy, Willian Benard III Lamarcus lived motionless. The prince, age three, rested in bed, dressed in lovely medieval clean, stylish clothes. Queen Claudia had been called to assist the awakening of the child.

Once inside the room, Leila placed the cage on the bed and gradually opened the little door. The Red Scorpion didn't move. It stayed in the center of the cage waiting. Inside the room the silence intensified as a soft beat occupied their minds. Few minutes went by, few thoughts ran through, then a little noise arose. The scorpion began to exit the cage.

The action attracted everybody's eyes. No one dared to exercise any movement. The Red Scorpion walked leisurely in the direction of the cage's small gate and exited onto the bed. Then, inch by inch, climbed the boy's body. It strolled slowly across the child and stopped over the child's chest. The scorpion lifted its tale and clapped his stinger, turned around, and went back to the boy's feet. There, the wonder happened. The scorpion bit the right foot of the prince.

King James and his wife Claudia held their breath nervously, quite terrified about what could happen next with their child. They felt helpless.

Instantly, after the assault, a thick mist covered the bed, forming a solid white steam which began to spin gently and turned around and around until it spread in the air and vanished. The child simple disappeared with the mist.

On the bed remained the scorpion that magically, engaged into a curious development. Its red color began flashing slowly, then fast, the red seemed to vanish and arrived again, brighter than before and it converted into magnificent crystal—the Red Talisman.

The spectators watched this metamorphose in astonishment for they would never have an explanation for what just happened. They all exchanged glares and engaged into the radiance of the Talisman.

No words disturbed the impeccable instant for no one knew what to say. The wonder remained consuming the seconds inside the room, filling the space with absenteeism of actions. They all needed to confront a novel fact in order to face the new reality—a touch of magic or another surprise.

After this first disclosure, Leila spoke. She decisively faced the children and uttered, "Now, we know the scorpion is the Red Talisman. It was never a real animal, but a Leedrofic Adaptation."

Furiously the king asked. "Young lady, where… is… my son?"

For Leila, the tension of the moment disappeared. Her brain became aware of evidences she never knew were hidden inside her mind. She quickly, pointed to Lucas, "Here…. He is your son."

"What…?"

"Lucas Lambert is your son Willian Benard III Lamarcus."

"No. This is impossible," said the king.

"Your Majesty, you are going to hear a long story. The most unique story you could ever expect. Magic has saved your son."

Mystically, Lucas also became aware of the legitimacy of his existence. Like light striking his brains, he remembered that Limbo Rock—the dragon—once called him prince. Consciously, he began to talk, "Leila is telling the truth and I can prove it. Your Majesty, please take me to the library and I'll show you that I am your son."

King James Lamarcus frowned doubtfully. His eyes flashed out his entire agony. *This must be a nightmare,* he thought.

"James…" uttered Queen Claudia, "We don't have anything to lose. Listen to the boy."

"Okay, Claudia. Let's go to the library, however; you all should know that today… this young lady will not fool me."

The king exited the room in fast fashion and after him went Queen Claudia and the children. Leila delayed exiting the room for she had to secure the Red Talisman. Like before, she fetched from the air a red velvet box, placed the Talisman inside it, dropped the box into the leather bag she always had with her and walked after them.

At the library, she reunited with the children to witness what Lucas would do to prove to the king he was his son. Of course, Olivia, Tess and David crashed into a confused state of mind where the surprises stopped being enjoyable. They felt scared.

The lovely library held a tenacious silence that ended when King James asked, "Young boy, here we are. Why should I believe you're my son?"

Lucas walked to one of the book shelves and grabbed a book. Calmly, he returned to the king, and opened it. He confidently turned over some pages and stopped. He looked at the king and read. "Long ago, in the year 1571, a jeweler named Graindel, crafted the Lamarcus' noble ring. This ring was commissioned to King Kleber Lamarcus in Malta Febre, before Malta Febre became part of the Normabell Province. A magician named Elber Liche gave it the enchantment it now has."

"How did you know this was written in this book? Only the queen and I knew that."

"How shouldn't I? Perhaps because it's true, I'm your son."

Solemnly, Lucas moved close and showed his right hand to the king. "Please…. Place your ring on my finger. We will see… if it fits me."

"Young boy," cried the king, "This ring is the most impressive jewel my family ever possessed. It only sizes the finger of a genuine Lamarcus. And you do not belong to this lineage."

"Then… Your Majesty… don't hesitate to prove it."

Unconvincingly, King James Lamarcus gazed around. He urgently looked at Leila. "Don't fool me young lady, for if you do… today… I'll get rid of you… forever."

"I understand, Your Majesty."

The king looked at Lucas and buoyantly said, "If this ring fits you, then yes… I will have to accept you're my son. But I am confident this is not going to happen."

"I understand, Your Majesty," responded Lucas.

Captivated by his own curiosity, King James Lamarcus removed the ring from his hand and pushed it on one of Lucas's fingers. The opulent expectation framed an enigmatic enchantment. Enchantment that went on until the ring sparkled a tiny illumination and magically shifted from a big size to a small size; fitting Lucas' finger perfectly as if it was never on another hand.

Queen Claudia covered her mouth with her hand as tiny tears clouded her eyes. She remained shocked for few seconds, then she stepped forward and hugged Lucas. "It's true. You're our son—Willian! Oh, God Eller! Thank you! This is incredible!"

The king also admitted the truth. He had no power to deny it. Half happy and half perplexed, the king moved on and also hugged Lucas. He held the hug for some seconds. He waited so long for that moment.

"Welcome Prince Willian Benard III Lamarcus. May God Eller, always bless you."

For the first time in his entire life, Lucas felt so important. He sensed the legitimacy of his existence happening in front of his eyes. And silently commented, *how did the dragon know it?*"

"Young lady," called the king. "Tell me why my son was taken from me. Where did he live during these eight years?"

Courageously, Leila started to disclose all the information she had installed in her mind. "A few months before your son

Willian turned three years old, Jardel Caponette and Orca Cinfera, succeeded in finding the way to the Calvendra Forest where the Suarcileu Tabernacle had been placed many years ago. They went there, broke the spell that protected the entrance to the Tabernacle and stole both Talismans. With the Talismans, they obtained the power of Karobaf, which involves energy from the moons. Only these crystals had the transparency to identify such a power."

"You're telling me that Jardel Caponette and Orca Cinfera used energy from the moons to harm my son?"

"Yes, Your Majesty. Marco Prado Cashemire is an amazing scientist, magician, and mathematician. He spent his whole life studying the moon's energy and he also created lots of spells. He had more crystal balls in his archive than we have fingers in our hands. In one of his crystal balls, he saw Jardel Caponette and Orca Cinfera with the Talismans. He is the only magician who saw it."

Queen Claudia, suddenly added, "Jardel Caponette is an evil man. Nothing merciful would come from his soul. I know. I almost married him."

"That's true," replied Leila, "He desperately wishes the title of *king* and his ambitions have no limits. That's why he went so far."

"All this happened because of one man's ambition?" asked the king.

"Yes, Your Majesty. Nothing else than that," commented Leila.

A slight silence ran through them as their minds couldn't stop being busy with so many remarks. Leila continued releasing information.

"After discovering that Jardel Caponette and Orca Cinfera had the Talismans, Marco Prado created a crystal ball just to follow their movements. He succeeded in setting the crystal ball in motion. So, by watching them, day by day, Marco Prado discovered their intentions. Jardel Caponette wanted to harm Queen Claudia, because she had chosen to marry you. He wished to acquire the Cordavia Province by marrying her."

"Of course, he needed Cordavia and the noble title," added Queen Claudia.

"That's right," replied Leila. "And their second objective was a revolutionary war. They wanted to keep the conflict between the provinces."

"Now, I see that ambitions always crafted their actions, but explain to me why they didn't kill my son? Why they preferred to keep him trapped in this dark course?"

"Oh, they planned to kill Prince Willian, but magic didn't let it happen."

"Oh…! Between this whole commotion my son was taken away to be protected?"

"That's right," answered Leila.

"Who helped us in this magic ordeal?"

"Sir Marco Prado, my father, and Magno Dreepel. The father of David Dreepel."

King James turned his head to look at David. "Did you know this?"

"No, Your Majesty. I am hearing of it now, for the first time. And I think not even Leila knew anything until now."

Leila moved her head in agreement. Once again, she explained, "With the help of Marco Prado Cashemire, David's father and my father conceived a Leedrofic Adaptation Child. A fake child. Then, using magic to be invisible, my father and David's father entered the castle and swished the Leedrofic Child with the real one.

King James eyed Leila with his mind in disarray. For him this was too much of a fairy-tale. He needed to know more.

"Okay, they saved my son. For eight years my wife and I, have thought we lost our son because of the work of magic and now you're telling me that… a *work of magic* has saved him?"

"Believe it or not, Your Majesty. This is the truth."

"Explain it better, young lady," said the king.

"Your Majesty, this is how everything happened. Jacira Caponette disguised as a servant entered the castle with the scorpion. At night she went to the prince's bedroom and let the scorpion bit him. Because the child was a Leedrofic, the scorpion could only put him to sleep."

"This happened here in my castle?" asked the king

"Yes. On that same day, Jacira Caponette left the castle with the scorpion. She returned to the Rastaga Woods and gave it back to Orca Cinfera. Orca tried to convert the scorpion back into a Talisman and he couldn't. At that moment, he found out something went wrong. He consulted one of his crystal balls and discovered the child was just sleeping and knew that if the scorpion bit the child again; the spell would be lifted. That explains why Jacira Caponette spent eight years of her life babysitting the scorpion. And because of the power of the Talisman, Orca Cinfera never knew the child was a Leedrofic Adaptation."

"Where did they take my son? We have lost eight years of his life."

"Your son was taken to Nordache, 333 years into the future and was raised by a family named Lambert."

"Why? Why this? Why in the future?"

Leila sensed how hard it was for the king to understand what had happened. His frustration seemed overwhelming. Magic had never been his favorite subject and now all of this. Leila didn't know how far she still had to go. She quietly eyed David Dreepel. David said nothing. Lucas shook his head giving her his support. They had experienced a lot to stop right now.

Even though Leila noticed the complications of the story she was telling, she moved on. She kept revealing to the king all the Aliel girl guarded inside her mind. Because of the magic of it, she wouldn't be able to stop what she was doing. The intriguing secrets flashed quickly inside her mind to be told.

"Your son became part of an experiment. Mr. Nicolas Toscapela and Mr. Magno Dreepel spent time together studying the possibility of folding time. They shared their discoveries and finally, Mr. Toscapela proved the theory and developed the Surdrape Time Fold Passage. With such dominance traveling to the past or future became possible."

"Ah, Mr. Toscapela…," uttered the king. "I never liked that man. Now, I can see why he always could appear and disappear furtively, like our moons in the sky?"

"He used the Surdrape Time Fold Passage for the first time with himself, then with your son. Imagine… by taking Prince Willian into a distant future, he would not have to hide him from Jardel Caponette or Orca Cinfera."

"Young lady," started the king, "Hypothetically you are telling me what magic can *be* or *do* under the sky and above the ground.

Nevertheless, I want to know why 333 years in the future?

"That... I don't know, Your Majesty. Only Mr. Nicolas Toscapela would be able to give you an answer for such a question."

"James," uttered Queen Claudia, "Let's accept whatever hides behind it. We have our son back. Let's be grateful."

King James Lamarcus, breathed in slowly. He glanced around shaking his head. "Fine, Claudia, let's be grateful. We will organize a feast for tonight. I am inviting my lords and knights and we will celebrate the return of my son. Is that okay with you, young lady?"

Leila silently approached David and whispered something in his ear. Following that she said, "Your Majesty... yes, it is okay, we will be here. However, we must leave now. We need to go back to Lili Sandra to find out how we can rescue Queen Naelia from Rastaga Woods."

"Too much magic for my taste," said the king. "Young Lady, you do what you have to do. But my son is not going."

"Oh, no... Your Majesty, with all my respect, I must go," stated Lucas.

"Your Majesty, may I speak?" asked David Dreepel."

"Yes."

"We're here fulfilling a journey. You can't intervene in the fruition of such a crossing, because the future of your aristocracy depends on it. We will be back for the celebrations. But we must leave now."

"Your Majesty," cried Lucas. "I have to finish this crossing, for in it lays the future of My Jupiter."

"So, Queen Naelia is alive?" the king asked.

"And her husband, too. King Duayne Cashemire," explained Leila. "He is at the Astafe Castle in Lili Sandra."

Queen Claudia approached Leila and the children. "Leila, please go. I trust you. But please come back for the feast."

"I will," responded Leila.

After that, Leila and the children exited the Bacellar Castle. Outside it, David made the line on the ground, articulated the preamble, uttered the three magic words and to Lili Sandra they went. Back at the Astafe Castle for what? For what was yet to come.

CHAPTER
20

WHILE LEILA AND THE children were in Bonahunta, Marco Prado Cashemire had a vision in one of his crystal balls. Vachal Maglaja, Leila's father, swiftly appeared and spoke with him. After helping Leila and the children, Vachal Maglaja used his magic to communicate with Marco Prado.

His face emerged inside one of the crystal balls that was on top of the table at Marco Prado's work place. And when Marco Prado saw it, he immediately stopped what he was doing and got closer.

"Vachal Maglaja?" Marco asked himself, "What a pleasure having you here in my humble archive. How can I help you?"

"I came to tell you that Jardel Caponette and Orca Cinfera are no longer a threat to you. I sent them to a Tundra Cristronela, in the deepest part of Rastaga Woods. A place where magic has no power. Only some magicians from outside can help them and to figure out how to find *such a magician*, will take at least one hundred years."

"Thank you. This indeed is lovely news."

"I thought so."

Vachal Maglaja's face took the whole size of the crystal ball and he moved his eyes and mouth when he spoke.

"Marco… there is another thing I have to tell you. Your brother is blind because of magic. He is not ill. Jacira Caponette forced a spell on him. The spell can be lifted. Go to see Jacira. She is still there, in the yellow house, on Pedra Vestida Street."

"Another great news," replied Marco Prado. "My brother was a good king and deserves to reign again. If he could go back, oh… the people from Jarmyra Province would be very happy."

"Don't worry, he will rule again, soon. However, before this happens, other things need to take place. The urgent matter is the amalgamation of the Talismans. Please go to the Astafe Castle and help Leila. She and the children must make it happen and then, they must return the new Talisman to the Suacileu Tabernacle."

"If I find out how to do the amalgamation of the Talismans, you can count on it. However, I don't know anything about it," added Marco Prado.

"That's why I am here. I am going to refresh your mind. There are great revelations behind the Talismans. Revelations that will make even you very happy."

Marco Prado didn't say anything. He just kept his eyes on the crystal ball. Then confidently, Vachal began to coach him in how to help Leila and the children. He spoke with strict exactness and intact clarity. It was so wonderful the way the amalgamation of the Talismans would happen that Marco Prado listened questionless and with vivid fascination for being part of it. When Vachal Maglaja finished, he asked, "Do you have any question?"

"No. I understood what should be done."

"Good. I count on you on this."

The crystal ball began blinking its colors and Marco Prado realized that his meeting with Vachal Maglaja was ending.

"Wait a minute," said Marco Prado. "I do have a question. Are you coming back?"

I will, but not now. Until the APERAGLA tiger is alive, I cannot come back. This is the price I have to pay to have undertaken this delegation."

"I understand," added Marco. "Thank you for choosing me to assist in the amalgamation of these Talismans. I will do my best."

"I know you will. You are a great scientist and unique magician. One day you will be the number one on this planet. Keep up the good work."

Following that, exactly like he showed up in the crystal ball, Vachal Maglaja disappeared. Marco Prado remained quiet for another minute, thinking about this remarkable vision.

After Vachal left, Marco Prado opened the Bá-Onadi book and looked for blind spells. He found out that there were three ways of making a person blind—by magic. He carefully read about them. At the end of his reading, he called Moreno, his assistant and they went to the yellow house on Pedra Vestida Street to look for Jacira Caponette.

Once there, they knocked at the door. No one answered. Marco Prado used magic and opened it. Inside the yellow house, they found Jacira Caponette underneath the dining table. She had been reduced to a size of a cat. Marco Prado looked at her and laughed.

Then, he grabbed her from the floor and placed her on top of the table.

"Marco Pardo… who would think that you would be the one coming to visit me after your brother left this house?"

"Yes…. Who would think that a witch like you would be reduced to the size of a cat? Life is really full of odd surprises, right?"

"You didn't come to laugh at me. What do you want?"

"I know you're responsible for my brother's misery. You made him blind."

"How did you find out it was me?"

"Birds talk. And I have one in my crystal ball that doesn't fly, but loves to talk. And right now, you will be the one replacing that bird. You will talk." While saying that, Marco Prado took her by the waist and put her inside his leather bag.

"No…o…o…! Please, take me out of here." she screamed, but no one listened to her.

A few minutes later, inside the basement, Marco Prado took her out of the bag and placed her on top of one of his working tables. Jacira Caponette looked around curiously.

"So, this is where you have been all this time?"

"Hmm, hmm," added Marco.

"Where are we?"

"The basement of Loyporcha Magic School."

"My son looked for you everywhere, except here in the Loyporcha Magic School. He would never imagine the school would go this far to hide you."

"There are lots of things that I do that he would never imagine. I see him inside one of my Chrystal balls quite often."

"You're lying," replied Jacira Caponette.

"No. I'm not. But now, let's talk about my brother. According to Bá-Onadi book, there are only three ways to make a person blind by magic. One is with 165 POTION which involves dead bats in the preparation of it. The second is the KIARA MOON INCARNATION. The magician has to utter the five magic words at midnight under the Kiara full moon. Then, the last one is the incarceration of the LINAC COABINA BUTTERFLY."

"Wow… you have done your research," said Jacira.

"Tell me which one you used to harm my brother."

"No. Making King Duayne Cashemire blind, turned out to be one of my greatest accomplishments. I am not going to throw it away because you're asking."

"I will bring you to dust if you don't help me lift this spell. Think about it, because at the end, you will lose more. It's true, my brother will never get his sight back, but you will be particles inside a trash can. And life will not stop."

Jacira Caponette crossed her arms and walked cautiously over the table between all the material Marco Padro had scattered around. She even kicked some small articles with her little boot.

"Your son and Orca Cinfera will never come back. I think you should know that. The APERAGLA Tiger trapped them into a Tundra Cristonela in the Rastaga Woods. They will need an outside magician to free them, but… it will take—"

"Like *we magicians* always say; A HUNDRED YEARS to find one," added Jacira Caponette.

"Yes," replied Marco Prado. "And… please don't say—*we magicians*—because you are no longer a magician."

"It's true. My son, with his ambitions, ruined my life. I shouldn't have listened to him."

"Your son would destroy My Jupiter if we do not stop him. You know that."

"What do I get if I tell you what you want to know?" asked Jacira.

"Nothing."

"Oh… you have to give me something."

"You deserve nothing."

"I am going to ask for something simple. I promised."

"For example?"

I don't want to be a human. I want to be an animal; a cat."

Marco Prado looked at her and laughed tapping the table repeatedly. He laughed and laughed until he couldn't anymore.

Jacira Caponette walked closer. "I don't see what is so funny. I was a good magician and I still have my brain. Make me a cat, let me live here, and you take good care of me."

"You're joking, right?"

"No. Why should I? And I can help you create these spells you do. I have an amazing extra sensorial perception that travels beyond infinity."

"A cat?"

"A cat with the brain of a fantastic magician. I became a bad magician because of my son. Now, I can see I was wrong. I know that even if I manage to have my power back, the Loyporcha Magic School will never forgive me. I am your last option to cure your brother and you are my last hope to do something positive for the sake of magic."

Marco Prado remained quiet. His mind worked at full speed. To lift the spell Jacira plunked on his brother, he had to agree with her. And it was true what she had asked was not complicated.

"Okay. A cat?"

"Yes."

"What kind of cat?"

"A beautiful black cat with lovely green eyes."

"Fine. Tell me what magic did you use to harm my brother?"

"Wait a minute. I am going to tell you what magic I used and where you can find what help you to lift the spell. But this must happen my way."

"Jacira, don't play with my patience," replied Marco. "Be quick."

"Fine. First, I am going to tell you the magic I used. Then you make me a cat. After that, I'll tell you the rest."

"How? You're a cat. You do not speak."

You will make one of my nails bigger than the others and I will always be able to write with it. This is how I am going to help you with your work."

"A cat that can write?"

"Better than a talking cat, no?"

Marco Prado breathed in slowly. "Okay. Let's do this," he finally said.

Jacira then added, "I used the incarceration of the LINAC COABINA BUTTERFLY."

Marco Prado exchanged glances with her. He thought she was really smart in choosing the Linac Coabina. She used the butterfly… the most clean and sophisticated method. He walked away from the table and grabbed a book of spells he created. Then, flashing purple lights out of his eyes, he looked to Jacira Caponette and uttered nine strange, long words.

A crucial silence took over the basement and the power of it traveled over and above the planet. It went on transcending time and space, swirling inside lost craters and around big moons. Jacira Caponette, withdrew from the table in the form of miasma and a gorgeous black cat appeared in her place. The cat stood on his legs elegantly, stretched gracefully, glanced around, and walked to Marco Prado.

The cat used its paw to secure a piece of paper and with its right little long nail wrote: The Linac Coabina Butterfly is trapped inside a wishing well in the Rastaga Woods. You enter the woods, cross the first bridge, turn left, walk about twenty feet and the well will be there, behind a small log house.

Marco Prado quickly grabbed his leather bag, opened a closet located at the corner of the basement and took out his new crystal ball, Nackivela. Marco Prado dropped the crystal ball inside his brown leather bag, put on his long winter coat and called his assistant.

"Moreno, I am going to Astafe Castle and I don't know when I will be back. Keep an eye on this cat."

Immediately the cat walked over to one piece of paper and wrote another thing on it. I am not THIS cat. Is PICACHÚ.

"What is PICACHÚ?" asked Marco Prado.

The cat wrote: Picachú is my name. It means Goddess in, Rucharci.

Marco Prado turned to leave and the cat jumped off of the table. The cat looked for a corner to lie down. When it found one, it curved around her legs and closed its eyes to sleep.

Marco Prado took one slight moment to observe the cat. He felt sorry for Jacira Caponette. Again, he opened the closet in the corner of the basement, removed a comfortable yellow blanket out of it and silently, tossed it to the cat.

Picachú happily jumped on the blanket. "Miau!"

Marco Prado took it as... *thank you.*

"So long, Picachú," he said walking away.

"Miau!... Miau!... Miau!... Miau!"

Marco Prado interpreted this as: So... long... Marco... Prado.

CHAPTER
21

AFTER DRAWING A LINE on the ground—David Dreepel, Leila and the children, jumped over it and arrived in Lili Sandra. They landed in front the Astafe Castle. Together, they took an instant to contemplate the castle; their home in the Province of Bonavery. Then they climbed the castle stairs and entered it.

Inside they found, King Duayne Cashemire, Mrs. Marcela Maglaja and Marco Prado. When Leila saw Marco Prado she quickly commented,

"You…here? I thought you didn't want to leave the school basement, because of Jardel Caponette."

"This was before the APERAGLA tiger appeared. Jardel Caponette and Orca Cinfera are no longer a threat to me."

Leila then looked at her mother. "Mother, I saw dad. He is the APERAGLA tiger."

Marcela Maglaja contemplated Leila with a sweet smile on her lips. For a moment, Leila wondered why her mother showed no surprise.

"Mother… you know that, don't you?"

"Yes, Leila."

"Unbelievable! You hid this from me?"

Marcela Maglaja came closer. "Leila… my dear… in magic the impossible happens because the magician's keep secrets. If everything lies opened, there is no fantasy and only *fantasy can* shape creation. The absence of fantasy can destroy illusion. I was not allowed to disclose the APERAGLA Tiger Enigma to anyone. Not even you."

"Leila, your mother is right," replied Marco Prado

"So, my dad's gone to never come back?"

"No. He will be back when the tiger is gone. The tiger has five lives."

"Is the tiger a Leedrofic Adaptation Animal?" asked Leila.

"No, Leila. The tiger is not a Leedrofic. The tiger is a Patronage Spirit. Such a spell demands a vessel, a chosen devoted authority to give strength to the transformation. And in magic, the connection established between a spirit and an authority is called, Trossál Integraty. That means, the years involved in this magic must be respected by both the magician involved in it and the legion of sorcerers responsible for it. One day the tiger will be gone."

"But… you have no idea when it will be over."

"That's right."

Leila wiggled her head frustrated. She really wished her father could be around. "Magic… sometimes…. Sometimes the cruelty in it makes magic hideous. It's like having a power and not the right to use it."

"In magic, Leila," added her mother, "*Regulations* are in fact what shield the conception of any fabrication. In all of it, there is little to explain and a lot to believe."

Leila took a moment to reflect on what her mother said. She couldn't stop thinking of her father.

"Leila," called David. "We need to find out how to rescue Queen Naelia before it gets dark. It is already three o'clock."

"Yes, David. We must focus on it."

"Where's Tess?" asked Olivia.

Everybody looked around and noticed the absence of Tess. They only became aware of it now and had no idea how long she had been gone. Concerned about Tess' whereabouts, David Dreepel began to move upstairs to check the bedrooms. He climbed the first three steps when Mrs. Clenilde walked into the dining room. She immediately found out they were looking for Tess.

"Don't worry," said Mrs. Clenilde, "Tess is okay. She went to the cave to see Limbo Rock. Inbacula is with her,"

"Oh… okay," replied Leila. Everybody exchanged glares and breathed in, comforted.

"David," said Olivia, "I think you should ask Inbacula for the Titleless Book, so we can check if Mr. Nicolas Toscapela left something there about entering the Rastaga Woods safely."

"There is no need for that. I think the answer will be in one of my crystal balls," added Marco Prado, now moving close to Leila. He had been away from Leila and the children speaking with his brother.

For a slight moment Leila eyed Marco Prado inquisitively and he expected it. Leila sensed a strong energy around her. She could smell Marco Prado had something bizarre going on. Calmly, Leila moved toward him and spoke into his ear.

"Marco Prado, tell me why are you here?"

Without delay, he answered with his lips also very close to her ear. "Well… Leila, new things happened after you visited me. Important affairs that must have our full attention."

"That's Fine with me," responded Leila. "But not now. Perhaps tomorrow, because now, I must find out how to rescue Queen Naelia. And I need to do that before we return the Talismans to the Suacileu Tabernacle. My dad told me that."

"It is precisely about *that*, we need to talk," said Marco Prado. "After his performance at the Bacellar Castle, your father visited me. Not physically, but through one of my crystal balls."

"He, did?"

"Yes."

"Why?"

"Everything has to do with the Legend of the Talismans and he wants my help."

Leila remained silent. She observed Marco Prado. On that instant, Inbacula and Tess walked in.

"I am glad you are back, Tess," commented Leila. "Next time, please let we know you'll be visiting Limbo Rock. We were looking for you."

"I'm sorry, Leila. I'll be careful next time."

"Okay. Now, children let's move and sit at the dining table and listen to what Sir Marco Prado has to say. After saving us at the

Bacellar Castle, my father visited him through a crystal ball. And this is unusual."

"Through a crystal ball?" asked the children in harmony.

"Kiulaya…," said Marco Prado. "My favorite one. I created it in 1639 when I was only twenty-seven years old. It is my second crystal ball. Made of Quagmire type of magic, which consist of echoes of incantation spells, combine with earth's rock made with symbolic properties, and the participation of clear, archaic spiritual forces. Kiulaya is the eye opener of great generations."

The children immediately took a seat at the enormous table and attentively crossed their arms. They seemed to be crashed into episodes of wonderment. As expected, Leila and her mother also accommodated themselves for the show. King Duayne Cashemire exited the room to go upstairs to rest. Mrs. Clenilde helped him climbing the stairs.

"Please, Sir. Marco Prado, tell us what my father whispered when he appeared in your crystal ball."

Marco Prado raised his head and said, "Vachal Maglaja, unexpectedly popped inside Kiulaya and began to speak with me. He told me to come here to see you and the children. He said I don't have to hide anymore, because he had sent Jardel Caponette and Orca Cinfera to a Tundra Cristonela, located at the end of Rastaga Woods; a place where magic doesn't work. It will take at least one hundred years for them to find out how to escape from it."

"Did you know my father was the tiger?" asked Leila.

"No. But I knew that *he*, as Vachal Maglaja would come back at the right time. And he did."

"What else did he say?"

"He instructed me to set the Talismans one next to the other. The purple one at the left side and the red one at the right side. Then David Dreepel must say the word which will activate the power in them."

"But I don't know *that* word," added David.

"You will know it at the right time," said Marco Prado. "Next... Lucas, Olivia, and Tess also will say a word. If each one of you say the right word, the Talismans will begin their amalgamation. They will become one crystal. The union of the Talismans must happen, otherwise, David Dreepel will not be able to finish his journey."

"Why didn't my father tell me that? Why you?" asked Leila with frustration tempting her voice.

"Because when the Talismans were locked, the power will activate Nackivela."

"Who is Nackivela?"

"My new crystal ball. I created it two months ago and until today I was not able to make it work. Your father said that with the amalgamation of the Talismans, Nackivela will be activated and it will unveil accuracies we need to know."

Leila glanced around. She wanted to see the crystal ball in action. Slowly she uttered, "So... there are more secrets."

"Yes, Leila."

"God Eller... have mercy! I feel happy that I have the Red Talisman with me instead of having left it at the Bacellar Castle."

"That's phenomenal," uttered Marco Prado. "Because I also have brought the purple one. The one Professor Coorbell gave to me for shelter."

"Yes, but you'll need the crystal ball, Nackivela," replied David

Dreepel. "Did you bring it?"

"Of course, my dear, David" responded Marco Prado, with terrific enthusiasm flashing out of his eyes. He walked away from the table. Marco Prado went to the living room where he left a big, brown, leather bag. Inside it was, Nackivela.

Marco Prado returned to the dining room with the crystal ball in his hand. It was the most beautiful crystal ball the children had ever seen. It had the size of a full moon when the full moon appeared in a modest size. That means, not small, and not big, just clear and precise. The natural shining of it made you believe that dust of any kind will never stick on it.

Marco Prado, carefully, set the ball on top of the dining table. "Meet Nackivela—my last creation," he said proudly. "The universe mind. However… I couldn't grasp the right allure from any moon, to activate the enchantment of it. I hope the Talismans will break the quiescence of such a creation."

"If my dad told you the power of the Talismans will activate it. Believe. My Dad never lies."

"There is something I don't understand," said David, "What is going to lock the Talismans?"

"The Triquetra," added Marco Prado.

"What is it?" Inquired Olivia, intriguingly. She desired to see the ball in action.

Mrs. Marcela Maglaja jumped to answer the question, then hesitated…. She let Marco Prado do that.

"The Talismans hold the elements which control the power of My Jupiter aristocracy. They embrace the creation, the secrets, and the expectations indorsed by the Triquetra Supremacy."

Marco Prado paused to see the faces of the children. But at the moment, no questions distracted their minds.

Marco Pardo began, "The Triquetra is a unique symbol which unifies the Talismans. It carries the power reserved for one jurisdiction. Such dominion has been reserved only for a few aristocrats. When the two crystals joined in amalgamation the Triquetra will magically appear to forever lock them.

While the children quietly imagined the Triquetra Symbol, Leila exited the table to go to the leaving room looking for her traveling bag. She grabbed the bag and returned to the dining room. Silently, she took from inside it the velvet box she fetched from the air, to keep the Red Talisman safe.

"Here is the Red Talisman," she finally said while giving it to Marco Prado.

Marco Prado opened the box and held the crystal in his hand. He was mesmerized by the beauty of it. The other one was already on the dining table. Solemnly, Marco Prado inspected them. Both crystals were remarkably identical, they only differed in colors. One…was purple and the other one was red.

The Talismans were the size of an egg, oval shaped and both had a little hole on the edge, indicating it would be possible to hang them as a necklace from the neck.

"Please, Marco Prado, let's do what my father instructed, because we do not have much time. I promised King James Lamarcus, to be back at the Bacellar Castle for dinner. He decided to celebrate the returned of his son and invited his lords and knights for the feast. Aside from that we need to go to the Rastaga Woods to rescue

Queen Naelia."

"Yes, Leila," answered Marco Prado.

Cautiously, he placed the Red Talisman to the right side of the purple one. Then he waited. Everybody paused for the moment. No words had been said and no movement had been made. Their eyes held suspense in sharp standings. Time passed through and minutes touched eternity. Only their optimism remained vivid.

Afterward and miraculously, David Dreepel uttered a word. His lips moved saying, "CONTROL…!" Following that, without any explanation, Lucas articulated, RAIN…! Olivia replied, FIRE…! and Tess added, WIND…! And for the moment the children could only watch the Talismans. It seemed that even though there were no more words to be said, their minds kept repeating.

CONTROL, RAIN, FIRE, WIND.

CHAPTER
22

PROGRESSIVELY, BOTH CRYSTALS SHRANK until they acquired the size of a coin and the purple and red colors simply, disappeared. They remained small for a few seconds, then they blended, expanded again and regained the size of a pear. Magically, wind, fire, and rain, played inside it. At the end of such a phenomenon… gradually, the colors reemerged without mixing. Half of the new Talisman was purple and half red. Another lapse of time glided by and in the center of it appeared the Triquetra Symbol.

The symbol flashed back and forth as if some unique energy activated into it. While the Triquetra Symbol moved inside the new Talisman, the Nackivela crystal ball began to illuminate and some motion propagated inside it. Everybody moved closer to the crystal ball, even Mrs. Clenilde and Mr. Inbacula did it, too.

Inside the crystal ball, they saw Jacira Caponette on top of the table at the basement of Loyporcha Magic School.

"Jacira Caponette?" uttered David.

"Yes," said Marco Prado. "I went to the yellow house on Pedra Vestida Street and picked her up."

"I shrank her to protect us," added David.

"I know. That's why she is small."

"But I thought my power would last only one minute."

Leila quickly eyed David. "Hmm…. Apparently not. Look at her. She's still small."

David exchanged glares with Leila. His words floated in the air, almost senselessly. "But it was like that with the dragon, right?" He added. "My power only worked for a minute."

"No David," replied Olivia, "With you, the power works differently, because we walked out of Bonahunta City with the dragon in the size of a dog. It was Mr. Nicolas Toscapela, who changed his size into the size he is today."

"Correct," everybody agreed on that.

"David…," explained Marco Prado, "You will be an outstanding warlock. Exactly like your father."

"I don't even know my father, Sir. Marco Prado."

"Patience… rushing toward the future is dangerous. You can miss pieces of the present."

"Can you bring Mrs. Caponette back to her original size? I feel sorry for what I have done to her."

"No need for that," added Marco Prado. "She is no longer a human."

"What?" shouted Leila and the children in conjunction.

"Now she is Picachú; a lovely cat."

"You turned her into a cat?" asked Mrs. Marcela Maglaja.

"She asked me to do that. I just compromised. I wanted to find what kind of magic she used to harm my brother. She is the one who made him blind. When she knew about my wish, she asked me to turn her into a cat because she no longer wanted to be a human. Now, she's a cat which can write and possesses a smart brain."

Next, they saw her inside the crystal ball, as a cat, jumping off of the table and walking to a corner of the basement. David Dreepel gave Marco Prado a severe long look, disapproving his action.

"Hey, she asked for it. And I'm going to take good care of this cat. I'm a good person."

The images from inside of the crystal ball, exited and nothing else happened. Showing Jacira Caponette in the school basement seemed to be a prelude, just something to prove to Marco Prado his crystal ball was working.

Marco Prado felt happy and gratified. He officially, skimmed his right hand over the crystal ball to activate its energy. He seemed eager to enjoy the next revelation. No one said anything. They just stared at the crystal ball. Swiftly, a white fog began to take over the space inside the ball and gently, it spread apart. When the fog disappeared new images arrived. These new images moved around showing pieces of previous time twenty-eight years ago in 1626.

Two girls of the same age, twelve years old; were riding horses. One girl was white and the other black. Suddenly, the white girl fell down and rolled down the mountain to the foot of the valley. The black girl could not climb down into the bottom of the valley to help her friend. In desperation, she begged to God Eller for assistance. Immediately, a brown middle size dragon appeared. The dragon spoke with the black girl through thoughts. She jumped on it and the dragon flew her down to pick up her friend.

The dragon flew both girls out of the valley and dropped them in the center of Nordache. On that day, Nordache was having a flower festival and there were flowers all over the main street. King Jordan Cashemire and his wife Queen Leonor Cashemire came to the main street to enjoy the festival. The dragon landed in the center of the street and delivered the girls safely. The entire city stopped their activities to see the dragon with the girls.

"This is my daughter," said Inbacula. "The black girl is my daughter."

"Really, Inbacula?" replied Marco Prado.

"Yes, this is my daughter Analia and Princess Naelia Cashemire."

Leila eyed Inbacula thoughtfully. She wondered for an instant. "Do you remember when this happen?"

"I do," responded Inbacula.

Why is Nackivela showing this to us?"

"The Talismans, Miss Leila." added Inbacula. "Behind this incident lives the origin of the Talismans."

When Inbacula talked, the events inside the crystal ball stopped and when he was silent, the events re-started. Nackivela kept showing the same story.

The girls were so thankful to the dragon that spontaneously, they ran away, took a flower and returned to give it to the dragon. One flower was purple and the other red. The girls held the flowers up to the dragon. The dragon brought his face closer, puffed hot air from his mouth and burned the flowers. Magically, in Analia hand, appeared the beautiful crystal Purple Talisman. And in Naelia's hand was the Red Talisman. Inside the crystal ball the images uniquely disappeared behind the fog and the crystal ball once again remained quiet.

"This is indeed the origin of the Talismans," said Leila. "Inbacula, I didn't know your daughter and Princess Naelia grew up together."

"My wife and I worked for King Jordan Cashemire. We lived in the Shelicart Castle and since my daughter was the same age as Princess Naelia, they used to do things together."

"What happened with the Talismans after the dragon created them?" asked David Dreepel.

Marco Prado Cashemire answered, "Years ago, when your father, Magno Dreepel, was doing some excavation in Dunes of Gargatuela, he found an archaic book which spoke about the legend of the Talismans. The legend talked about the first black girl riding a dragon, revealed the two flowers and the creation of the Talismans by the dragon."

"If my father found the book, the Loyporcha Magic School new about the myth?"

"That's right, David," said Marco Prado. "The book became property of Loyporcha Magic School and since then every magician has studied the legend. No one ever expected that one day it would become a reality."

"No one ever considered the authenticity of such a tale," added Mrs. Maglaja.

"Inbacula, please tell them what happened next," said Marco Prado. "You know it better than I, because you where there."

Inbacula moved his head affirmatively and proceeded, "When the administrators of Loyporcha Magic School became aware of what happened at the flower festival, in Nordache, they sent Professor

Olimpio Piarato to the Shelicart Castle to speak with the king. The school decided to retrieve the Talismans.

"Why?" asked Olivia.

"For the safety of it," responded Marco Prado.

Inbacula continued his revelations. "After Professor Olimpio Piarato explained to the king about the legend, he also informed the king the Talismans needed to be taken to a safe place, because in them rested the power which would one day protect the aristocracy of the planet."

"Oh... the girls had to give them away!" Uttered Tess quite disappointed.

"Yes," replied Inbacula, "However, the king had decided that only the girls would choose the future of the Talismans. Obviously, after taking the girls into the labyrinths of the legend, Professor Olimpio Piarato, convinced them to let the Talismans go to the Suacileu Tabernacle."

David quietly, reflexed in the legitimacy of the story. Then confidently, added, "It is great to know the girls departed from them, otherwise... the Lamarcus aristocracy wouldn't be here today.

"Perhaps not," added Mr. Inbacula, "But three months later, my daughter contracted a strange fever and died. According to the legend without a soul the Talismans would not transport any power. Therefore, one day, the dragon would select a soul for the vigor of such a myth and my daughter was the chosen one."

"Naturally, Analia was the special girl in this myth," added Tess. "Now things make sense. I finally understand why Analia knew so much about dragons. She was the first black girl to hide a dragon. That's why she could help us with Limbo Rock."

A tenacious and long silence traveled through the dining room. Everybody took the time to review all they had seen in the crystal ball and also Mr. Inbacula's narrative. They felt sorry for Inbacula. He had lost his daughter because of a legend.

At that moment the children began to realize everything happened for a purpose. Naelia… Tess… the Purple and Red Talismans…and the Red Scorpion. Nothing had been misplaced and the whole purpose was to protect the aristocracy of My Jupiter. Perhaps, the eminent secrets—in precise way… are indeed, the magic of it.

As if magic was still around, Olivia went on and said, "The origin of the Talismans motivated my curiosity. I want to know more."

In the trajectory of this unique instant, words gained the utmost power to forge any wishes. Olivia wanted to know more and the power of the Talismans would provide more. Suddenly, a silhouette of a twelve years old girl became visible in the room. It was Analia. She appeared and spoke through her thoughts. Everybody could hear her.

"Hello, everyone. I'm here to help. Limbo Rock and I are going to Rastaga Woods to rescue Queen Naelia. I am the one who stole the Purple Talisman from Orca Cinfera and brought it to Queen Naelia. By wearing the Talisman on her neck she became invisible for all the dangerous magicians who live in the Rastaga Woods. I took care of her there during the eight years. She slept for eighteen months because of me. Since the Rastaga Woods is in Bonahunta, I will bring her to the Becellar Castle. Then Limbo Rock and I will go to the Suacileu Tabernacle in the Calvendra Forest.

"How?" asked David Dreepel. "The forest is too far."

"Limbo Rock and I will travel the sky. Dragons have the power to transcend time, and spirits have the ability of emerging at any time.

In fact, David Dreepel didn't know dragons had power to transcend time. But it didn't matter, because there were lots of things he didn't know.

Analia got closer to Marco Prado and said, "You, Sir Marco Prado, don't have to worry about the Linac Coabina Butterfly. Before I leave Rastaga Woods I will go into the wishing well to free her. And as soon as she flies away, your brother will see again.

"Is Limbo Rock the dragon who helped you save Princess Naelia?" asked Tess.

No, That was Figu Galapu. He is also a Cordente Dragon. The same legion of dragons, but not like Limbo Rock.

Following that, Analia spoke to her father. "Dad, I will not come again. I am a fairy tale, the soul of this legend and I will be forever at the Suacileu Tabernacle. Don't be sad. I will be happy there. Figu Galapu, the dragon has allowed me to have my mother there with me. So, I will not be alone."

Her image mystically started to exit. It moved back slowly until it left the walls of the castle. Inbacula had tears running from his eyes. Everybody was silent for an entire minute to glorify the moment. They lowered their heads and thought about Analia.

When, Leila spoke, she said, "We must get ready to return to the Bacellar Castle for the feast with King James Lamarcus, and then returned the Talisman to the Suacileu Tabernacle. It is almost four o'clock."

As Leila returned her attention to the pending tasks, an unusual affair took place inside the Astafe Castle. A tenacious noise made their heads turn around and look outside. An avalanche of thunder and lightning flashed in the sky of the Newzuma Valley. The windows of the castle, mysteriously, began to close. Nackivela, the crystal ball, which remained on top of the table lighted up and another set of images emerged behind the clear, shining crystal.

Everyone shifted their attention to the crystal ball, once again. They carried an intense desire to watch the enactment. They stayed close together assisting the revelations. To their surprise it was the city of Nordache, in the year 1646. There were soldiers fighting on the streets. Jardel Caponette and Orca Cinfera created an army of Leedrofic soldiers and attacked Nordache. The soldiers of King Duayne Cashemire couldn't kill the enemies, because the swords went through their bodies without harming them. Thousands of people from Nordache had died.

Jardel Caponette and Orca Cinfera, entered the Shelicart Castle and with magic, Jardel Caponette lifted King Duayne in the air and sent him many times against the wall. He did it repeatedly; One... two... three... four... five times, until the king had blood all over his body and couldn't stand on his feet. He was on the floor bleeding and left there to die.

Jardel Caponette kidnapped Queen Naelia and her two daughters, Princess Laura and Princess Clea. They covered their faces and took them out of the castle. In a carriage, they ran across the city and penetrated the woods behind the city of Nordache. Deep in the woods, Jardel Caponette stopped the carriage, pushed Princess Laura and Princess Clea out of it and order two soldiers to stay behind and kill them.

As soon as the carriage disappeared between the trees, an old man, dressed in a long white tunic, wearing sandals, and carrying a lovely cane, appeared from nowhere. He brought with him a legion of phantoms which apprehended the soldiers and made them run scared until they fell into precarious abysm. The ancient man was no other than Mr. Nicolas Toscapela. He uncovered the girl's faces, held their hands, said his magic words, and jumped the line.

In the crystal ball the images disappeared and words began to float inside it. They floated and floated until they wrote: The girls arrived in Nordache in the year 1979. Precisely 333 years in the future and were raised by the Viglianco family.

Evidently, every person in the room read the words. Truly speaking, some of them... twice. Then, they looked at each other, more confused than ever. They crashed into a bizarre state of mind and slowly walked away from the table. Even Marco Prado, Mrs. Marcela Maglaja and Leila, had sunk into profound silence. Vachal Maglaja said the crystal ball would unveil accuracies they needed to know, but this...? Viglianco family...?

The absence of words bounced against the castle walls and intensified the noise of the surreal reality. Time needed to run to make the unbelievable—believable. Time had to pass to connect—what was disconnected.

After such a bizarre silence the only person who dared to act was Olivia. She walked to the center of the room. She looked intently at everyone, raised her head up high and spoke.

"If what this crystal ball just said is true, I.... I... am Princess Laura. Queen Naelia is my mother, King Duayne Cashemire my father, and Sir Marco Prado is my uncle.

No one had the courage to challenge such a statement. Truly speaking, *yes*... Olivia's words didn't fit in the moment, or the moment rapidly, became too unreal. However, crystal balls only show meaningful accounts. Evidently, after such revelation, their thoughts would struggle to process the facts.

Then, in reverence of what the crystal ball showed them, Tess... who understood little about the intricacy of such a fairy-tale, stopped carrying on her wonder and also claimed her title. She confidently, moved close to her sister.

"And I.... I am Princess Clea."

CHAPTER
23

THE SINGULAR REVELATION INTUITIVELY changed the viewpoint of all expectations that for so long had been placed in their minds regarding David Dreepel's journey.

Leila and the children from the very beginning had submerged themselves into a crossing, chock-full of bizarre surprises. Through the adventure, they got use to these wild encounters, naive believes, and unpredicted outcomes. They never expected *episodes from the past, merging into a distant future, and returning to their present.*

Without warning, facts from the past aroused quickly, bringing the full understanding that a distant future, indeed, linked their existence. Until this day, they had played their roles innocently, trying to just survive.

David Dreepel's journey held more secrets and dangerous endeavors; more perplexities than realism. Now, for the sake of having peace of mind, everyone examined the room. Their eyes glanced around furtively. They witnessed the windows of the castle purposefully opening as if they never had been closed. And the magic of it… would remain imprinted in their minds.

"Marco Prado," said Leila, "Did you know this?"

"This, what? That Olivia and Tess were Princess Laura and Princess Clea?"

"Yes."

"Of course not, Leila. But your father told me that the crystal ball had revelations that would surprise me. I believe he was talking about this disclosure."

Marco Prado approached his nieces and hugged them. "I have no words to express my happiness. Knowing you are both alive is the greatest blessing God Eller could ever give to me. My brother will drop on his knees."

Happiness floated inside the dining room in such a lovely commotion, that words ran away and tears soaked their eyes. These eight years of magic, protected their identity and the existing aristocracy of My Jupiter. Amazing…!

"Leila, what's next?" asked David Dreepel. "They found out who they are. Now, what about me? Who am I?"

"David…, you're asking a question that I cannot answer," responded Leila. "I believe that after we have that feast with King James at the Bacellar Castle, probably the next revelation would be about you. Remember, from the very beginning, this was nothing else than your own journey. Mr. Toscapela told me everything is about you."

Marco Prado approached Leila and David. Calmly he said, "David, eventually, you will have answers for your questions. Be patient. And another thing; I want to go to Bonahunta. You must find a way to bring me and my brother with you."

"I don't know if it would be possible. The Surdrape Time Fold Passage has rules. I don't know how many people I can bring with me."

"That's right," added Leila. "Me, David, Lucas, Olivia, and Tess are already five people and two more will make seven. Can you transport seven people at one time, David?"

"I don't know."

Intuitively, Marco Prado added, "I know Mr. Nicolas Toscapela left instructions regarding that supremacy. Please, David, review the rules."

"Okay, Sir Marco Prado, I will check the Titleless book."

"Thank you, David. I will expect the best, for Mr. Toscapela always surprises me."

Leila spoke again. She informed David that they must began the preparations to return to Bonahunta. She quickly fetched from the air a bigger velvet box for the Talisman. She placed the new Talisman inside it and dropped the box into her leather traveling bag. Carefully she secured the bag across her shoulder and turned around to leave the room. However, before she walked away Marco Prado asked for one more favor.

"Leila, please…, talk to the girls and asked them to wait until we're all in Bonahunta, to disclose to my brother who they are. Let's wait for him to have his sight back."

"Fine, I'll do that."

David left the dining room and went to the kitchen. He asked Inbacula for the book. They sat at the long kitchen table. Together, Inbacula and David opened it. The first page sent them to page

46. There they found the answer. Yes. In the supremacy of this transportation, David would be able to transport exactly seven people; no more.

Around 5:30 p.m., Marco Prado, King Duayne, Leila and the children stepped outside the Astafe Castle to again depart from Lili Sandra. Resolutely, they positioned one next to the other, held hands, jumped the line and arrived in Bonahunta.

On this pleasant afternoon the sky of Bonahunta had no gray clouds and it displayed a tenacious, vibrant blue. In front of the Bacellar Castle, they enjoyed a soft breeze blowing through the land, refreshing the ambience while carrying away a delightful smell.

Shortly after their feet touched the ground, Tess looked up. She felt the presence of the dragon. "Look Leila, Limbo Rock is coming."

They all raised their eyes. Even King Duayne Cashemire looked up instinctively, then realized he had his vision back. Happiness masked his face as he dropped to his knees, raised his arms and thanked God Eller.

When Olivia and Tess saw it, they ran to him. "Dad," they cried out loud.

King Duayne looked at them in astonishment. "Laura?... Clea?..."

"Yes, brother," added Marco Prado. "And to make things even better, you can see them. Jacira Caponette will never harm you again. I promise."

"Oh brother, thank you. I always knew you would do anything under your power to help me. Thank you so much." King Duayne hugged his daughters as tears filled his eyes.

The dragon landed in front of the castle and slowly lay down.

Queen Naelia and the specter of Analia were on top of him; however, only Queen Naelia was visible. Unhurriedly and with wonder zooming from her eyes, the queen climbed down off of it. Her daughters and husband immediately, ran to meet her. They embraced each other mutely, happily, and thankfully. The moment belonged to them only, but Marco Prado, Leila, David, and Lucas, experienced the genuine emotion which enwrapped them. And as an act of sympathy, their eyes moistened, a little bit, for the Cashemire's; one of the greatest aristocracies of My Jupiter.

All of a sudden, King James Lamarcus and Queen Claudia arrived at the door of the castle. They were delighted when they saw King Duayne and Queen Naelia. They rushed down the steps to welcome them.

When Leila saw King James, she rushed to him. "Your Majesty," she said, "I am so sorry that we have the dragon here in front of your castle. He brought Queen Naelia, from the Rastaga Woods. He will leave soon."

"No, Miss Leila. It's okay. The dragon can stay if necessary."

"Thank you. But it's not necessary."

While everybody began to walk inside the castle, Tess moved toward Limbo Rock. She stepped closer and spoke.

"Are you coming back?"

"No, Tess."

"Why not? I love you."

"I love you, too."

Almost crying, she asked the dragon to bring his head close to her. Gently, she kissed Limbo Rock's forehead. The dragon gave away a tender glance, flipped the wings and flew away.

At the Bacellar Castle King James Lamarcus, his lords, and knights, started the celebrations. In the huge dining room, tables had been arranged; one next to the other and flowers of different colors decorated the center of each table. They expected fifty people and of course, now they had three more; King Duayne, Queen Naelia, and Marco Prado.

At 6:30, everybody walked to the dining room where they spent some time sitting down, drinking good wine and talking. As soon as King James ensured all his lords and knights had arrived, he informed them about the finding of the Red Scorpion and the returned of his son, Prince Willian. As expected, the news shocked the entire Lamarcus' court.

Without any hesitation, King James told them in detail how all this happened and that Prince Willian had been in Nordache under the care of the Lambert family, 333 years in the future.

After that, Marco Prado spoke on behalf of his brother King Duayne Cashimire, his wife and daughters. He explained that Jardel Caponette ordered two of his soldiers to kill the princesses. The reason they are present today, was because they had been saved by Mr. Nicolas Toscapela.

"Like Prince Willian," said Marco Prado, "Princess Laura and her sister Princess Clea were also in Nordache under the care of Viglianco family, also 333 years in the future."

Following these revelations, the king exercised the ring enchantment so he could prove that Lucas Lambert was, without doubts, his son Willian Benard III Lamarcus. The tales involving Prince Willian and the two princesses, formulated lots of questions and concerns among the lords and knights of King James Lamarcus.

King James spent seven years killing magicians, then all of a sudden magic gained his utmost reverence in the process of accepting an estrange young child as his son.

All people who were present saw the ring shrinking to fit Lucas' finger. Furthermore, they believed that shrinking a ring could also be a work of *magic*.

Dinner was served with elegance and ostentation. The king wanted to show his happiness without modesty, because for eight years sadness lived inside his castle. Finally, it was time to leave the past behind.

When dinner was over and the servants began to clean the tables to serve dessert, Lord Ferdinand Lamarcus, the brother of King James Lamarcus, took the floor. He calmly said, "Your Majesty, I think we may need to investigate more about all these new occurrences. Do not forget that through magic, anyone can take the place of Prince Willian."

The entire court eyed Lord Ferdinand inquisitively. *How he had the courage to distrust the legitimacy of the king's ring?*

Since no one spoke, Ferdinand added, "I am Lamarcus and the king's ring will fit my finger, as well. What if magic maliciously made it fit the finger of this young boy to confuse us?"

A quiescent moment arose and quickly intensified the perplexity of the imminent matter. The wrong concept of magic could destroy the night. And for this reason, Lucas decided to say something.

"Lord Ferdinand, I have no intention of misleading this court. I am here just living my life. The ring has an enchantment which is part of its own creation. Yes, it's magic, however, not for people to play with it. The enchantment in this ring is genuine."

"How do you define GENUINE?" asked Lord Ferdinand.

"INDISPUTABLE. And the opposite of such a word—is exactly what sustains our conversation, right now. Why don't you challenge me? Bring out anything you have in mind. A unique question or… a date… I don't know… anything."

Lord Ferdinand eyed the king for his approval. King James Lamarcus looked at Lucas and saw Lucas was confident. King James Lamarcus nodded his head indicating to his brother to go on.

Lord Ferdinand took a moment to think. His mind traveled fast on nearby roads. It looked for events or stories, incidents or misfortune, trapped in any significant past. He chose the year, 1645, Prince Willian was two years old.

After standing from his chair, Lord Ferdinand said, "I have thought about something. Like you have said Prince Willian—a unique question. If you answered it right, I'll never doubt you're Prince Willian."

"Okay," said Lucas.

Lord Ferdinand then explained, "In the year 1645, when you were two years old, for the first time I took you to the Ganbari fair. You had been inside the castle for almost a month, with a bad cold. When you got better, I convinced your mother to let me take you to the fair. I thought some fresh air after almost thirty days inside the castle would be good for your health. However, as soon as we stepped a foot outside, we had to returned to the castle. What had happened was not my fault, but it made you furious. We had to cancel our activity and return to the castle. You told me you would hate me forever."

The Lord made a brief pause. He felt the whole court was eager to see the end of it. Peacefully Lord Ferdinando proceeded. "Prince Willian, tell me what happened on that day that forced us to return to the castle."

Lucas stood up, opened his arms, closed his eyes and brought a soft and noiseless rain over the dining table. Instantly, everybody stood up and moved away from the table to avoid getting wet. Lord Ferdinand and Lucas were the only ones who remained close to the table.

"That's right. *Rain* is the answer," said Lord Ferdinand. The Lord walked around the table and stopped next to Lucas. "Prince Willian, forgive me."

"No, you're defending the Lamarcus'. I would have done the same."

"Are you a magician?" asked the lord.

"No," answered Lucas. "I brought the rain with the power of my heart and soul."

"Where did you learn to do that?"

"Oh, my lord…! It's a long tale. When our relationship gets stronger, I'll tell you the whole story."

Obviously, the tiny rain only stayed for a minute. The king ordered the servants to serve dessert in the next room, in the entertainment room. Quietly, they all moved to the entertainment room and while waiting to once again be seated, some lords come close to Prince Willian to ask questions about the future.

Lord Eduardo Linnar was the first one. He approached the prince and said, "Prince Willian, regarding these 333 years in the future, tell us about it. What can you remember from there?"

"Almost nothing," answered Lucas. "Only one thing remained in my memory."

"Then tell us about it?"

"Airplanes. I remember the airplanes."

"What is it?

"An incredible form of transportation. It is a man-made type of thing and we can get into it and fly."

"What?"

"We can get inside it and fly up on the sky."

"Describe it."

No... I am going to draw it."

Lord Linnar brought what Lucas needed and Lucas drew a beautiful airplane. His drawing of the airplane passed from hand to hand and became the topic among the lords and knights. Then, Lord Linnar and Lord Mathew Calbazar decided to approach the two princesses to also ask them about the future.

"Princess Laura," said Lord Calbazar, "Please tell us what do you remember from the future."

Olivia moved her head trying to bring back some memories.

"Only one thing," she said.

"What is it?"

"Cars. They are spectacular!"

"What do they do?"

"They are similar to carriages. They have four wheels, but they are not pulled by horses. People get into them and drive them."

Both lords shook their heads negatively. "If they are not pulled by horses, how do they move forward?"

"They moved by a power called gasoline."

Lord Calbazar shook his head confused. Then said, "And you,

Princess Clea? Do you also only remember one thing?"

"Only one thing."

"What is it?"

"Dinosaurs."

"There are dinosaurs in the future?"

"No. Toy dinosaurs, made by plastic."

"What is plastic."

Tess frowned her nose. "Plastic…. Plastic…. Is a…. Is everything in the future."

Lord Linnar and Lord Calbazar exchanged a suspicious look. They thanked them and walked away. For the rest of the night, until they moved to the dance square, the subject matters disturbing the court was *airplanes, cars, and plastic.*

Leila, Marco Prado, and the children approached King James and explained to him they had to leave. Their last mission was to return the Purple-Red Talisman to the Suacileu Tabernacle and they must arrive there before midnight.

The king got the attention of all the guests and explained to them why Leila, Sir Marco Prado and the children would be leaving. When the king mentioned the Purple-Red Talisman, some lords asked to see it.

"Are they as the legend says?"

"Yes," answered Marco Prado. "But now it is only one. We saw the unification of them in the Astafe Castle in Lili Sandra. It was a striking transformation."

"Can we see it?"

"I don't know. Ask Miss Leila, she has it."

Leila opened her bag and grabbed the velvet box. She brought it to the table, opened it, and exposed the beautiful oval Purple-Red Talisman with the Triquetra inside it. The lovely crystal passed from one hand to another all over the lords, knights, kings and queens. While the Talisman moved around, inside it, the triquetra exercised its forever movement. The beauty of it left the court in wonder for they never imagined the striking splendor of the crystal.

When the Talisman returned to Leila's hand, she grouped the children and with Marco Prado, they exited King Lamarcus' Court. The celebration at the Bacellar Castle extended until the early hours of the morning. At midnight, everybody stepped outside to watch the Otela Moon exiting the sky of Bonahunta. It would be another seven years for that moon to return.

At the end of the night Lord Eduardo Linar, Lord Ferdinand Lamarcus, and Lord Mathew Calbazar walked together to a carriage which remained outside waiting for them. They had come together. Inside the carriage Lord Mathew, asked, "Do you believe in this future tale? Airplanes, cars and plastic?"

"Of course not," answered Lord Mathew Calbazar. "These children are very intelligent and have an extravagant imagination. Everything plastic? Cars without horses? Airplanes as flying transportation? Impossible. Only birds can fly."

"You're right Mathew. These children possess an atypical brain and exceptional imagination. So exceptional, that I think they can backward the future and perhaps forward the past—as easy as— they shaped the present with lovely fairy tales. And in all sense, we… have the magic of it."

DAVID DREEPEL

Lord Ferdinand then added, "Like Elber Liche, the magician who enchanted the Lamarcus' ring, once said, "EVERYTHING, that—at any given moment begins inside a mind—is indeed magic.

CHAPTER
24

MAGIC WILL ALWAYS HAPPEN in the edges of art. It will constantly play its game with the unknown and will move furtively from place to place, grasping forceful energies. It will project clear light and darkness and will subsist in the core of any abstraction. Behind everything lays the mind with its own mysteries. Minds will hold compelling images connected to any sort of reference. Through the time and space the POWER works. And through the creation the IMAGINATION controls.

The Leda Formosa Valley belonged to the Province of Cordavia, and about thirty-seven impressive, colossal mountains shaped the valley. A huge dense forest, known as the Calvendra Forest, sketched the enormous space around the valley and in those woods, forceful rivers, great waterfalls and dangerous grottos, outlined the land. The valley remained constantly covered by a solid milky mist that moved slowly around... up... and down... concealing the highest peak of the region.

Exactly at the center of the valley, emerged the distinctive and magnificent Mount Mascratti. It was an extraordinary elevation in the territory. At the bottom of Mount Mascratti, lived a secret entrance to a quite impressive tunnel. This underpass zig-zagged toward the left, then right, and finally, exposed an atypical, massive crystal door. On the other side of this crystal door rested the Suaceleu Tabernacle.

On the same night King James Lamarcus celebrated the return of his son, Leila, Marco Prado, and the children, arrived in the Leda Formosa Valley. They left Bonahunta exactly at 11:45 p.m. and one minute later touched the soil of the valley. The stillness of the place made them feel eerie. As if they were the only living things on the face of the planet. The Valeria moon just exited the sky over the valley and the next moon, the Otela, didn't arrive yet.

David Dreepel was the only person moving around fearlessly. As he advanced, he moved his arms in the air, trying to spread apart the dense milky mist that obstructed their view. Following David, came Marco Prado, then Leila, Olivia, Tess, and Lucas.

Concerned about where they might end, Marco Prado said, "David, I hope you know what you're doing. Are you sure we're walking in the right direction?"

"No, I'm not. But my entire life depends on what could possibly be, after this deep fog. None of you need to come with me. If Leila wishes, I can deliver the Talisman by myself."

"I am okay, David. We will move on together."

They proceeded, trespassing the mist without knowing where they would end. In front of them could be anything, a river, an abyss or perhaps, a dangerous cave, but at the moment, nothing scared David Dreepel. And for another fifteen minutes they went deeper into the milky fog experiencing nothing but the desire to find what they wished—the Suacileu Tabernacle.

After walking for another ten minutes, a clear light appeared in the sky. They looked up and instantly, knew the Otela Moon had arrived over the valley. As of a *magic touch*, they saw the vestige of something huge. It was Mount Mascratti there imperatively present.

Miraculously, all the fog moved behind them, shielding their presence in the valley. The gorgeous mountain was located in the center of the land and it was more than 20,000 feet high. None of them had ever seen anything as high as it towered above them.

Quietly they looked up in full admiration. The moment seemed itself magic. Snow wrapped Mount Mascratti in such a perfect manner that it appeared the mountain never—in any time of the year—would stop being white. Beautiful pieces of ice artistically cut and meticulously mounted one on top of the other, decorated the surface of it. In pure silence; it told: *Forever snow… forever white… forever ice pieces of crystals. Nothing would tempt with the glory of such a creation.*

The Otela moon, known as the moon full of surprises was, fairly silent, illuminated the sky and guarded the next little surprise. Even though Mount Mascratti was covered by ice, the ground had no snow flakes. The bottom of the mountain remained green, and the lovely flowers, here and there, vividly conserved their beautiful colors. The special place seemed to have an endless touch of divinity.

The minute they finished contemplating Mount Mascratti and

advanced forward, they saw two dragons and a tiger guarding the bottom of the mountain. At the right side it was the dragon Figu Galapus, and on the left side stood Limbo Rock, and in the middle, the APERAGLA tiger. Indeed another great surprise.

As they got closer, the tiger began its transformation. Vachal Maglaja once again appeared in front them.

"Dad," uttered Leila, "Do you live here?"

"Yes, Leila. Until the tiger finished its lives."

"The tiger has more than one life?"

"Five. And it already died in two."

Together they entered the tunnel which was going to bring them to the huge crystal door. Vachal Maglaja walked in front guiding them. When they saw the door, Vachal Maglaja said, "There is no key to this door, just walk through."

The size and height of the space on the other side of the crystal door overwhelmed them. They turned their heads to look up and felt like tiny ants, compared to the extravagant elevation of the walls. They were inside of the tabernacle, which was located underneath Mount Mascratti and had lights of its own. They were the reflections of 2,889 thousand pieces of crystals that meticulously, screened the walls.

Impressed with the remarkable aspect of it, they walked through, looking around, enjoying the luminosity of the wall. Then, at the end of this rounded astronomical chamber, rested an exquisite, transparent, long table, and a pleasant forty-two year old man occupied the lovely transparent chair behind the table.

The man had refined blond hair, which fell elegantly along his shoulders. He had a pleasant face, with clear hazel eyes and a soft kind look. He wore a sophisticated purple tunic with wide, long sleeves.

When Vachal approached the table with the visitors, the man gave away a sweet smile. He calmly, stood up and walked to the front to meet with the newcomers.

"Dear friends," said Vachal Maglaja, meet Sir Magno Dreepel."

"My dad?" replied David Dreepel.

"Yes, David," answered Vachal Maglaja.

The man advanced and shook hands with each one of them. He didn't hug David. He only held his hand a little bit longer. According to the code of manners, the guardian of the tabernacle should not exercise any kind of emotion.

After this cordial introduction, Sir Magno Dreepel asked, "Leila... my dear, may I have the Purple-Red Talisman?"

"Yes, Sir."

Leila opened her small travel bag that she always kept across her shoulder, took the velvet box out of it and handed the box to Sir Magno Dreepel.

Silently, Sir Magno Dreepel opened it. For some seconds, his eyes contemplated the oval Talisman with the Triquetra inside it constantly moving in a comfortable, eternal orbit. Sir Dreepel removed it from the velvet box. After holding the Talisman in his hand for another second, he looked up at the crystal wall behind his table. Solemnly, he lifted the Talisman in the air and it immediately exited his hand. The Purple-Red Talisman elevated up high, traveled toward the left and stopped in the middle of the wall. It twisted a little and plugged into a space between the other crystals.

"There... is where it belonged," said Sir Magno Dreepel. "Thank you, children… for bring it back."

"Children," called Marco Prado, "Inside these walls, in each of these crystals lives all the energy magic needs. The tabernacle is the heart of any illusion. Every crystal guards something; a spell, a recipe, an enigma, or a presage. All that, for one reason or another, relates to the unnatural."

"How many spells do you know by memory, Sir Marco?" asked David.

"745," responded Marco Prado.

"And how many did you create?"

"125."

"And are they here, in these crystals?"

"Yes, they are."

"Can you find in which crystal are they?

"I don't think so. It's the first time I have entered the tabernacle. I don't know."

"Yes, David," answered Sir Magno Dreepel. "He can find these crystals. The magician can always assess his crystals. Lift your finger Marco Prado and think of one of your spells."

Marco Prado, proudly, did just what Sir Magno Dreepel had said. In less than a minute, from the wall came a piece of crystal in the form of a sphere. It traveled down, flashed its energy until it stopped in the hand of Marco Prado.

"Wow… this is very cool," said Tess.

"Which spell is this?" asked David.

Marco Prado took a moment to study the lights of the crystal. Then he said, "It is the one which activated Kiulaia. The crystal ball that showed who came here and stole the Talismans."

"Ah… the crystal ball that showed Jardel Caponette and Orca Cinfera with the Talismans," uttered Olivia.

"That's right," answered Marco Prado.

"And how did they find it?" asked Olivia. "Mount Mascratti is totally covered by a mist. Then, there are two dragons and a tiger outside guarding the entrance to it. Without mentioning the massive crystal door which seems impossible to trespass if your intentions were not good?"

Instead of Marco Prado, Sir Magno Dreepel answered. "Children, before… we didn't have the dragons and the tiger outside. It was only an eagle. For many years, a special eagle with magnificent black eyes guarded the bottom of the mountain. Aside from that, the crystal door opened differently. It opened with a light flashed from the eyes of the eagle. Orca Cinfera is a great magician. He once belonged to the Strauda Legion of Light Magicians, and was as brilliant as I am."

"Oh!" uttered the children. "He used to be a good magician."

"Yes. I have spent a long time in the Dunes of Gargatuela studying the land and digging for any kind of archaic objects. Three months after I arrived there, on one afternoon, I was walking along the beach when, suddenly, I witnessed a big change in the land. The ocean disappeared and a man appeared on the sand. Then, the sky also modified and it became very dark, and the moon descended from above in the form of a woman."

"God Stambulo and his lover?" replied Marco Prado.

"Yes. And they saw me," continued Sir Magno Dreepel. "God Stambulo spoke to me. He asked me to return to my tent and to stay in it for three days until he returned to the ocean and the moon to the sky. Then he advised me to keep digging in the sand of Gargatuela, for I would find a book which will explain how to exercise the amalgamation of the Talismans."

"Oh! You spoke with God Stambulo?" asked Tess.

"I did. And because of it, a few months later, I found the book which indeed described how to unify the Talismans. I brought the book to the Loyporcha Magic School."

As a brief silence ran through, the children tried to picture the Dunes of Gargatuela in their minds. And they remembered it.

"According to what you just said, no one knew the Talismans needed to be blended to protect the aristocracy of this planet, correct?" stated Olivia.

"Correct, Olivia. And because I found this valuable book, on this year… the Loyporcha Magic School granted me the award of Magician of the Year. Something that infuriated Orca Cinfera and Jardel Caponette. We were almost the same age and had enjoyed the same classes. They couldn't manage not to be offended."

"That's why they hate you and wished to harm the union of the provinces?" commented David Dreepel.

"Yes," replied Vachal Maglaja quickly, "They are jealous of everybody… me, Marco Prado, Sir Magno Dreepel, Professor Coorbell, and others."

Leila desired to know more. She looked at her father and remarked, "Even though they hated everybody, how did they manage to find the Leda Formosa Valley and enter the Suaceleu Tabernacle? Strong magic always guarded the valley and only strong magic would carry the power to disclose it."

"They found this *Strong Magic*," said Sir Magno Dreepel, "And this happened eight years ago, when the guardian of the tabernacle was Professor Julian Coorbell, the father of Professor Breno Coorbell. Jacira Caponette graduated from Loyporcha Magic School with high qualifications. She has an outstanding, brilliant mind. Her son Jardel Caponette convinced her to help him and Orca Cinfera to find the tabernacle. This is how everything began."

"How did she help them?"

"She went to a village called Dergata and convinced Juliet Sarmaira, an old, extraordinary witch to join them in the search. Juliet Sarmaira gave Jacira Caponette a middle size black caldron from an ancient age and an eye of a night bird—an eye of an owl. Only a magician with a sharp mind could control the eye of a night bird. Jacira Caponette succeeded with the task."

Magno Dreepel silenced and glanced around. He enjoyed the expression he saw in the children's faces. Calmly, he proceeded.

"The way the eagle guarded the tabernacle was, by detecting when intruders approached the valley. The eagle could see activities from miles away. When the eagle saw people coming, it immediately, used its power to create lots of different paths around the valley and sent to the air an annoying energy which confused peoples' minds. By walking through these paths, with the eerie noises, intruders got lost and arrived in the Calvendra Forest behind the valley. Some people could never exit the forest and died there."

"We're talking about a forest bigger than some provinces," commented Marco Prado.

"That's right," affirmed Sir Magno Dreepel. "Jacira Caponette used the spell Sarmaira gave her and with the eye of the night bird, caught every fake path the eagle created and trapped them inside the black caldron."

"How clever!" uttered, Leila.

"Absolutely," responded Sir Magno Dreepel. "Of course, the last path was the right one. The one that put them here in the front of Mount Mascratti. And once here, she exercised the power of the eye of the night bird and killed the eagle. A tenacious sharp sword, appeared into the air, advanced toward the eagle and abruptly, cut off his head. Orca Cinfera grabbed the eagle's head, awakened the power of the eagle eyes and opened the crystal door."

"This is unbelievable!" exclaimed David Dreepel. None of the crystals attached to these walls could do anything against them?"

"No," answered Marco Prado, quickly.

"Why, not?"

"These crystals are the heart of magic, not weapons. They have been created to store magic secrets and power."

"I think sometimes—Magic… loses the *magic* of it," replied Lucas, with frustration bouncing inside his mind.

"A few months later," added Marco Prado, "I saw all that happened, through my Kiulaia Crystal Ball."

David Dreepel felt uneasy about these occurrences. Curiously, he inquired, "How did they find the Talismans? They were here, mixed with 2,889 of other pieces?"

"Oh, they did it easily. Once they were inside of the Tabernacle, Orca Cinfera and Jardel Caponette forced Professor Julian Coorbell to exit the Talismans from the wall and when the professor placed the Talismans in their hands, Orca Cinfera used the night bird eye to kill him. Before they left, Orca Cinfera took the fire ring with him. Cinfera cut Professor Coorbell's finger off to have the ring."

"That simple?" asked Lucas.

"Yes. When they were inside, unfortunately, their mission had no obstacles," explained Vachal Maglaja.

While the children reflected in the opulence of these surprising fairy tales, Vachal Maglaja said, "Leila, I think you did an amazing job protecting these children. You were wonderful. However, I want you to know that if I didn't appear at the Bacellar Castle that afternoon, Jardel Caponette and Orca Cinfera would have killed you all. You would have had no means of magic to fight them. That is why, Sir Magno Dreepel sent me. High spirits told him to send the tiger to protect the Red Scorpion."

"Oh… he sent you?

"He did. That's how the tiger lost his first life. Every time the authority appeared physically, the tiger died. I am the authority. And every time a family member of the authority sees the tiger, the authority must manifest."

"Thank you for coming and save us. I knew I was in big trouble."

They all took a moment to analyze and understand the covenant property of the APERAGLA Tiger delegation. This piece of magic really involved integrity and sacrifice.

"Is your ring the Fire Ring?" asked David Dreepel.

"Yes," responded Sir Magno Dreepel.

They all swished their eyes to the ring. It was a beautiful gold, ruby ring, showing some crossed swords on one side and a magic ministry emblem on the other side.

"How did Loyporcha Magic School retrieve the ring?" inquired David.

"Orca Cinfera and Jardel Caponette underestimated the power

of the ring," said Sir Magno Dreepel. "Orca Cinfera tried to place the ring on his finger, but he couldn't. Three days after they entered here and stole the Talismans and the ring, a red bird appeared at Loyporcha Magic School. It was 9:30 in the morning. The bird flew straight to the library and landed on top of the long table the professors used for meetings. At the moment, sixteen professors were sitting at the table to discuss who would be the next guardian of the Tabernacle. I was among these professors."

"In three days they had known what had happened here?" asked Leila.

"They did. Professor Breno Coorbell used to speak with his father, through a crystal ball almost every other day. He saw his father's death on the next morning. They had no idea who had attacked the Tabernacle; however, they recognized something needed to be done quickly in order to protect it from the Draba Legion of Dark Magicians. Imagine if they enter here?"

"Oh... it would be the worse day for magic," added Marco Prado.

"That's right," replied Sir Magno Dreepel. "When Professor Breno Coorbell arrived with two other professors to retrieve the body of his father, Julian Coorbell, they found the vacant space in the crystal wall and realized the Talismans, also had been gone."

"How was the ring recovered?" asked David with interest and curiosity.

"The red bird flew to the center of the table at Loyporcha Magic School. As soon as the bird landed on the table it converted into a ring. We... the professors, understood what we had to do. One by one we grabbed the ring and tried to wear it. Every time we did it, the ring caught fire and returned to the center of the table. After twelve professors, I took the ring and without any problem placed it on my finger."

"Wow...! Amazing...!"commented, Tess. "The ring chose you as the new guardian."

"Exactly. The ring can't exit from my body. The only way a person can take it off of my finger, would be by killing me and cutting my finger off."

David Dreepel watched his father. His father seemed calm and confident about being around them. David wished he could know more about himself. He decided to change the course of their conversation.

"Where is my mother?" David Dreepel asked.

"I don't know. She left with you and I never saw her again."

"You're my father and never knew how I grew up?"

"No,"

"Who am I? Am I a Leedrofic Adaptation?"

"No.

"Oh... I know what you are," cried Lucas. "I always knew. David... you're a grasshopper."

When the word GRASSHOPPER hit the walls of the Tabernacle, one crystal exited from its place and created an avalanche of small pieces of glass that instantly converted into a huge transparent wall which separated David and Magno Dreepel from the others.

David Dreepel and his father suddenly, had been put in another compartment. They sat at a small table that occupied the center of the chamber and waited to see what would be next. They looked at each other with serious expression ornamenting their faces. They didn't know what was going on. They appeared to be troubled with the startling wall, as well. Then after a few minutes went by, David felt eager to control the situation and confidently he did.

"Talk," said David. "I want to know who am I and why I am here on this journey."

"You're David Dreepel, my son," answered Sir Magno Dreepel. "I never knew the whereabouts of your mother after she left with you. And as far as I know… you have asked for this journey. This is all that I know."

"Do you know Mr. Nicolas Toscapela?" asked David.

"I do."

"Where is he?"

"I don't know. He also left. I believe he is on another planet."

"Another planet?"

"Yes," replied his father, "Let me show you what I found written in one of these pieces of crystals, stored in these walls. I found it when I was reading about my duties as a guardian of the Tabernacle."

His father lifted his hand and picked one crystal from the wall behind him. He expanded the crystal and showed David what was written on the surface of it. The writing addressed David Dreepel:

Dear David Dreepel, when you find this note it is the end of your journey. However, I decided to grant you one last favor. At this time, you will be eager to know me better because you have questions. You wish to find out more about yourself. To come across my world, you must decrypt an enigma. There is no magic in it. You must use your brain.

When you complete the five challenges, there will be no way to try it again. Good luck.

Last Link MDDD

Finding the Planet

Surprising Light

Chose the Animal

Two Words LR

CHAPTER
25

"TO FIND WHO I am, you must decrypt this enigma." Again… and again… these words repeated inside David Dreepel's mind, constantly enlarging his frustration and constantly diminishing his hope.

Magno Dreepel remained next to David trying to help. He used his knowledge to guide David throughout such a trial. After spending some time reading the enigma over and over, Magno Dreepel spoke. "David," he said, "Think about what became intrinsic relevant for the final of your journey?"

"Relevant?" repeated David.

"Yes. For example: when you arrived here, at the Tabernacle, what was your utmost wish?"

David thought for a split second. His mind brought him back to Nordache, Bonahunta, and Lili Sandra. *What was my utmost wish?"* Without hesitation he stated, "Find who I am."

Magno Dreepel briefly, evaluated the answer. Decisively, he

added, "In that case, encountering me here and meeting me turned out to be meaningful."

"Absolutely," added David speedily. His mind carried the weight of such a reality. He always desired to meet his father. While looking at Magno Dreepel abruptly, David stood up. "*LAST LINKING MDDD*... this link is us... right? *Magno Dreepel and David Dreepel*"

His father stared at him and smiled. Their names indeed solved the first mystery. Instantly, they began to believe that the enigma might not be as hard as it seemed.

Magno Dreepel once again engaged in his inquiries. He felt excited about this whole enigma game. After examining the next challenge, assuredly he said, "Now David, what can be the planet in connection with the journey? Think about the word *planet*. How many times had it appeared during your journey? Why did it appear? And who mentioned it."

David submerged into deep thoughts. He revised things they had done and challenges they had faced. He went back to Bonahunta and thought about his experience there. He almost died in that city and on that day Mr. Nicolas Toscapela came and named the dragon.

Happily, David uttered to his father, "Oh... you're brilliant. When Mr. Nicolas Toscapela named the dragon Limbo Rock, I was not present, however my friend Lucas told me what happened. Mr. Nicolas Toscapela named the dragon Limbo Rock, because when the dragon stretched back to change size the dragon reminded him of people dancing on the beach, on a planet called—Earth."

"Outstanding memory, David," commented Magno Dreepel. "Earth must be the planet."

"Oh... certainly," exclaimed David. "Earth must be it, because no other planet was ever mentioned during the journey."

David expressed contentment as he began to believe that somehow… he would succeed in cracking this paradox. He carefully began to think about words, places, and even smells related with their quests. Suddenly, he realized everything was always precisely connected. Nothing, survived senselessly.

"I have the rest of it," he said. "If we're right with the planet, the animal will be DRAGON… and the two words… LIMBO ROCK; the name of the dragon. It makes sense, doesn't it?"

Magno Dreepel quietly examined the connections between the planet, the dragon, and the dragon's name and he agreed the relationship among them, held solid connotation. "David… I think you got it."

Nevertheless, David Dreepel had four challenges solved, there was one left… SURPRISING LIGHT. At the moment David decided to think about the magic involved in the journey. Anything related with, spells, lights, surprises and everything responsible for wonders, or odd encounters and unique words that had been said.

He thought and thought and cleverly, remembered something very trivial. Leila many times mentioned the Otela Moon, as the surprising moon. She always emphasized in the word *surprising*. And for the wonderment of it, the Otela Moon just arrived over Leda Formosa Valley. It cannot be just a coincidence. With great excitement David said, "The Otela Moon. This moon is the source of the surprising light. I must believe in it."

Looking at David, Sir Magno Dreepel added, "I think you have it all. You decoded the enigma, David. And the reason I am confident about such a discovery is because everything ended here at the valley. I am here, the dragon is here, and the Otela Moon. This is not a coincidence. A coincidence does not work like that."

"The dragon must be the relationship with the preamble I will need for the transportation to the planet Earth. It has to be Limbo Rock. I am going outside to talk to him."

"Are you sure about that?"

"I am."

"Be careful…, if the animal is not the dragon, you will never have another chance."

"I know. But I have strong feelings that he controls this power."

David and his father walked for the Tabernacle exit, crossed the huge chamber, passed the massive crystal door and arrived outside. No one saw them. They were disguised by the crystal wall which separated them from the others.

On the other side of the wall remained Vachal Maglaja, Marco Prado, Leila, Olivia, Tess, and Lucas talking about crystals and spells. They had no idea where David and his father went, but they knew they had a lot to catch up.

Outside, David stopped in front the Mascratti Mountain and looked up. The Otela Moon showed its presence by sending down a bright, silver light over the valley. Of course, it was the surprising light.

Expectantly, David Dreepel placed himself in front the dragon. He had to talk to Limbo Rock. Though, he realized that only Tess and Inbacula could hear the dragon. He eyed his father, walked closer and whispered in his ear, "Before… the dragon never spoke with me. I could never hear him."

Magno Dreepel remained silent. His mind ran back to explore

the sense of it. In reality, if David cannot hear the dragon, why make the dragon the significant animal in the enigma? Magno Dreepel had an incredible mind. He quickly recognized that such a matter, DAVID NEVER BEING ABLE TO HEAR THE DRAGON, probably persisted throughout the journey, exactly for this moment to confuse David. Confidently, Sir Magno Dreepel said, "Today the dragon will speak with you and you'll hear him. Trust me."

David Dreepel gave one last look to his father and returned to talk to Limbo Rock. First, he eyed the dragon sincerely. Then in a gentle tone of voice spoke. "Limbo Rock, I have to travel to the planet Earth and I believe you handle the preamble for this transportation. Please… help me?"

Slowly, Limbo Rock raised on his feet. He blew some fire out of his mouth. "Dear David Dreepel, and future warlock, what makes you think I can help you?"

"Oh… I can hear you."

"Thank the Otela Moon," said the dragon. "The moon full of surprises."

"For some reason," explained David, "My creator made you the significant animal in the enigma he left to me. Wouldn't it be enough for you to help me?"

"Oh… your creator," replied the dragon. "People with imagination. *Imagination* David, transcends spaces and your creator has an impeccable mind."

"I need to find out who I am. There is this slight idea that I am a grasshopper. I need to know more."

"And because of this *slight idea*, you want to travel to this far planet to have a meeting with your creator?"

"That's right."

"What…if what you find doesn't please you?"

"What… if it does? Don't you think I have the right to know?"

The dragon walked a little bit farther. Playfully, blew fire from his mouth. Dragons transcend time and dragon's mind possess the cosmos energy. Its sagacity can glide the past, present, and future. Dragons can obtain unique evidences which belonged to pieces of times. The dragon contemplated David's wish. *What would happen with these children if David didn't find out who he is?* The dragon thought. *Until now, David Dreepel had been the reason for this journey.* Limbo Rock found his answer. He will use his ascendancy to help David.

Limbo Rock returned to David. After eyeing David for a couples of minutes, he said, "David Dreepel, I will help you if you promised me that you will come back—no matter what."

"I promise."

The dragon brought his face very close. "Be careful about what you promised, David Dreepel. Promises can be a cruel snare in your fortune. Some of them can fetch the downfall of all your ambitions."

"Why are you telling me that?" asked David impatiently.

"Because you must come back and study to becoming a magician. The peace among the three provinces depends on you."

"Oh…! Now… you can see the future?"

"I am a dragon. Dragons transcend time and my mind can glide the past, present, and future. On the day King James Lamarcus almost killed you, Tess went alone to the Rastaga Woods. On that day she spoke with her mother, Queen Naelia and retrieved the Purple Talisman."

"I know that story," added David. "She saved my life."

"Yes. However, an invisible witch plunked a course on her. On that day, Tess inhaled a Teenalfa—a tiny bug, the size of sand grain. It will be mutating inside her. Tess now belongs to this bug. The bug will never harm her if she does not fall in love; nevertheless, if she ever gives her heart to a prince, she will die. The bug will kill her."

"How do you know this?" asked David.

"I am a dragon. I am a legendary animal. My existence comes across lots of prophecies."

David silenced. He looked to his father trying to see if he would bring in some comment.

"He can't hear me, David," said the dragon. "At this moment, only you can hear me."

"How can I help Tess? I thought the amalgamation of the Talismans will take care of the peace above the provinces."

"It will keep them unified, but in peace... is another story."

"Okay. What can I do to help?"

"Tess, who is Princess Clea, will be responsible for the peace between Province of Jarmayra and Bonavery. She will fall in love with Prince Eduard Montanara. She has to marry him for the great future of these two provinces."

"But if she falls in love she dies—how can this happen?" asked David.

"That's why you need to come back. The eye of the eagle which had been buried by Jacira Caponette, will became a beautiful black and white stone. Only this stone will make the Teenalfa disintegrate without harming Tess. And you, David Dreepel, will be the warlock in charge to find the Tupinambaz."

"Oh! Tupinambaz is the name of the stone?"

"Yes, because your creator named the Eagle Tupinambaz and I don't think he would resist keeping the eagle's eyes hidden forever. The power of the eagle's eyes will haunt him endlessly... until he decides to write about it," explained the dragon.

"According to you, I am going to graduate from Loyporcha Magic School?"

"Absolutely."

"Well... that's good news. Because I want to be a magician."

"If you come back. You will be one of the best warlocks of this planet and during this time, I will be asked to be your Dragon Lord and I will accept the position."

"Everything you are telling me seemed—"

"I know... bizarre," finished the dragon. "Your only concern at this moment revolves around your needs to go to planet Earth to meet with your creator. I am going to help you."

"Do you think I'll recognize him when I see him?"

"You'll even know his name."

The dragon stepped away from David, opened one of his wings, using the edge of it, traced a line on the ground. David Dreepel knew what would happen next. The dragon would exercise the preamble for this transportation. Quietly, David approached the line.

"David Dreepel, remember... no matter what, you must return," said the dragon. "You will not recollect this conversation we just had. But I do want for you to remember one word."

"Okay, Limbo Rock. Tell me the word."

"TUPINAMBAZ."

"Great... you can count on it."

DAVID DREEPEL

"Then… good luck, young warlock."

The dragon stepped back and exercised the preamble.

In the name of what I can control. The ability of having the power of imagination, esoteric code D.D., two seconds fragmentation and incorporation, space, time folder, the future, City of Miami, State of Florida, Country United States, Continent North America, Planet Earth, Milky Way Galaxy, year 1979.

CHAPTER
26

"DELIGHTFULLY, DAVID DREEPEL CROSSED the line and appeared in downtown Miami, in front of the public library. As soon as he saw the library building, he knew he had to go inside. David quickly, entered the library, climbed to the second floor and walked straight to the back of the room. In a quiet corner, he came across a middle size, rectangular table, and behind it, sitting on a chair he found what he was looking for—a twelve-year old boy.

There were books, papers, pencils, and a computer on the table. David Dreepel stopped a few distance from the table and quietly, observed the boy. David waited until the boy saw him.

The boy had a smart, cheerful face, black hair, light brown eyes, and captivating lips. It didn't take long for him to lift his head and see David. For a few seconds, the boy remained speechless. Then he kindly uttered, "David Dreepel…?"

"Mathew Espada…!" replied David.

"So, you decoded the enigma?"

"Yes. Two of the challenges wrapped some unique mysteries, but the others... very easy."

"Tell me the easy ones," said Mathew Espada.

"When I decoded the planet, the animal and the last two words, just popped out... immediately. Mr. Nicolas Toscapela named the dragon Limbo Rock because of a song he heard here, on the Planet Earth."

"It had to be Toscapela and the dragon, right?"

"I am not here to answer your questions. You are the one who will tell me everything I want to know. Why this persistent mystery with the grasshopper? Am I a grasshopper?"

Mathew Espada answered boldly. As if he had nothing to hide. "In the sense of creativeness...YES. In the sense of magic...NO."

"Can you please, explain it better," asked David.

"I don't have to explain anything to you. Remember, I am your creator. You should not have come."

"Please...," replied David, "Tell me why this innocent and puzzling grasshopper is in my pathway? It must be an eloquent reason attached to it."

"Wow... David Dreepel...! I'm proud of you. I made you intelligent and sophisticated. Look how you talk, *eloquent reason*. Politely."

David remained quiet. He wanted just to wait hoping Mathew would talk.

"Okay," said Mathew. "Everything started when I was in fourth grade 1979. My teacher, Mrs. Katia Tornnel asked us to write a short story about an animal. I arrived home and told my mother. My mother wanted to be a writer and was working on her first novel. She had notes and names written down for future books. When I told her, I had to write a short story about an animal, she told me to look in one of her folders, because she once had to do the same and she wrote a lovely short story about a grasshopper. She advised me to read her story to get some idea."

"Oh… it was your mother who created the grasshopper."

"The first one, yes," answered Mathew Espada.

"There is more than one?" asked David.

"No. Listen to what happened. I looked at my mother's papers and found the grasshopper story. In her story, she was a doctor who came home late at night, after long hours of working, took a shower, put on her pajamas, brushed her teeth, and climbed into her bed to sleep. She turned off the light and a grasshopper that was on the edge of her night table, began to sing. My mother immediately, turned on the light. The grasshopper stopped singing. She turned off the light and again… the grasshopper started singing. This activity repeated for at least four times. Light on, quiet grasshopper, light off, singing grasshopper. This course of action speedily, infuriated my mother and she decided to take control of the situation. She turned the light off, grabbed her slippers, on the darkness of the room, followed the music of the grasshopper and quickly, turned on the light, saw it, and smashed it with her slipper."

"She killed the poor grasshopper?" asked David.

"She did," replied Mathew. "And like you said, *poor grasshopper*, because she felt exactly like that—guilty. She couldn't sleep. She began to think that perhaps the grasshopper was an opera singer and was just practicing his number and she killed him. She imagined that when she died and passed to a grasshopper's land, they will kill her with their slippers; exactly like she killed this poor singer. She spent quite a time imagining unpleasant episodes of punishment, because she murdered a grasshopper inside her bedroom. After hours of remorse, she finally slept."

"What happened with the poor grasshopper?" asked David.

"It died. I read her story and the grasshopper died. In her story, that was it."

"What do you mean, in her story?" asked David.

"Because I wrote the same story. I just copied it. I made a few changes, but not much. For example: I was not a doctor. I was just a kid, ten-years old. Then, instead of my slipper, I killed the grasshopper with my tennis shoes. However, I did something interesting. Something my mother never did. I gave the grasshopper a name. I went to the list of names my mother had for her future books and I chose one. I picked DREEPEL."

"Dree... pel?"

"Yes. Just Dreepel," repeated Mathew Espada. "And surprise... surprise... my story was the best short story and I had to climb to the cafeteria stage and read it to the whole school. My mother came to the school for the event and discovered I had stolen her grasshopper story. I received a lovely small trophy."

David Dreepel remained silent, wishing that he was not that grasshopper. "What happened next?" he asked.

"My mother felt disappointed with me. She decided that I did not deserve the trophy. She went to speak with Mrs. Katia Tornnel. She told my teacher that I stole her short story and that I do not deserve to be the winner, because it would not be fair with the other students. My lovely teacher told my mother, that I was very intelligent, a problem-solving child. Then she explained to my mother, that I had a problem… I had to come up with a short story about an animal… and I did it well, in my own way. End of the discussion."

"Just like that?" commented David. "Another dead grasshopper?"

Mathew breathed in deeply. "I wished it ended, like that, but no. My guilty nightmares never abandoned me. The grasshopper was living inside my mind, torturing me. I began to see it inside my small trophy and it started talking to me. It didn't die, and it had a name—Dreepel. I didn't hit it hard enough. The grasshopper asked me to write another story. Something with more details and long… A journey."

"Ah… That is why Mr. Nicolas Toscapela always said I asked for this journey. Then, I am a grasshopper."

"No….The grasshopper inspired me to create David Dreepel, but you're not a grasshopper."

"All right, supposedly you're right. How will you explain it to me, in a way, I can understand my existence?"

"When the grasshopper began to talk to me in my imagination, I spoke with my friends Lucas and Olivia, because I didn't know what to do with it. I constantly had words messing with my thoughts. Lucas and Olivia really loved the idea that I had a grasshopper living inside my mind. They became fascinated with the flow of it and encouraged me to write a journey for Dreepel. Under such a concept everything started. The whole thing became an interesting game… a piece of fiction."

"I believe that to exit the grasshopper from your mind, you killed it again," added David Dreepel.

"No… Lucas, Olivia and I started working together. Olivia decided I should select valuable and interesting books, place the grasshopper inside a library and give it the power to read fast. When the grasshopper had acquired enough education, I would let it chose its destiny. As soon as this day arrived, the smart grasshopper decided to be human and… a magician."

Promptly, David added, "Ah…! Now, I understand, why hypothetically… the grasshopper was the inspiration for my existence."

"The moment we gave the grasshopper, education… first… and last name…you had been born and the grasshopper became an animation."

"Indeed, good job. Even though you chose the Medieval Era… the 333 years into the future matched the year your grasshopper short story had been written."

"Exactly."

"Who had decided to introduce Lucas, Olivia, and Tess into the story?"

"Lucas did. He asked to be a character in the journey and I agreed. By exchanging ideas, we all decided that Olivia, her sister Tess, and I, should participate in the journey, too."

"You became Nicolas Toscapela, right?" said David.

"Right," replied Mathew Espada. "It was also Lucas' idea. He found it interesting to have the creator inside the creation. And when David Dreepel appeared at Dunes of Gargatuela, and for the first time, uttered his name; automatically, he became part of his own magic. He inherited what belonged to him; his journey."

"AUTOMATICALLY," asked David.

"Yes. Because at this point you had already read thousands of books. Your knowledge had transformed you."

"Yes, but in Nordache, when Lucas, Olivia and Tess met me... they first saw a grasshopper. Then in Bonahunta when King James Lamarcus was going to kill me, again appeared the grasshopper, and later on, at the Dezatela Desert, it was the grasshopper which brought the scorpion from underneath the boulder. Who am I... hmm?"

"Like I already said, in the sense of creativeness, *yes* you're a grasshopper. In the sense of *magic, no.* And as an author, I kept the grasshopper as your savior. David Dreepel's benevolent savor. The only mistake I made was allowing you to come to Woodmera; because Woodmera is my *secret place...* a spot inside my mind where I go to disconnect from my routine and live an extravagant fantasy. You found it. I never thought that when you reached the Suacileu Tabernacle, you would choose to meet me instead of going on and finish your journey."

"Oh... you thought that by meeting my father, my existence would be glorified?"

"Yes," answered Mathew Espada. "It should have comforted you. I shouldn't have created the enigma or let you meet Magno Dreepel. I regret I did that because now, you will not finish your journey and this makes me sad. Very said."

"What?"

"You cannot finish your journey. All the people you left in the Suacileu Tabernacle, will be there trapped forever, because you violated my space."

"Oh…no, I will be back and I will become a magician. You can't interfere in it."

"How I cannot? I am your creator."

"Yes, but now you're not the only one in control. You have created strong, rational characters and amazing pragmatic animals that— through magic— they became as powerful as you are. Animals that can transcend time."

"Oh… again, talking about the dragon. I can see that he brainwashed you about the future he sees. You're so naive, David. The dragon has nothing to help you to go back and finish your journey."

"You're right, he did tell me something about the future; however, I can't remember a whisper of it. But I remember the word he told me to not forget."

Mathew Espada laughed mockingly. Then calmly, he said, "Okay, tell me. What is it? Because there is no word… in the face of this planet… that can bring you back to My Jupiter.

David Dreepel turned around, waved his hand, and said,

"TUPINAMBAZ"

CHAPTER
27

"DAVID DREEPEL RETURNED TO the Suacileu Tabernacle. He landed rashly, outside it, rolling over the ground until he stopped at the feet of the dragon. Quickly, Limbo Rock rose up from his feet.

"Young warlock, glad to see that you came back."

David stood up, replacing his medieval hat back on his head. "Yes, I did come back. And thank you, Limbo Rock. You have saved me."

"Did I?"

"Yes."

"How?"

"The word TUPINAMBAZ."

The dragon moved his head showing contentment.

"How did you know that?"

"I am a dragon. Dragons are magic. We're legendary reptilians above average intelligence and we possess intuitive power."

DAVID DREEPEL

"Of course."

"Have you met your creator?"

"I did," said David Dreepel.

"How was it? Are you a grasshopper?"

"No. The grasshopper was the inspiration for my existence. That's all. Then as magic works, later on it became my savior. In conclusion, for the sake of magic, I am David Dreepel"

"Are you happy with the outcomes?"

"I am. I had an interesting encounter."

"I'm glad you're happy with the truth. Now young warlock, go and take care of your journey. You must finish it."

"I understand," replied David.

"You have to return Olivia, Tess, Queen Naelia and King Duayne to the Province of Jarmayra, to the Shelicart Castle. The girls need to focus on their education for they are princesses. Lucas should return to Bonahunta to the Bacellar Castle, where he will start his training as knight to also becoming a fine prince. You and Leila will remain in Lili Sandra to initiate your classes at Loyporcha Magic School. Do you understand how the rest of your mission would be?"

"I do."

"David… delay nothing in these matters. The Otela Moon will change phases in two days. After that you will lose your supremacy to use the Surdrape Time Fold Passage. You must act now to finish your journey. Good luck."

"Yes, Limbo Rock. Consider everything done. And again, thank you for helping me to return."

"Oh… thank you for having returned," said the dragon.

David Dreepel walked into the Tabernacle and stopped in front

291

the transparent table where everybody was seated, even his father had returned inside to join them. The huge crystal wall that elevated to separate David and his father from the others, had vanished from the chamber.

"David, where have you been?" asked Olivia. "We have been here waiting for you."

"I quickly went to a secret place to find out who I am."

"Are you a grasshopper?" asked Lucas.

"No…. The grasshopper indeed was the inspiration for my existence, but I am not an animal, I am David Dreepel."

"Cool," uttered Tess. "I knew it."

While the conversation was going on, Magno Dreepel and Vachal Maglaja, suddenly stood up. They knew time was running against David. If he didn't return to Lili Sandra now, he may never end his journey.

"David," said his father. "It's time to leave. From now on, you cannot delay your tasks. In magic, time means… *past* and *future*… alongside. The *present*…an instant energy."

Magno Dreepel walked around the table and shook hands with everyone. Following that, Vachal Maglaja guided them out of the Tabernacle. Once outside, Vachal Maglaja hugged his daughter. Then began his transformation and returned to his duty which was being the APERAGLA Tiger.

The children said good-bye to the tiger and dragons and prepared to leave. Solemnly, they held hands. After hearing the preamble said by David, they crossed the line and arrived at Lili Sandra.

They landed in front the Astafe Castle at 2:00 a.m., under the Ophela Moon. The whole city rested quietly, as if the new moon had nothing dangerous behind its existence. Leila, Marco Prado and the children climbed the steps of the castle and entered it. Leila always opened it with the flash neon she exercised from her eyes.

As soon as they walked into the living room, Inbacula and Mr. Clenilde came. They left their beds to welcome them. Inbacula and Mrs. Clenilde, helped them by providing some candles to light their way upstairs to their bedrooms. Everybody was so tired that going to bed and having some decent sleep turned out to be the most convenient thing to do at such a time.

On the next day, after breakfast, David walked to the kitchen and asked Inbacula to bring the Titleless book. David wished to check the preamble of the Surdrape Time Fold Passage, before they left Lili Sandra. When he first read it, the book said they all needed to be together for the transportation to work, but now David realized coming back from Nordache, it would be only Leila and him.

When he and Inbacula opened the book, the first page sent them to page 113.

On page 113 they read: David Dreepel, at the end of your journey, the preamble and the magic words for the transportation will be the same. You and Leila will return to Lili Sandra safely. There is no need to change anything. After reading this page, burn the Titleless book. There is nothing more in this book that you should know.

Leila and the children got ready to leave. Time was running fast and they shouldn't play with it. First, they would stop in Bonahunta, to drop Prince Willian at the Bacellar Castle. From Bonahunta, David transported King Duayne Cashemire, Queen Naelia, Princess Laura, and Princess Clea to Nordache to the Shelicart Castle.

When everything was in place for the trip, Leila said, "Children, it's time to leave. Please say goodbye to Inbacula and Mrs. Clenilde."

Obviously, the moment brought tears to the eyes of the children. They did not want to leave; however, they understood that nothing could have been done differently. If they did not return to their new lives, nothing they had experienced would ever make sense.

While putting on her coat, Olivia asked. "Leila, are we going to remember the moments we have shared?"

"You will Olivia; however, not as Olivia."

"Are we going to forget, David Dreepel, you, and Limbo Rock?"

"No. You will remember everything that happened on this journey as episodes of your childhood. Not as Olivia, Tess or Lucas."

"I think magic is more complicated that what I imagined," added Lucas. "That's why I want to be a knight, then king."

"Mr. Inbacula, thank you for everything," said Tess. "My sister and I will never forget that your daughter Analia saved our mother."

"Thank you, Princess Clea. I also will never forget you."

Lucas walked to Marco Pardo and hugged him. "You... Sir Marco Prado will do something for me. Can I count on it?"

"Even though I don't know what is it, yes. You can count on me."

"When my father decides to marry me away, I want one of these crystal balls you have in my palace, so... I can find the right princess."

"Deal.... I'm going to create one especial crystal ball for this matter."

Perhaps, moments like these should never ended; nevertheless, reality tells another story and a few minutes later they left Lili Sandra behind.

David Dreepel conducted his last tasks with such precision, that he even managed to not cry, when he said goodbye to his friends. Inside his heart he kept the hope that one day—in a near future—they will meet again. For now... their time together was over. For now... their expectations belong to another scope with new prospects and fancy dreams. On one side stayed great aristocrats and on the other side superb magicians. David and Leila returned to Lili Sandra to the Astafe Castle and found Marco Prado still there.

"Oh, Sir Marco Prado, are you still here?"

"Yes, David. I decided to waited for your and Leila's return, to make sure everything went well. Now, that you're back I can go home."

"Wait a minute, Sir Marco Prado," said David. "Why don't you stay here with me and Leila. Move your laboratory from the Loyporcha Magic School to the castle. We have a basement, and an attic. You can choose."

"Are you serious about that?"

"Of course. This castle is huge and here you'll not be alone. At the end of each day, you'll have someone to talk. Even during the day, because Inbacula and Mrs. Clenilde are always here."

Marco Prado looked at Leila. He studied her face. "Are you okay with it, Leila?"

"Marco Prado... this castle is not mine. Of course, it will be a pleasure having you here."

Inbacula, who was present and heard the entire conversation, just asked, "Sir Marco Prado, where do you want your laboratory? In the basement, or in the attic?"

Smiling, Marco Prado answered, "Basement, Inbacula. I like basements."

Standing to go to Loyporcha Magic School to start packing to move, Marco Prado stopped and said, "David, I forgot to tell you something. I have a servant and a cat."

"No problem, bring them. Ah... the cat is Jacira Caponette, right? The woman I had to shrink. The woman who became a cat."

"Yes. That cat, Picachú."

David smiled shaking his head. "Picachú is welcomed here. Bring her."

Following this conversation, Mrs. Clenilde arrived in the living room, bringing with her three things. Two lovely grey caps with the name of the school, beautifully engraved on it. LOYPORCHA MAGIC SCHOOL OF LILI SANDRA. One cap for Leila and one for David. Then Mrs. Clenilde gave David a thick book. The BÁ-ONADI magic book. Its cover was made of leather and the letters customized in gold. Under the tittle appeared the personalization. DAVID DREEPEL.

The Loyporcha Magic School was located about two miles from the castle, so Leila and David could walk to the school if they wished. After dressing into their new caps, the three of them, David and Leila, together with Marco Prado walked to the school.

As soon as they climbed the stairs, Professor Coorbell and Leila's mother, joined them. Professor Coorbell took David around the school and showed him every corner of it. In two halls David saw pictures of his father on the walls. He also saw Vachal Maglaja's picture among the great magicians.

After showing David the whole school, Professor Coorbell, took him to his office. There was something David needed to know. As soon as they sat comfortable in front of each other, Professor Coorbell said, "David, today you will take the NURCUÁ test. It's a test every student must take in order to be accepted in the school. Don't worry about the test, because with the knowledge you already have, you'll passed it without any problem."

"Yes, professor, I'd like to take the test."

Following this conversation, David signed a couple of papers and they exited the office.

"Now, David, I'm taking you to the student chamber, located in the second floor; where lives your *Good Luck Charm Animal*—your Mascot."

"Animal?"

"Yes. Every student has an animal as his assistant. This animal will keep the schedule of your classes, will ensure you have all the books you need, will keep track of your grades, etc."

David smiled. He never expected that.

"Your Mascot has been chosen by Mrs. Cornelia De La Tress Vilavaldi, the founder of Loyporcha Magic School. Her spirit comes once a year and selects the student's Mascots. She investigates the life of each student to protect the integrity of the school. She always picks the right animal for each student. If the student disliked the animal, it can be changed; however, it never happened."

"What animal do I have?" asked David, eagerly.

"Oh, I don't know. However, I have asked to be your Pilot Professor. This is why I'm here to introduce you to your Mascot. Only your Pilot Professor is able to see and hear your Mascot like you do."

David wiggled his head surprisingly. He felt excited about the school treacheries. Professor Coorbell and David Dreepel entered the students' chamber. The huge room had all the walls covered with beautifully crafted small drawers.

"Okay, David Dreepel, call your drawer," said the professor.

"How?"

"By saying your name. First and last name."

David articulated: DAVID DREEPEL.

Instantly, all the drawers moved toward the left, shifted up and down until the one with his name stopped exactly in front him. Without hesitation David opened it. The drawers only opened half way. After a few seconds a charming grasshopper appeared inside the drawer.

"Oh,...a grasshopper?"

"Don't you like it?" asked the professor.

"Oh... I love it."

"Then, talk to him."

The grasshopper was standing elegantly on his two legs. Silently, David admired it. He was fascinating with the surprise. Eyeing the lovely grasshopper, David said, "I am David Dreepel. Do you have a name?"

"I do," answered the grasshopper. My name is Lost."

"Lost?" repeated David.

"Yes. My creator said I was trapped between two dimensions; that's why... Lost."

"I know from where you came from", said David."

"Mr. Mathew Estrada said you would recognize me. He talked to me after you left."

DAVID DREEPEL

"Oh! I can see he did. By allowing you to be my Mascot, he knew I finished the journey, right? I am glad he understood the magic of it and I am glad that this time he didn't try to kill you when you were singing."

"I heard that story, too. Cold heart."

"Yes. Welcome to my life. And now… let's contemplate my future. Where is the schedule of my classes?"

"Give me a minute, sir. I'll be back."

Lost turned around and disappeared in the deepest part of the drawer. As fast as he vanished, he arrived again. "Sir David Dreepel here is your schedule." He gave David a piece of leather with the schedule written on it.

David took the piece of leather, read the schedule, and smiled happily. Today he will only have the NURCUÁ test. If he passes it, tomorrow he will start his classes.

"Thank you, Lost. I'll see you tomorrow. I always will come to say 'hi'."

"Thank you, Sir Dreepel, and good luck on the test."

David felt excited about what he was about to start. He hoped he would be as good as his father was, and as creative as Marco Prado became. His life just began. Walking next to Professor Coorbell, David brought to his mind the image of Mathew Espada, the person in charge of such a dimension.

Happily, he whispered, "THANK YOU."

****

Two years later, 1656, a fourteen-year-old boy was walking over the Dunes of Gargatuela. He wore elegant medieval clothes and was alone. The isolated place told him anything he should have known. He advanced over the sand deeply connected with his mind. He knew, he was starting a new journey. A journey called; HUNTING THE TUPINAMBAZ.

An ancient man dressed in a stylish white tunic that tenderly, brushed the fine beige sand, appeared walking over the sand. His hair, in catches, covered his shoulders as it moved gently, with the breeze which blew through the land at the moment. His mysterious blue eyes openly, delivered a peaceful look. On his right hand he held a lovely wooden cane, wore sandals on his feet and seemed familiar with the environment around him.

The ancient man stopped in front the fourteen-year-old boy and asked, "Who are you?"

"I'm David…. David Dreepel."